Wrongful Secrets

Donald Gorman

*Mary —
Thanks!
Enjoy the book!
— Donald Gorman*

authorHOUSE®

AuthorHouse™
1663 Liberty Drive, Suite 200
Bloomington, IN 47403
www.authorhouse.com
Phone: 1-800-839-8640

© 2008 Donald Gorman. All rights reserved.

No part of this book may be reproduced, stored in a retrieval system, or transmitted by any means without the written permission of the author.

First published by AuthorHouse 7/24/2008

ISBN: 978-1-4343-9428-6 (sc)

Printed in the United States of America
Bloomington, Indiana

This book is printed on acid-free paper.

Table of Contents

Chapter 1 Hell Shack 1

Chapter 2 The Man in the Fireplace 26

Chapter 3 Surprises 55

Chapter 4 Purely Innocent Guilt 78

Chapter 5 When Something is Wrong 105

Chapter 6 You've Been Very Bad! 128

Chapter 7 Chilling Coincidence 156

Chapter 8 Separating Good From Evil 182

Chapter 9 Entanglements 208

Chapter 10 Unique, Indelicate Hunger 223

Chapter 11 Alarming Behavior 247

Chapter 12 Compulsion and Combustion 277

Chapter 13 Punishing Yourself 301

ABOUT THE AUTHOR 323

"...Abandon all hope,
All ye who enter here!"

--Dante
The Inferno

Chapter 1
Hell Shack

Eight or nine flickering candles pierced the darkness. Two small oil lamps added a dim, murky glow to a portion of the dismal surroundings.

Music blared from a portable cassette player. The Foreigner tune sounded tinny and inadequate coming from the outdated device.

"It's freezing in here!" she commented through chattering teeth. She shivered in her heavy winter coat. She wrapped her arms tightly around herself for warmth.

"Cold as ice," he poked. "Just like the song that's playing."

"Very funny, Rich!"

"Hey," another girl noticed. "There's a fireplace in here!"

"I know."

"Well, can't we start a fire or something?" she suggested.

"We'd have to go out and gather some firewood," Rich said. "We don't want to do that every time we come out here. Plus, we don't want anyone to see smoke coming out of the chimney. If anybody finds out we're here, they're bound to do something about it."

"This is probably trespassing," another boy said.

"But, I'm freezing to death," she reiterated.

"Don't be a wuss, Kim," Rich said. "Suck it up. It's warmer in here than it is outside. Have another beer. That'll help."

She took the bottle he handed her. "Can't we cover up that hole in the window at least?" she asked.

Another boy lit a joint. He took a deep hit. "Here," he offered while holding his breath. "Get some of this in you. That'll warm you up."

She took the rolled paper and put it to her lips.

"And, it's so dirty and cluttered in here," another girl complained.

"I told you it was a mistake to bring girls here," he reminded. He exhaled a cloud of smoke which curled around in the scant light of the lamp.

"Oh, I wouldn't say that," Rich smiled.

"Really, Rich!" she said. "You're such a pig!"

"Shut up and take a hit, Cheyenne."

"Speaking of which," he said. "Where's Trixie?"

"I think she went upstairs, Bill," Kim said. "She went with Frank about twenty minutes ago."

The boys shared a glance and a chuckle.

"Don't be like that," Kim said. "They just went to talk."

"Of course," Logan replied sarcastically. "They needed a private bedroom so they could just talk."

"You're a jerk, Logan!" Cheyenne declared.

The boys laughed.

Wrongful Secrets

"So, how did you find this place?" Kim asked, hoping to change the subject. "And why do you call it 'Hell Shack'?"

"This place has been abandoned for years," Bill explained. "We've always known about it. But, we only thought about using it as a party spot last spring. It's in a great location. It's far enough into the woods that it's private. But, it's not so far that it takes long to walk here."

"Aren't you afraid the cops will find it?" Cheyenne asked.

"They're not too likely to even look for this place," Rich said. "As long as we don't cause any trouble."

"Or do anything to get noticed," Logan added. "That's why we don't want to use the fireplace. We only use this place to get drunk or high on the weekends. And we don't mean nobody no harm. It's just a place to party."

"But, what is this place?" Cheyenne asked.

"It used to be somebody's house," Bill replied. "It was more out-in-the-woods when it was first built in the 1800s. The town of Spruce Valley has kind of encroached on it over the years. Someone's bound to buy this property up eventually. But for now, it's a great party hangout."

"It was built by a small-time farmer named Mortimer Hilzak," Rich explained. "Even now, people call this The Hilzak Place. That's how we came to name the little house 'Hell Shack'. It's a bust on his name. One year, they had a real bad harvest season. It was a dry summer, and they didn't get many crops. With no food or income from their crops, they went hungry. The family was starving, and there was nothing Mortimer could do. His two daughters died of measles or something."

"Oh no," Kim said sympathetically.

"According to the legend," Logan continued. "They had no food or money and nobody was willing to help them. I guess Hilzak didn't have many friends. Mortimer went berserk and chopped his wife and son to bits with an axe."

"That's horrible!" Cheyenne exclaimed.

"Then, he hung himself in the bedroom," Logan went on. "Nobody's lived here ever since."

The girls exchanged a fearful glance.

"Some people say the place is haunted," Rich said in a playfully taunting voice. "Some say that on a night like this, you can still see the ghost of Old Man Hilzak creeping slowly up the stairs with an axe in his hand."

"Stop it, Rich!" Kim demanded.

"You're just making that up," Cheyenne theorized bravely.

"Sometimes," Bill teased. "You can hear the voices of his daughters calling for food or help. Occasionally, you can hear the screams of his wife...just like she screamed as he chopped her to pieces!"

"You two aren't funny!" Kim scolded.

"Seriously, Bill," Cheyenne asserted. "If you don't stop, I'm leaving! It's cold and dark and spooky enough in here without you making it worse."

"Okay," he said. "I'll be good."

The music had stopped. The tape was over.

In the insufficient, flickering light, the silence was exceedingly eerie.

Moments passed. The silence grew thick.

"Oh, my God!" he suddenly called out in panic. "What's that? Over by the stairs!"

The girls screamed. They spun around to face the staircase.

They stared in fright.

Then, they breathed a sigh of relief.

"Richard!" Kim scolded. "That's not funny! Stop laughing! It's not a joke! I swear I'm going to leave if you don't cut it out!"

"Alright," Rich said as the laughter subsided. "I'm sorry."

"You girls need to lighten up," Logan said. "We're here to have a good time. We've got beer. We've got pot. In a moment, we'll have music again. We have all night to enjoy ourselves."

"Then, stop trying to scare us," Cheyenne asserted.

"Listen," Logan said. "It's early January 1984. It's the start of a brand new year. It's *our* year. We'll be graduating high school in just a few short months. Then, it's off to face the world. We've got our whole lives ahead of us. All you have to do is…"

He was interrupted by a scream.

Everyone froze.

"Did anybody else hear that?" Logan asked.

"It sounded like Trixie!" Cheyenne said.

She followed Bill and Rich as they ran toward the stairs.

Kim and Logan stayed behind. They anxiously watched their three classmates quickly ascend to the second floor.

"What do you think happened?" Kim asked.

"Who knows?" Logan shrugged. "It's probably nothing."

A few moments later, three boys walked down the stairs.

"Fine!" he called angrily back behind him. "I'll be down in the front room! Come back down when you come to your senses!"

"What's going on, Frank?" Logan asked.

"Oh, it's nothing," he said. "Me and Trixie were fooling around in the bed. I went for her pants. At first, she was into it. Then all of a sudden, she flipped out and started acting like I was doing something wrong!"

"Oh!" Kim gasped. "Trixie! You're an ass, Frank!"

"I didn't do anything!" he insisted. "I'm telling you! One minute she was into it, the next, she's practically screaming rape! That girl's screwed up!"

"Maybe I should go to her," Kim suggested.

"Cheyenne's up there with her now," Bill said. "What the hell, Frank? What's wrong with you?"

"I'm telling you," he persisted. "She was into it! Then out of nowhere, she turned cold on me! She's a drunken bitch! That's what I get for going with a tease!"

"Shut up, Frank!" Kim ordered. "I'm going to go see if she's okay."

She bounded up the stairs with a flashlight in her hand. She followed the voices to a small bedroom. She shined the light into the room. There were a few candles offering a feeble light of their own.

Cheyenne was sitting on the bed. Her arm was around the shoulders of a pretty girl who was gently sobbing into a wad of tissues.

"What happened, Trixie?" Kim asked as she cautiously entered the room.

"Oh, my God," Trixie sniffled. "I really liked him! I really liked him! Everything was going great. We were making out on the bed. Then, he tried to unbutton my shirt. I pulled away and told him to stop. He promised to be good. We started kissing again, and he went right back to my shirt! I told him to stop! He promised he would! Then as soon as I kissed him, he's trying to reach into my shirt! I told him to stop! But every time I let him touch me, he'd start again! Then, he went for my pants! I told him to stop, but he wouldn't! He just held me down and kept trying to pull my pants down! That's when I screamed! Oh, my God, Kim! He tried to rape me!"

Kim sat on the bed. She took Trixie into her arms. She allowed her friend to cry on her shoulder.

Downstairs, Rich said, "I didn't want to say anything while Kim was in the room. But admit it, Frank. There's no way Trixie wanted you to do what I saw you doing when I came into that room."

"Of course not," Frank declared. "By the time you got there, she was already freaking out! But, I'm telling you! When we started, she wanted it! Actually, I'm starting to think maybe she planned this thing from the beginning. She was trying to make me look like I'm the ass! She set me up! The worthless little slut!"

"Oh, don't even start, Frank," Bill argued. "You're hyper even when you're sober. Right now, you're drunk and you're being your typical asshole self! She was kicking and screaming and you wouldn't stop! You were holding her down! We had to drag you off her like a little punk!"

"Jesus, Frank!" Logan spat with an accusatory tone. "I'm the one who told you about this place! You're going to ruin it for everybody!"

"She got me all worked up," Frank defended. "Then she pulled the rug out from under me! How's that *my* fault? A guy's got needs!"

Donald Gorman

"You don't *need* to…" Bill began. Then he said, "Oh, never mind! I've got to go outside for a minute. This beer's running right through me. And it *is* cold tonight."

"I have to go too," Logan said.

"Damn," Rich added. "Now you got me started. We'll be back in a minute, Frank. Stay downstairs, and see if you can stay out of trouble while we're gone."

"No problem," Frank said. "I don't want nothing more to do with that bitch tonight."

He sat on the dusty, cold chair. It was hardwood. It was uncomfortable.

He watched the three boys leave the room. The chair creaked as he bent down to take a beer from the cooler. He twisted off the cap. The icy, smooth contents poured easily down his throat.

It was sweet. It was soothing.

He chugged half the bottle before setting the glass container on his knee.

He glanced around. It was dark and dreary.

Lamps and candles did little to illuminate the filthy, decrepit, ancient surroundings.

Most of the room remained obscured by a discomforting darkness.

He was already in a bad mood. The daunting stillness didn't help.

He lit a cigarette. He took a drag. Angry thoughts nagged him like an unsympathetic mother.

What was wrong with everyone?

Why was Trixie turning on him? They'd gone out four times, for God's sake! Well, kind of. They'd made out with each other four times.

Wrongful Secrets

What was her problem? What did she want from him? Did she come here just to start trouble? Did she go upstairs with him just to screw with his head?

Why was everybody taking *her* side?

She's the problem! Not him!

He took another drag of his cigarette.

Then, he heard a noise off in a dark corner. Over by the stairs.

He perked up. He looked around.

"Who's that?" he called out.

There was no reply.

He stood up. "Girls?" he called. "Trixie? Is that you?"

The silence grew thick and disturbing.

He stood up. He slowly lifted an oil lamp from the table.

"Logan?" he shouted. "Bill? Answer me, Rich! I ain't in the mood for games!"

Not a sound could be heard.

He took a step toward the source of the noise.

"Come on, guys!" he ordered. "Quit messing around!"

The floor creaked eerily as he crept cautiously over to the stairwell. He kept a vigilant eye on his dismal environment. He was careful not to trip over the chucks of wood and debris that littered the floor.

He couldn't see more than three feet in front of him. Furniture seemed to be everywhere. He could almost make out the banister just ahead of him.

"Hello?" he called out. "I ain't playing with you, assholes!"

Silence seemed to close in on him like an army of jet black panthers. He was almost at the stairs.

He turned. He gasped!

He was staring into the intimidating glare of an older man. The deep, maddening snarl on the man's face was accented by the dim, haunting glow of the lamp. The man was dressed in clothing that had been outdated for a hundred years or so.

He held an axe in his menacing fists.

Frank screamed. He jumped with a start.

He stumbled backwards into some piece of furniture? Was it a sofa?

He fell to the dirty, cluttered floor.

There was a stabbing pain in his hand. He must have cut himself on something when he fell. It was bleeding. However, it was just a small flesh wound.

He glanced nervously back toward the staircase. Everything was dark. Whoever he had seen was gone.

Could it have been…???

No! That's impossible!

Isn't it?

He couldn't see. Everything before him was shrouded in pure darkness.

Then, it occurred to him that he had dropped his oil lamp and cigarette when he fell. He couldn't see them. He groped around the floor with his hands.

He didn't find them.

So, he turned around.

His jaw dropped when he saw a raging fire spread rapidly through the cold, dry furnishings in the room. Apparently, he'd knocked over a table with another oil lamp and four lit candles on it.

Wrongful Secrets

"What the hell?" he gasped.

Quickly, he leapt to his feet. He ripped off his heavy leather coat. He began a desperate attempt to beat the flames down.

"Help!" he shouted. "Help! Fire! Come quick, everybody! Fire! Fire!"

The three boys ran into the room.

"Oh shit!" Logan gasped.

"What the hell did you do, Bentworth?" Bill shouted.

"Never mind that now," Frank replied angrily. "Help me put out the fucking fire!"

The three boys cursed at him as they all did their best to contain the growing blaze. They used their coats and whatever they could find. Their efforts seemed to be in vain. The furious flames engulfed more of the room without hesitation. The boys had no choice but to retreat as the angry, threatening blaze forced them back without mercy.

"It's not working!" Logan observed anxiously.

"The whole place is made out of 100-year-old, dry wood," Bill pointed out as he swung his coat at an encroaching fire. "Face it! This place is going to go up like a match! And there's nothing we can do about it! Thanks a fucking bunch, Frank!"

"Get screwed!"

"Where are the girls?" Rich asked. "Are they still upstairs?"

"Damn it!" Frank gasped. "I forgot about them! We got to get them out of there!"

"The fire's already heading up the stairs!" Rich shouted.

"Shit!" Frank grumbled. "That's alright! I'll get them out!"

"How?" Bill asked.

"I'll manage!" Frank insisted.

He made his way between fierce, tall columns of fire. The dancing spires of taunting yellows and ravenous orange and red taunted and lashed out at his face. He tried to shield himself with his arms. He cautiously navigated a narrow, jagged path toward the stairs.

The other boys tried to find their own path while calling out to the girls.

"Kim!" they called. "Trixie! Cheyenne! Fire! Girls! Fire! Girls!"

"Damn it!" Frank snarled. "I can't even get near the stairs! The fire's too damn hot! It's all over the place!"

"I can hear them screaming!" Logan observed. "They must be trapped!"

"We got to get them out of there!" Bill commanded.

"How are we going to do that, Ambrose?" Rich asked. "We can't get near the fucking stairs!"

"We can't just leave them here!" Frank demanded. "This whole thing is my fault!"

"You got *that* right!"

"You're not helping, Ambrose!" Rich spat.

"We can't stay here!" Logan advised. "If we don't get out of here now, we'll never get out!"

"What about the girls?" Rich insisted.

"We'll have to deal with them from outside," Logan said. "Come on."

Four boys made their way carefully between the hostile, consuming flames. They left behind the menacing crackle of the blaze and the terrified screams of the girls.

With great difficulty, they pushed their way out of the burning building. They coughed against the smoke inhalation.

They coughed and wheezed as they stood in the cold safety of a thin blanket of snow.

The following day, four boys were seated at a booth in a diner.

"We have to go over this one more time," Frank said. "We have to make sure nobody screws this up when the cops talk to us."

"Are you sure the cops even *will* talk to us?" Logan asked.

"They're bound to," Frank said. "They'd be fools if they didn't."

"How would they even know about Hell Shack?" Logan asked.

"Do you think the girls are really...?" Bill started. He cleared his throat before concluding, "...you know, dead?"

"Don't be a moron, Ambrose!" Frank snapped. "Of course they're dead! There's no way they could have gotten out of there alive! I can still see Trixie's face in the window when we were calling to her from outside. She looked so absolutely horrified!"

"I know," Logan grumbled. "They all looked scared to death! I only saw them for a second or two. But, I'll never forget the terror on their faces as long as I live!"

"I'll be hearing those screams," Frank added. "The fear in their voices. I called up for them to jump. I told them to jump! I would have caught them! One at a time, of course. But, I would've done it!"

"But, as soon as we started to call up to them," Rich reminded sadly. "Flames surrounded the window like a picture frame. They all disappeared a moment later!"

"And all that was left were the screams," Frank muttered. "The horrible, endless screams!"

"So, what the hell happened, Bentworth?" Logan asked. "You still haven't told us how you managed to burn down Hell Shack and kill three of our friends."

"Shut the hell up, Tetweller!" Frank threatened. "I told you it was an accident!"

"Yeah," Bill said. "All you told us is that you saw something. But, you didn't tell us what you saw."

"Never mind," Frank mumbled. "It isn't important."

"Not important?" Logan argued. "You took out Hell Shack and three really hot-looking girls! How is that not important?"

"I'm warning you, Tetweller!" Frank snarled. "It was an accident! Don't joke about it! Trixie was my fucking girlfriend!"

"Then, why did you try to rape her?" Logan pushed.

Frank jumped out of his seat.

Rich quickly rose to his feet. He caught Frank by the shoulder.

"Easy, boy," he cautioned. "If we start fighting amongst ourselves, we'll all end up in jail. We have to keep a united front. Remember? That's why we're here."

Frank took a moment to calm himself. Then, he sat down.

"I didn't try to rape nobody," he quietly insisted. "I'm telling you, Trixie wanted it when we started! She just freaked out in the middle, and it was hard for me to slam on the brakes. Especially, since I was drunk."

"Then, why did you torch up my favorite party spot?"

"That's enough, Tetweller!" Rich intervened. "If you don't keep your mouth shut, *I'll* put your lights out for you! Do you understand?"

There was an uneasy pause.

"It was an accident," Frank finally defended. "Everything last night was one big accident. The only thing you've got to remember is that I got my cousin Al to vouch for us. We can say we were all over at his garage last night from 8:00 'til 1:00."

"You mean Cole's Garage over on Railroad Ave.?" Bill asked.

"Yup," Frank nodded. "We helped him fix a few cars. Then, he had a quick backyard barbeque. That's why our coats smell like a forest fire."

"A backyard barbeque in the middle of January?" Bill asked.

"It's not that unusual for Al," Frank explained. "He's a nut about things like that. The cops in this town know him. They'll understand. Man! Everything's coming together! Even God's on our side. We even got a couple more inches of snow early this morning. That should cover any footprints evidence the cops may have had. I tell you… if we stick together, we'll be in the clear!"

"Right," Logan said in an uncertain tone. "But, is your cousin going to stick to his story when he finds out our Cracker Jack box came with a surprise inside? You know, three girls who didn't used to be so charred and crispy?"

"I explained everything to him," Frank said. "He knows about all that."

"So, we're really in the clear?" Bill asked.

Donald Gorman

"As long as we all stick together," Frank said. "Remember: Cole's Garage on Railroad Ave. from 8:00 'til 1:00 with my cousin Al. We worked on a few cars. Then he cooked up some chicken and sausages on his grill."

"What kind of cars were we working on?" Rich asked. "The cops will want to know some of those little details."

"Let's see," Frank rubbed his chin. "He had a Honda Civic on the rack. Then, there was a Ford Taurus and a Chevy Malibu."

"I don't know nothing about cars," Bill said. "Suppose they ask me for details?"

"We had you holding a flashlight," Frank said. "And running for socket wrenches and stuff. You'd know how to do that, wouldn't you?"

"I guess."

"Good," Frank smiled. "So, we're covered."

"I still want to know what you saw," Logan persisted. "You know, just before you torched up the place."

"Will you let it go, Tetweller?" Frank argued. "What does it matter?"

"I'm kind of curious myself," Rich added.

There was a tense pause. Everyone waited for an answer.

Frank felt the pressure. Finally, he weakly offered, "I just saw…a guy. A man. An old man."

"You saw an old man?" Bill asked anxiously. "In Hell Shack?"

"Yeah," Frank stammered. "He was sort of carrying… an axe."

"You saw an old man carrying an axe?" Rich asked with uncertainty.

"Just for a second," Frank explained. "Then, he just sort of…disappeared!"

"Disappeared?" Rich pushed.

"I know it sounds crazy…"

"Old Man Hilzak?" Bill gasped. "You saw the ghost of Old Man Hilzak?"

"I saw something," Frank insisted. "But, just for a second."

"Oh, you're so full of shit, Bentworth," Logan scoffed. "He didn't see anything! He torched the place on purpose to cover up what he tried to do to Trixie."

Before Frank could respond, Rich jumped in. "Let's not even start this again," he averred. "It doesn't matter what Frank saw or didn't see. He didn't torch the place on purpose. It doesn't matter how we got here. The important thing is that we're here now. And like it or not, we're here together. At the very least, we're all guilty of trespassing, and probably more than one partying offence, not to mention manslaughter. If the cops want to rag on us, they can try to jack it up to a more serious murder charge. They're probably going to throw arson into the mix, too. This ain't no game, my friends! We're talking jail time here! We either hang together or we hang separately. Does everybody understand?"

"Yes," said a humble chorus of three.

"Good," Rich said. "Now, see if you can flag down a waitress. I need more coffee."

"Well, well, well," said an authoritative voice from behind. "Frances Bentworth, Richard Kirsch, Logan Tetweller and William Ambrose. Fancy seeing you four boys together in a diner bright and early on a fine Sunday morning like this."

The boys turned to face the two men in uniform.

"Actually," Logan confidently corrected. "It's about noontime, Officer Woods. But, who's counting? How are you, Officer Farley?"

"Wonderful," Farley grunted.

"I'm glad we found you all together," Woods said. "That'll save us the trouble of having to hunt you all down. Your mother told us you'd be here, Frances. We'd like to talk to you."

The boys shared a nervous glance.

"Certainly, Officer Woods," he said. His tone was polite almost to the point of being condescending. "What can I do for you?"

"As if you didn't know," Farley said.

"Ssshhh, Ed," Woods cautioned. "I'll handle this. Do you mind telling me where you were last night, Frances? Say, between the hours of 11:00 to 1:00?"

"Sure," he said. "We were all at my cousin Al's last night. Alan Cole. He owns Cole's Garage on Railroad Ave. We were just hanging out. We helped him with a few cars. He's a bit backed up on his work load. Why?"

"You weren't with Trixie Sinclair last night?" Woods asked. "Isn't she your girlfriend? Your mother says you two have been spending a lot of time together."

"Yes," Frank admitted. "She's my girlfriend, sort of. We've gone out a couple of times. But, we're not like 'engaged' or anything. She said she had something to do last night. And I figured she'd be bored at the garage. Why? What's this all about?"

"She was at the old Hilzak place last night," Woods said. "Didn't you introduce her to that place? That is a favorite party hangout for you boys, isn't it?"

Wrongful Secrets

"We've been there," Frank said reluctantly. "And sure, I took Trixie there once or twice. But, I wasn't there last night."

"Then, why was she there with a couple of her girlfriends?" Woods asked. "That's primarily a *guys'* party spot, isn't it?"

"We've known about that place for a while, boys," Farley informed them. "We know you guys are regulars at that old place. We've seen you. We left you alone 'cause you really weren't causing any harm. We figured you were the ones leaving empty beer bottles behind. We didn't really press the issue yet because you're usually not bad boys, you only go in small groups and you don't go up there too often. Still, we figured we'd keep an eye on you."

"Listen, officers," Logan asked. "What's this all about?"

"The old Hilzak place burned down last night," Woods said. "Trixie Sinclair, Kimberly Johnson and Cheyenne McCall were trapped inside. All three girls died in the fire."

"Trixie's dead?" Frank gasped.

"And, you had nothing to do with it?" Farley asked.

"Have a little compassion, pal!" Frank snapped. "She was my girlfriend!"

"It's like he said, officers," Rich reiterated. "We were at his cousin's garage last night. We were nowhere near the old Hilzak place."

"You really want to stick to that story?" Woods pressed.

"It's the truth!" Frank insisted.

"Why don't you boys just own up," Woods suggested. "We don't think you set the fire on purpose. We're sure it was an accident. Just admit it. You were there just having a few beers, you were a little tipsy, you knocked over an oil lamp or some candles or something, and the fire got out of control before you could stop it. All the dry wood and debris in that old house, it was sure to go up like a tinderbox. The whole thing was an accident. We'll go easy on you if you just confess. I'm sure any judge will feel the same way."

"Better Manslaughter than Murder," Farley added.

"How do you know the girls didn't go up there alone?" Bill asked. "Maybe they set the fire accidentally, just like you said."

"No," Woods shook his head. "The girls were upstairs. The fire started downstairs."

"Maybe it was the wind," Bill persisted. "The wind could have knocked over candles or whatever. Some of the windows are broken in that place."

"Just admit it," Farley ordered. "You boys were there last night!"

"I'm sorry, Officer," Logan said. "We were at Cole's Garage."

"Cole's Garage?" Woods said with a hint of doubt. "On Railroad Ave.?"

"Maybe Trixie was there with someone else last night," Frank said sadly. "Maybe we weren't as close as I thought. We'd only gone out a few times."

"And, where can we find this Alan Cole if he's not at the garage?" Woods asked.

"He lives just about four blocks up the street," Frank said. "773 Railroad Ave. It's a big white house with his black Dodge Ram parked in front when he's home."

Wrongful Secrets

"Well," Woods said with uncertainty. "We'll check your story. I still think you'd be doing yourselves a favor if you just own up to the truth right now."

"We've told you the truth," Logan said.

There was a tense pause.

"Okay," Woods sighed. "We'll look into it. We're sorry for the loss of your friends, boys. Stay in town. I'm sure we'll want to talk to you again."

"Where would we go?" Rich asked.

The cops glared at him. They gave each boy an authoritative glance. Then, they turned and left the diner.

As the glass doors closed, the boys heaved a sigh of relief.

"I hope we're doing the right thing," Bill said.

"Do you want to go to jail?" Frank asked.

"No."

"Then, we're doing the right thing."

"I don't like this either," Rich said. "But, Frank's right. This is the only way."

"Do you think they believed us?" Bill asked.

"If Al holds up our alibi," Frank said. "They'll have to believe us."

"Right again, Frank," Rich nodded. "Of course they didn't believe us. But, if Al comes through, we're in the clear. Those cops will have no choice but to leave us alone. The only question is: Can we trust your cousin, Bentworth?"

"Sure," Frank smiled. "He always looks out for me. He's a good man."

"I still don't like this," Bill said.

"Nobody likes this, Ambrose," Logan asserted. "But, we have no options here. We're going to be graduating high school in just a few months. Then, we have our whole lives ahead of us. Our lives and our futures depend on us sticking together and staying out of jail. We shouldn't all have to pay the rest of our lives for one stupid mistake Bentworth made on a drunken Saturday night."

"Watch your mouth," Frank warned.

"Oh relax, Bentworth," Logan said. "I'm on your side. We have to stick together for the sake of our futures. We could all have great things in store for us. I already know what Bentworth is going to be. An actor! That was quite a performance you gave, Frank. 'Trixie's dead? *Gasp!* Maybe she *was* cheating on me! Maybe we weren't as close as I thought! Boo Hoo!' That act deserves an Oscar."

"Hey," Frank argued. "That wasn't an act! Sure, there was a 98% chance Trixie was dead…"

"98%?" Rich interrupted. "You saw her face in the second floor window just before the flames closed in around her!"

"I know!" Frank spat. "I was there! But even though her mother told me on the phone that she never came home last night, I still wanted to hold on to a little bit of hope that somehow she survived! I know it was crazy, but I didn't want to believe she was gone! Hearing it from the cops destroyed my last hope! Trixie's dead! So are Kim and Cheyenne! They're all dead! And I killed them!"

No one dared to speak.

"And, it hurts knowing that Trixie and I weren't as close as I thought," Frank continued. "She proved that to me last night, too!"

Still, nobody said a word.

"I'll never forget her face in the window," Frank went on. "So beautiful, helpless and terrified! And the flames surrounded her before I could move! She disappeared, and all I could hear was the screams! The horrible, endless screams! The last thing I saw before I had to turn away was…"

He stopped himself.

"What?" Rich asked. "What was the last thing you saw?"

Frank took a deep breath for courage.

"You're going to think I'm nuts," he said. "But as the window was engulfed in flames, I saw Hilzak's face!"

"Hilzak?" Logan scoffed. "You saw Old Man Hilzak in the flames?"

"I know it sounds crazy," Frank insisted. "But, I saw his face right in the middle of the fire! He looked right at me! It was as if he knew the fire was my fault! He looked right at me, and I swear he said, 'Some people never die! Some things never end!'"

"He said what?" Logan questioned. "I think you *are* going nuts, Bentworth. This whole thing is starting to get to you. Maybe you should go home and lie down."

"I don't care whether you believe me or not," Frank said. "That's what happened! I just…I've got to get out of here!"

"Sure," Rich said. He watched his friend stand. "That's probably a good idea. Just be careful. Watch your actions. Remember, we're all in this together."

"Don't worry about me," Frank said. "I'll be fine. I just need to be alone for a while."

He turned. He marched out of the diner with determination.

The three boys watched him leave.

When he was gone, Bill asked, "Do you think he's okay?"

"We can only hope," Rich said. "He just has to keep his head on straight. We all have to keep our heads together. We just have to stick to our story."

"That's cool," Bill said. "Don't worry. *I'm* not going to jail!"

Outside, it was cold and cloudy. A police patrol car was heading toward Railroad Ave.

"Do you think those boys were lying?" Farley asked.

"I'm almost certain of it."

"What about this Cole fellow?" Farley asked. "Do you think he'll hold up their story?"

"We won't know until we get there."

"We should have done something about that Hilzak house months ago," Farley said. "We knew it was unsafe. And high school kids shouldn't be playing around places like that. They should have better things to do with their time."

"We were kids once," Woods said. "We know what it's like. They weren't causing any real trouble. We would have had to chase them around, miss some late night movie marathons, deal with angry parents … it would have been a mountain of paperwork…"

"Yeah," Farley interrupted. "And look where it got us. Three dead teenage girls. We had to deal with angry parents this morning, didn't we?"

"And they're going to stay angry for a long time," Woods agreed. "I never thought I'd see something like this in such a small town. It really gets to you."

"Yes it does," Farley muttered. After a respectful pause, he added, "And, there were some land developers interested in that area, too. A story like this could drive away potential buyers. This town could use the money."

"Oh, the stigma of an incident like this may last a year or two," Woods imparted. "But, the almighty dollar will win out eventually. Don't you worry. That section of the hillside will get sold soon enough. Believe me."

"I still want to hear from this Cole fellow," Farley said. "Do you really think the boys were at his place last night?"

"Maybe."

"Do you think Cole would lie to protect his cousin?"

"Anything's possible," Woods said. "Only one thing's for certain. If he does, we may have to let those kids go. I hate to say it, but it's true. There's nothing we can do about it. If they all stick together, those boys might just get away with causing the wrongful deaths of three innocent young girls."

Somewhere on the street, Frank wiped his eyes. A tragic picture flashed through his mind. Those words kept ringing in his ears:

"Some people never die! Some things never end!"

Chapter 2
The Man in the Fireplace

"Mrs. Gould, isn't it?"

"Please," she said. "Call me Carol."

"All right," he said as he shook her hand. "You've done a magnificent job with this place, Carol. Everything looks wonderful."

"Thank you."

"Not too big," he continued. "Not too small. It all looks very elegant. How many rooms do you have?"

"We have thirty rooms," she said. "Not what you would call luxury suites, but every room is tasteful and comfortable. Through those doors we have a dining area. It's almost a small restaurant. Twenty-five tables that seat four people each. A small, intimate bar that's well stocked. It's not the fanciest place in the world, but we're proud of it."

"As well you should be," he nodded. "The place looks absolutely splendid. Even the lobby is spacious and beautiful. Does that fireplace really work?"

"Oh, yes," she said. "It's fully functional. We use it this time of year, too. We invite some of our guests to spend time down here on cold winter evenings. It's great to cozy up to a nice, warm fire on a cold January evening with a glass of wine or a hot cup of cocoa. This really isn't part of the lobby, though. We call it The Den. We've gotten some great compliments."

"I'm sure you have."

"You should join us one evening," she offered. "Tonight, perhaps?"

"Yes," the younger gentleman agreed. He put his arm around Carol. "We'd love to have you. It's the least we could do."

"Thank you, Leon," he said. "I may just take you up on that. I was just telling your wife what a splendid job you've done here."

"Thank you, Mr. Schumacker," he said. "We've done our best."

"There's no need for formality here," he said. "Call me Michael."

"We never would have been able to build The Hillside Inn without that loan, Michael," he said. "I can't tell you how grateful we are."

"I'm just glad everything turned out so well," Schumacker said. "And, I'm sorry it took me so long to get over to this part of town to get a look at the place. You've been open for about a year now, haven't you?"

"Yes," he said. "We opened a year ago this month."

"Congratulations, you two," Schumacker smiled. "I'm sure you'll have many happy years here."

"I heard you talking to Carol about the fireplace," he pointed out.

"Oh, yes," Schumacker said. "It certainly is a grand structure. It's a focal point in this big, beautiful room."

"It sure is," he agreed. "It's much bigger than…"

He stopped himself.

After an awkward pause, Schumacker said, "That's alright, Leon. You know I'm well versed in the history of this region. I'm well aware of what happened on this site. Is that what you were going to mention? The house that used to stand on this spot?"

"Yes," he admitted. "The old Hilzak house. It used to stand almost directly on this spot. In fact, our fireplace was practically built on the remnants of the old original fireplace. That was the architect's idea. I think he has a morbid sense of humor. Of course, our fireplace is much bigger than its predecessor."

"It would have to be," Schumacker said. "The old house wasn't very large. It was little more than a two-story shack. Do you know the *real* story of the Hilzak tragedy?"

"The *real* story?" Carol asked.

"I was fascinated by your notion of building the inn over the ruins of the Hilzak house," Schumacker said. "That's one of the reasons I considered the loan in the first place. I did some research before I approved the loan. Although rumors abound, the true story never made the headlines."

"What do you mean, Michael?" Leon asked.

"A lot of people," Schumacker explained. "Are under the impression that Mortimer Hilzak's wife and daughters died from some common ailment like the measles or smallpox or something. That, combined with a bad harvest supposedly drove him over the edge. According to the legend, he chopped up his son with an axe and then hanged himself in the bedroom."

"That's what we heard," Leon said.

"My extensive research revealed a different story," Schumacker imparted. "When they found Mortimer's body, it was discovered that he had a disease very similar to syphilis. That is the most likely reason for why he went mad."

"Syphilis?" Leon asked.

"His wife and daughters got very sick, alright," Schumacker explained. "But, it is assumed by the authorities that they did not die from their illness. And they didn't have the measles."

"You're kidding," Leon gasped. "His wife *and* his daughters? You don't mean…"

"Yes," Schumacker nodded. "According to the authorities. Old Mortimer was not a very nice or innocent man. In those days, you could get away with burying bodies without autopsies. Especially, if you had the right friends. He managed to get word to somebody that he'd buried his wife and daughters days before he chopped up his son."

"How gruesome!" Carol said.

"Apparently," Schumacker said. "He had friends that kept the story from getting publicized. And, it's remained a reasonably well-kept secret to this day."

"That's awful," Leon said. "And, you still gave us the loan after finding out about all that?"

"Sure," Schumacker said. "Why not? I love stories like that. Besides, that was nearly 150 years ago. Then again, that's not the only tragedy that occurred on this site."

"Yes, we know," Leon said. "Nineteen years before we opened the inn, the old Hilzak place burned down. Three teenage girls were killed in the fire."

"That's right," Schumacker expounded. "Evidently, some high school kids were using it as a hangout for drinking beer and partying. Nobody really knows what happened. But somehow, they accidentally set the place on fire. It's not surprising the place went up like kindling. All that old, dry wood. Frankly, it's more of a shock that the building hadn't already collapsed before then."

"Did anyone survive the fire?" Carol asked.

"It was suspected that three or four boys were with them when the fire started," Schumacker told them. "The boys were questioned, but never charged. Details are a bit fuzzy. The police at the time thought the fire was probably an accident. They figured whoever started the fire survived. But despite suspicions, nobody was ever charged for the tragic deaths of three girls who were only months away from graduating high school."

"That's very sad," Carol said. "I'd heard some girls died in the fire, but I'd never heard the whole story."

"That was in January 1984," Leon added. "Then one year ago, nineteen years after the Hilzak house burned down, we opened this place. It was almost exactly nineteen years after the tragedy."

"It was *exactly* nineteen years," a solemn little voice said. "The exact same week."

They turned to see the somber face of the young boy.

"How would you know, Adam?" Leon said. "You weren't even born yet. Mr. Schumacker, this is our son Adam. He'll be seven next month."

"Hello, Adam," Schumacker smiled. "Nice to meet you."

The boy looked directly up at the stranger.

"He doesn't like you."

"Adam!" Carol gasped. "That wasn't very nice! Tell Mr. Schumacker you're sorry this instant!"

"He doesn't like you."

"Adam!" Carol scolded. "What's wrong with you? I forbid you to talk to our guest that way! Tell him you're sorry!"

The boy just stared at the older gentleman.

"Adam…" Leon began.

"That's alright," Schumacker said. "Let him talk. Who doesn't like me, Adam?"

"My friend."

"Who's your friend?" Schumacker asked. "Why doesn't he like me?"

"He just doesn't."

There was a heavy silence.

Then, Adam turned and walked away.

"Adam!" Carol ordered. "You come back here and apologize!"

The boy just kept walking slowly toward the door.

"Adam!" Leon called.

"That's okay," Schumacker forced a smile. "Let him go. Believe me. It's fine."

"I can't tell you how sorry I am, Mr. Schumacker," Carol said nervously. "He never behaves like that. He's usually such a good boy. I don't know what could have gotten into him."

"It's fine," he repeated. "Really. Don't worry about it."

Donald Gorman

"It's not fine, Michael," Leon said. "He shouldn't have talked to you like that. Please accept our apologies. Something must be wrong. I'll talk to him."

"Believe me," he said. "Don't let it bother you. I know what boys are like. I used to be one."

"At the very least," Leon said. "Please accept our invitation to dinner here tonight as our guest. Everything is on the house."

"That's very kind of you," the old man said. "But, I really can't make it tonight. I have a prior engagement."

"That's a shame," Carol said.

"But, I may stop over later this evening for a glass of wine by the fireplace," he said. "If you plan on having a fire going. Say around 10:00 or so?"

"Absolutely," Leon said.

"And, my wife will probably be with me," he said. "If that's okay."

"We'd love to meet her," Carol said.

"Everything will be free for the both of you," Leon assured him. "We'll treat you both in grand style."

"Please don't make a fuss," he said. "It's not necessary. Just a nice glass of wine by the fire sounds wonderful. I'm sure it will be perfectly charming. My wife will love it."

"I'm sure she will, Michael," Leon said.

"Well, I must be off now," he said. "It's been great seeing you both again. And, I must say I'm very impressed with what you've done with this place. Everything looks so fantastic. I'm sure it will be a success."

"Thank you," Carol said. "It was nice to see you again too. We look forward to meeting your wife this evening."

"Yes," Leon agreed. "Thanks for everything."

Wrongful Secrets

"Good-bye," he said while shaking Leon's hand. "And to you too, Mrs. Gould. Perhaps I'll see you this evening."

"We hope so," Leon said.

He put his arm around his wife's shoulder as they watched the old man cross the lobby. The smiles never left their faces until their guest was out the door.

Then, they turned to each other.

"Well," Leon sighed. "That was a nice meeting, for the most part."

"I wonder what got into Adam," she said. "That was so unlike him."

"I'd better go have a talk with that boy," he said.

"No," she said. "Let me go check on him. Maybe he's not feeling well. Maybe something's wrong. Let me talk to him."

"Fine," he said. "I have some paperwork to catch up on anyway. Let me know how it goes. Okay?"

"Sure," she said. "See you later."

"'Bye, honey," he said. "And, be firm with him."

She nodded. She turned in the direction her son had taken when leaving the room.

Her expression was pensive. She wondered what could have been wrong.

She called her son's name. Then, she ran off to find him.

✦

He chopped an onion. He didn't even think as he did it. It was as if he'd been chopping onions all his life.

Then, he was chopping something else.

Donald Gorman

The sizzle of three frying pans were like music to his ears. The pans sizzled in harmony like tenors singing on stage.

C minor. It was beautiful.

He had no time to appreciate the sound. He was creating his own art...mixing ingredients in a saucepan. He had two more entrees to begin.

He poured the sauce into another pan. He set it to simmer on a low heat.

"How's everything going, Glen?" came a voice from behind.

He instinctively wiped his hands as he spun around. "Not bad, Mr. Gould," he said. "Everything's under control."

"Glad to hear it," he said. "The lunch rush is just starting."

"We're ready for anything," Glen assured him.

"Good," he nodded. "Keep up the good work."

"You bet."

He adjusted his chef's hat as he turned back to his cooking. Keeping an eye on a number of dishes all at once was second nature to him. Despite his young age, he was a master in the kitchen. It was a skill he enjoyed.

"I saw you talking to Mr. Gould," a voice observed from behind. "Is everything okay?"

He turned and smiled.

"Everything's fine, Dawn," he said. "How are you?"

"Busy," she said. "I wish the Goulds would hire more maids. It's hard keeping up with the workload. Half of the rooms just checked out. The people in the other rooms won't let you go in and clean right away."

"Welcome to the grand world of serving the public," he said.

"It's not so bad, I suppose," she shrugged. "I like cleaning. At least, it's a decent job for the time being. I wouldn't want to do it for the rest of my life, though. It can get so monotonous! And, I still don't see why we have to wear these lame uniforms."

"I think you look beautiful in your uniform," he said.

"Thank you," she said with a shy smile. "Still, these uniforms seem so unnecessary."

"If you'd like to take it off," he joked. "I'll guard the door for you."

"No, thank you," she said knowingly. "I have to get back to work. And, you have something burning on the stove."

"Nothing's burning," he informed her. "That's the sauce for the chicken. It's supposed to smell like that at this stage of the cooking process."

"It smells horrible!"

"Give it a minute," he said. "You'll think your nose died and went to Heaven."

"I'm not even going to pursue that line of thinking," she said. "I have work to do."

"So do I," he said. "More orders are coming in. But, don't worry. I'll talk to Mr. Gould about hiring more maids."

"Thanks," she said. "Do you think he'll listen to you?"

"I doubt it," he said. "I don't have much pull around here. I agree with you, though. There's not enough of you girls on staff for such a big place. You'd think with their money, the Goulds could hire more help."

"Where do you think they got that kind of cash at such a young age?" she asked. "They're only in their thirties, aren't they?"

"Mid-thirties, I'd guess," he said. "I can't imagine where they got their money from. It can't be from anything legal."

"By the way," she added. "Have you seen little Adam? His mother was looking for him."

"No," he said. "I've been busy in here all morning. I hope the kid's okay. He's been getting a little creepy lately."

"You're not kidding," she agreed. "He was such a doll when I started working here. But this last month or so, he just seems so quiet. So secretive. It seems like he's got something deep on his mind."

"He's too young to have anything on his mind," he said.

"Well, what do you think is wrong?"

"Who knows?"

"Mmmmm," she cooed. "You were right about that sauce! It's starting to smell wonderful now."

"See?" he said. "I told you. I'm a genius in the kitchen."

"I believe you."

"Maybe I can cook for you some night," he offered. "Hopefully, some night soon."

"Maybe I'll take you up on that some night," she smiled.

There was a pause.

"Well," she finally said. "I have things to dust and beds to make."

"And, I have chickens to fry," he grinned. "'Bye, Dawn."

"See you later, Glen."

He watched her leave. He shook his head with a smile.

Then, he turned back to his food. More than one dish was nearly ready to serve.

And, the sauce was just about done.

"Adam?"

He barely grunted a response.

"Please look at me when I talk to you."

He reluctantly tore his attention away from the toy trucks on the carpet.

"I want to talk to you, young man."

"What is it, Mom?"

"Why were you so rude to Mr. Schumacker this morning?" she asked.

"I dunno," he shrugged.

"That was mean, what you said," she told him. "Why would you say those things to a complete stranger?"

"No reason."

"Are you feeling okay?" she asked. "Let me feel your forehead."

She knelt beside where he was sitting on the floor. She reached out to him.

He tried to pull away.

"I'm fine, Mom," he whined.

"You're not warm," she observed. "Does anything hurt?"

"No."

"Then, what's wrong?"

"Nothing!"

"You never used to act this way, Adam," she said. "What's going on? Is anyone giving you trouble at school?"

"School's fine, Mom."

She stood. She looked down at her son.

"Maybe I should take you to the doctor," she suggested.

"I don't need the doctor," he argued. "Nothing's wrong."

"Then, why did you talk to that man that way?" she persisted. "You've never even seen him before. Why would you say those things?"

"It don't matter," he said. "I didn't mean nothing by it."

"You said your friend doesn't like him," she recalled. "Who's your friend?"

"Nobody."

"Adam," she said as only a mother can. "Who is the friend you were talking about?"

"Some guy," he reluctantly muttered. "A man."

"A man?" she asked. "What man?"

"The man in the fireplace."

"Man in the fireplace?" she asked with a puzzled expression. "Which man? Which fireplace? Are you talking about *our* fireplace? The one downstairs? In The Den?"

He nodded.

"When did you see a man in our fireplace?" she asked.

"You can't really see him," he explained. "He's just there. He talks to me."

"He's invisible?" she asked. "An invisible man in our fireplace talks to you?"

He nodded again.

A chill ran up her spine. Sure...lots of kids have imaginary friends. But, most of them are friendly. Most of them are only playtime companions.

Most of them don't tell you to insult random strangers.

She decided to postpone judgment until she got some answers.

"What does he say to you?" she asked.

"Nothing."

"Adam," she said firmly. "Please answer me. What does he tell you?"

The boy looked down at his toy trucks. He began to fidget a bit.

"Just stuff," he finally mumbled. "Stuff about this place."

"You told Mr. Schumacker that we opened the inn exactly nineteen years after the old Hilzak house burned down," she reminded. "Did your friend tell you that?"

"Yes."

"What else did he tell you?"

He looked up at her.

"He said teenagers were in the house that night," he replied. "He said they were doing bad things. One boy even tried to hurt a girl. And then, he lied about it. My friend doesn't like when people do bad things. 'Specially, if they try to hide it. That's why he was glad when Mr. Hilzak burned the place down."

"Your friend told you all that?" she asked.

"Yes," he muttered. "He didn't like Mr. Hilzak, either."

She tried to mask her growing concern.

"Does your friend have a name?" she asked.

The boy quickly turned his gaze back to the toys on the floor. He was silent for a minute. Then, he looked back up at his mother.

"Mom?" he asked meekly. "Can I play with my trucks now?"

She studied his face. The fearful look in his eyes made her nervous.

"Alright, sweetie," she said. "But the next time you see Mr. Schumacker, I want you to tell him you're sorry. Okay?"

"Okay, Mom."

She watched him play for a moment. A knot tightened in her gut.

Something was wrong! A mother always knows!

"I told you not to call me at this number!"

"This is important," said the voice on the phone. "That Canadian deal is going through now. I just got the call. If you want to take advantage of that shift in proceeds before Traeger gets his hands on it, you have to act immediately."

"Damn it!" he said. "I have plans tonight!"

"Suit yourself," said the voice. "If you want to let 40 million bucks slip through your fingers, it leaves more for me. I'm not going to let Traeger get that deal. And of course, if we all miss out, that money will be in Stockholm before dawn."

"I hate these deals!"

"You don't mind the cash."

"Even if we pull this off," he asked. "Won't Stockholm notice their missing that money? That's a sizable chunk of change."

"Sure," said the voice. "They'll miss it eventually. But, they'll never be able to trace it to us. Besides, all that money will be buried in a variety of stocks etc. before anyone figures it out."

"I still think this is too much to skim at one time," he said. "You're asking for trouble. Someone's bound to notice."

"It's all been taken care of."

"I know," he said. "That's what scares me."

"Come on, buddy," said the voice on the phone. "Don't flake out on me now. This is the big pay-off. People had to die to set this thing up."

"That's part of the problem," he said. "I never wanted it to go this far. I'm a banker, not a murderer!"

"Nobody's asking you to kill anyone," coaxed the caller. "All you have to do is make the transfer. Punch a few computer keys, and you're done. Now, come on! We have to act immediately. Are you in or out?"

He thought for a moment.

"Alright," he sighed. "I'm in."

"Good man!" said the caller. "Don't worry. Everything will go smoothly. You're doing the right thing. Call me in the morning."

"Sure," he said. "And, don't call this number anymore."

"Hey," said the voice. "After I get my slice of that 40 million, I won't even know you exist anymore."

"Did you talk to Adam?"

"Yes."

"What did he say?"

"He has an imaginary friend who lives in the fireplace," she told him.

"In the fireplace?" he said. "That's a new one. Oh well. It's not uncommon for kids to have imaginary friends. And, I guess even made-up people have to live somewhere."

"I'm a little concerned."

"Why?"

"Adam said his friend tells him things," she explained. "About the house. His friend told him that we opened this inn exactly 19 years to the week that the old Hilzak place burned down."

"So?" he asked. "Even if it's true, he could have heard that anywhere! From any one of 5,000 people. We chose this site on purpose. Remember? People talk about its history when they come through here. It's part of the charm of this place."

"He talked about the teenagers in the house," she said. "The night it burned down. He knew what the kids were doing. He said one of the boys tried to hurt one of the girls. He said his friend was glad that Hilzak burned the place down."

"You're making too much of this, Carol," he assured her. "Like I said...Adam could have heard all sorts of rumors from all sorts of people who have been parading through here this past year. Even if he made up some of his story, who cares?"

"You didn't see the look on his face," she pointed out. "Or hear the sound in his voice. He seemed scared."

"So, what are you suggesting?" he scoffed. "Are you saying the place is really haunted? Do we have ghosts living in our fireplace? Are they telling our son to go around insulting our guests?"

"Have you paid any attention to your son this past month or so, Leon?" she asserted. "Haven't you noticed he's grown quiet and withdrawn?"

"Are you blaming this on me now?" he argued. "I'm not spending enough time with Adam, and that's why he sees imaginary men living in our fireplace? Ghosts who tell him the same scary rumors that all our guests regurgitate?"

"That's not what I'm saying!"

"Are you saying this place really is haunted?" he continued. "Maybe that's my fault too!"

"Stop it, Leon!" she demanded. "I'm not blaming you for anything! I'm not saying the place is really haunted! I'm just telling you that I'm worried about Adam! It's not normal for a boy his age to act the way he's been acting lately."

"It must be the ghosts."

"This isn't a joke, Leon!"

"Listen," he said with a softening tone. "If the kid's been a little off lately, it's not that big a deal. Kids go through moods. Hell...we all do. Let it go. He'll get over it."

"Maybe you're right," she sighed. "Maybe I'm overreacting."

"I'm sure you are," he said.

He took her in his arms. He kissed her.

"It happens sometimes," he continued. "It's the sign of a good mother."

"It's just that he looked so sincere," she said as she held him. "He looked so frightened."

"Whatever it is," he assured her. "I'm sure it'll all blow over."

"I hope so," she said. "I'm still going to keep an eye on him."

"Fine. You do that."

"And as far as ghosts are concerned," she reminded. "You know very well there have been at least three sightings of an old man carrying an axe up the stairs. And, one guy on the second floor saw the image of a teenage girl. She looked like she was calling for help over by the window."

"And, you believe these crackpots?"

"They're our guests," she pointed out. "I don't want to call them liars."

"The stories are good for business," he said. "But, face it. Old Man Hilzak and those girls departed from this property a long time ago."

"I know," she said. "But, you've got to love a good, juicy ghost story."

"That's why we bought the place," he said. "Did you tell Adam to apologize to Mr. Schumacker?"

"Yes," she said. "Everything's taken care of."

"Good," he said. He let her go. "Then, I'd better get back to work before Old Man Hilzak comes in and chops off my hands."

"You're not funny, Leon."

Wrongful Secrets

"Rita?" he asked. "Have you seen Dawn?"

"I think she's still finishing up in Room 19," she said. "She should be another twenty minutes or so. Why?"

"I have her sandwich ready," he said. "I've been doing the same thing for her as I've been doing for you. Except she likes chicken salad instead of tuna."

"So, my sandwich is ready?"

"Tuna on whole wheat," he said. "Light on the lettuce and mayo. Just the way you like it."

"Thanks, Glen," she beamed. "You're the best!"

"Don't thank me," he said. "It still comes out of your salary. Mr. Gould is a stickler for making me keep a tab for the maids."

"You still make the best tuna in the state of Oregon," she said.

"Thanks," he said. "I wonder if I should hang around and wait for Dawn. I wonder what's keeping her. It's past 8:30. Is she pushing for overtime or something?"

"There's no point in hanging around," she said. "You can leave her food in the refrigerator and just leave a note on the counter. She'll find it. Or tell Sam to give it to her when she comes down. See? You don't need to stay here, unless you have some other reason to see her."

"Not really."

She studied his expression.

"Why, Glen Cummings!" she gasped with mock surprise. "Do you have a thing for our little Miss Dawn Wyler?"

"No."

"Oh, my God," she chuckled. "You do! You like Dawn! It's written all over your face! Wait 'til I tell her!"

"I do not," he insisted. "And, don't you dare say a word to her! You don't even know what you're talking about!"

"This is great!" she teased. "I can just picture the headlines in the tabloids."

"Tabloids?" he asked. "I'm the cook in an upstate Oregon hotel, and she's a maid. What tabloid could possibly be interested in us?"

"Still," she smiled. "This just makes my day!"

"There's nothing to get excited about, Rita," he insisted. "I just wanted to make sure Dawn got her food."

"Fine, Glen," she grinned. "Whatever you say. Thanks again for the sandwich, sweetheart. And don't worry. Your secret's safe with me."

She headed for the door.

He called after her, "Don't even start, Rita! There's no secret!"

She was gone.

He stood for a moment. He considered waiting.

After a moment's reflection, he put the sandwich in the refrigerator.

"Hey, Sam!" he called. "When Dawn Wyler comes down, tell her I put her food in the 'fridge. Okay?"

"Sure thing."

"Thanks," he called. "Good night."

"'Bye."

He put on his coat. He walked slowly out of the large kitchen.

"I hope this isn't too late for you."

Wrongful Secrets

"Not at all," he said. "It's only twenty minutes to eleven. It's the perfect time for a glass of wine by the fire. We're glad you could make it, Michael."

"Thank you," he said. "This is my wife, Olivia. And this is Leon Gould and his wife Carol. They own this inn."

"We're delighted to meet you, Mrs. Schumacker," Leon said. "We're glad you could make it."

"Yes," Carol agreed. "Please make yourself at home. Can I take your coats?"

"The pleasure is mine," she said. "And please call me Olivia."

"We saved some nice, plush, comfortable chairs for you over by the fire," Leon offered. "Take a seat. Would you like anything to drink? Wine? Cocoa? Anything you want is on the house."

"A nice glass of red wine would be wonderful," she said as she sat. "Thank you."

"Coming right up," Leon said. "Anything for you, Michael?"

"I'll have what my wife is having," he said.

"Fine," Leon said. "I'll only be a moment."

Carol returned from hanging their coats. "I hope we're not keeping you up," she said. "We're so happy you're here."

"I wouldn't have missed it," Olivia said. "You have a lovely inn. I was admiring it from outside. It's a beautiful building."

"Thank you," she said. "We're very proud of it."

"As you should be," Olivia nodded. "And this room is absolutely elegant. A roaring fire in a luxurious fireplace. Soft lighting. What could be better?"

"I'm glad you approve," she said.

"The atmosphere is marvelous," Michael said. "I could watch that fire forever."

"It's so cozy," Olivia said.

"Here's your wine," Leon said.

The Schumackers each took their drink.

"You're both so young," Olivia observed. "How could you afford to build a place like this at your age? You're only in your mid-thirties, aren't you?"

"I'm 38," he said. "Carol is 35. I've had a lot of business training. I got a job managing my uncle's company at an early age. It paid well. We saved. We had a lot of luck with the stock market. Life's been good to us."

"And, that loan from your husband didn't hurt," Carol added.

"Well, I was only too glad to help," Michael said. "It sounded like a solid business venture. You seemed like a good risk."

They shared a small laugh.

"Plus," Michael continued. "The notoriously macabre history of this location made the whole deal irresistible."

"That's right," Olivia nodded. "This spot was infamous for supernatural sightings of various members of the Hilzak family even when the old house was still standing. But since those girls died in that fire twenty years ago, their spirits have been reputedly visible as well. Have you had any sightings since you opened the inn?"

"Well," Leon reluctantly admitted. "There has been the occasional guest who has reported a momentary manifestation. Just a few. There has never been more than one person who's ever seen anything. So, nothing can be verified."

Wrongful Secrets

"That's bound to happen," Olivia said.

"It's great for business," Carol said. "Lots of people come here hoping to see something. And if they go home convinced that they saw Old Man Hilzak, I guess that makes their trip more memorable."

"And, if they tell their friends," Leon added. "That's all the better for us."

"Have either of you seen anything?" Michael asked.

"No," Leon said. "But, don't tell any of our guests."

They shared another laugh.

"Don't worry," Olivia said. "We won't spill your secret. Michael only asked because he knows I'm a nut for that sort of thing."

"So are we," Carol admitted. "That's why we chose this location."

"Everything is wonderful," Michael said. "Even the wine is excellent, by the way."

"I'm glad you like it," Leon said.

"It's all perfectly charming," Olivia smiled. "A beautiful evening by the fireside with a superb glass of wine. Lovely company. I'm very glad we came."

"Thank you," Carol smiled.

"Yes," Michael agreed. "You've done a splendid job. I think we can look forward to a...*OW!*"

Everyone sat up to see what had happened.

Carol stared in disbelief at her son. He was dressed in his pajamas. He was standing behind Michael's chair. A child's baseball bat was clutched in his hands.

"Adam!" she scolded. "Did you just hit Mr. Schumacker with your bat?"

"No."

"Don't lie to me, Adam," she pressed. "You're still holding the bat!"

"I didn't mean to."

"Why aren't you in bed?" she asked. "It's way past your bedtime."

"I dunno."

"Tell Mr. Schumacker you're sorry!"

"Sorry, Mr. Schumacker."

"That's okay," he said. "I'm sure it was an accident. I'm…*OW! OW!*"

"Adam!" his mother scolded. "You just hit him again! Twice!"

"No I didn't."

"Stop lying, Adam!" she demanded. "I saw you hit him! We all saw you hit him! Give me the bat!"

"But, Mom…"

"Don't argue, young man," she insisted. "Give it to me!"

"Okay."

She took the weapon from her son. "Does this have anything to do with that friend you were telling me about earlier?" she asked.

"Kind of."

"Friend?" Olivia asked. "What friend?"

"Adam has an imaginary friend who lives in the fireplace," Carol told them. "For some reason, this friend doesn't like Michael."

"Ah, yes," Michael nodded. "Adam has a friend. Your friend lives in the fireplace, Adam? Is he there now?"

"He's always there," Adam said. "And he's not 'maginary."

Wrongful Secrets

"It's awful hot in there now, Adam," Michael said. "How can he stand the heat?"

Adam shrugged.

"That's enough now, son," Leon ordered. "Tell Mr. Schumacker you're sorry. Then, it's back to bed for you."

"Sorry."

"That's alright."

"Randy Dalton," Adam said.

Michael's face turned white. His eyes grew wide. His jaw dropped.

"What did you say?" he stammered.

"Was Randy Dalton sorry, Mr. Schumacker?" Adam asked.

"Where did you hear that name, Adam?" Michael asked. "Was it your friend?"

Adam nodded.

"Listen to me, Adam," Michael said urgently. "This is very important. Who is your friend? Where do you know him from?"

Adam looked at Michael and pointed at the fireplace.

Everyone stared at the fire blazing gloriously in its home.

"This is no joke, Adam!" Michael insisted. "Who is your friend?"

"I told you already!"

Michael just stared at the boy in disbelief.

"I have to go to bed now," Adam said.

"I'll take him upstairs," Carol offered. "I'm really sorry about this, Michael. It's really late for Adam. He must be exhausted."

She handed the bat to Leon. She led her son to the stairs.

"We're going to have a long talk in the morning, young man," Leon warned. "I'm sorry, Michael. He's usually a good kid. Let me get you both another glass of wine."

"I don't think so," he said. "Suddenly, I'm not feeling so well. Maybe we should go."

"Are you sure?" Leon said. "You haven't been here long. Are you alright? Would you like to lie down for a while?"

"No," he said. "I'll be fine."

"What's wrong, Michael?" Olivia asked. "What did that boy say?"

"Nothing," he said. "It's alright."

"I'll have a good, stern talk with him tomorrow," Leon assured. "His overall behavior was atrocious!"

"Believe me," he said. "It's not that bad. I...I just wish I knew who this friend is."

"Who is that name he mentioned, Michael?" Olivia asked. "Randy Dalton, was it?"

"Nobody!" he insisted. "Forget you ever heard the name! I...I..."

He paused to take a few deep breaths.

"Maybe I can get you some cocoa instead of wine," Leon suggested. "Or something stronger, maybe? Would you like some aspirin?"

"On second thought," he sighed. "Perhaps I will have another glass of wine. It'll help settle my nerves."

"Absolutely," Leon said. "Anything for you, Olivia?"

"Another glass of that splendid wine would be lovely," she said. "Thank you."

"Certainly," Leon smiled. "I'll only be a minute."

When he was gone, Olivia asked, "So, tell the truth, Michael. What did that boy say that got you so upset?"

Wrongful Secrets

"Let it go, dear," he said. "It's not that important. There's just something creepy about that kid that I don't like."

"I have to agree with you there," she nodded. "The boy should not be hitting strangers with baseball bats. The Goulds are going to have trouble raising that boy. I can feel it."

Upstairs, Carol was tucking her son into bed.

"So, do you understand me, Adam?" she asked. "I don't want you to ever hit anyone with a baseball bat ever again. Do you hear me?"

"Yes, Mom."

"And, who was that person you mentioned?" she continued. "Randy Dalton?"

"I dunno."

"Adam," she insisted. "Tell me."

"He's somebody that man knows," he reluctantly imparted. "He did something bad to Randy Dalton, and he's keeping it a secret. He doesn't want anybody to know the bad thing he did to Randy Dalton."

"How do you know that?" she asked. "Your friend in the fireplace again?"

"He doesn't like when people keep really bad secrets," he nodded.

"Yes," she said. "You told me that. You know, you really upset Mr. Schumacker tonight. That was a very bad thing."

"I'm sorry."

"I want to hear more about this friend of yours," she said. "I want you to tell me the truth."

"I'm tired, Mom," he muttered. "I want to go to sleep."

Donald Gorman

She looked down at the boy. She brushed the hair out of his face with her fingers. She leaned over and kissed his forehead.

"Okay," she smiled softly. "We'll talk tomorrow. Good night. I love you."

"Love you, too," he said. "G'night."

She stood and walked toward the door. She took one last look at him before she left. She closed the door behind her.

The boy was alone in bed. He was in total darkness.

He opened his eyes. He listened.

"I'm sorry," he said. "I tried. I really did. You saw. I tried."

He pulled the covers tightly around him as he listened.

"Okay," he said. "I'll do better tomorrow. I promise."

The boy closed his eyes. He went to sleep.

Chapter 3
Surprises

The Hillside Inn was being pelted by large, heavy snowflakes in the morning. It was windy and cold. A few inches of fresh, white snow already blanketed the grounds. The authorities expected that amount to double by the time this cold front passed. This didn't even rate as a storm in this area. But, driving was still unpleasant.

Three men were shoveling the parking lot beneath a thick cover of clouds that were nearly as white as the untouched lawn.

Inside, it was much more comfortable.

Two people stood behind the long reception desk in the lobby. The man was even younger than his boss.

"Did your husband find you, Mrs. Gould?" he asked.

"No," she said. "Why?"

"I think he wanted to talk to your son," he said.

"Adam?" she said. "I can imagine why my husband wanted to see him. But, he seemed fine when I saw him at breakfast."

"Is something wrong with Adam?" he asked.

"Nothing we can't handle," she said. "Just a few minor behavior problems. He's been in a bit of a mood lately."

"I hope he's okay."

"I'm sure he's fine, Jeffrey," she smiled. "But, thanks for your concern."

A couple approached the desk. They appeared to be in their forties. They were bundled up in warm winter clothing.

The man placed a key on the counter.

"We'll be going out for the day," he announced. "But, we should be back in the evening. We might even have dinner here. The restaurant area looks wonderful."

"Did you have a nice stay last night, Mr. Rodriguez?" he asked.

"Yes," he said. "It's a beautiful room. Very plush. Thank you."

"Are you sure these rooms are safe?" his wife asked.

"Couldn't be safer," he said. "Why? Is there a problem, Mrs. Rodriguez?"

"No," she said. "It's just that I thought I saw something last night."

"What did you see?"

"I can't be sure," she said. "It was a bright light over by the window. It only lasted for a few seconds. It almost looked like a girl. A young girl. She couldn't have been twenty. She looked scared. It was almost as if she was calling for help. Then suddenly, she was gone."

"You saw a ghost, Mrs. Rodriguez?" he asked.

"She says she saw it," her husband smiled in disbelief. "But, I didn't see anything."

"You were in the bathroom," she defended.

"Of course, dear."

•

"It was there," she insisted. "I saw it!"

"Are you aware of the history of this location, Mrs. Rodriguez?" Jeffrey asked.

"Yes," her husband answered for her. "We heard about this place before we made our reservations. That's one of the reasons we chose this place. Teresa was hoping to see a ghost. She thought it would be quaint. I suppose she got her wish."

"Don't make fun of me!"

"There have been a few sightings of spirits, Mrs. Rodriguez," Jeffrey intercepted. "A few of our guests have reported seeing something. None of the reports have been confirmed. It's hard to verify such things. But, nobody has claimed to have interacted with anything they've seen. I can't completely deny that the inn is haunted. But, there doesn't seem to be any danger to anyone, ma'am."

"Thank you," she sighed. "That's very comforting."

"You're very welcome," he said. "So, you'll be staying one more night?"

"Yes," Rodriguez said. "We'll be checking out around 9:00 in the morning."

"Fine," he said. "Perhaps we'll see you at dinnertime."

"We're looking forward to it."

"Have a nice day," he said while waving good-bye.

"You were very good with that couple," Carol said. "I'd almost think you're used to working in haunted hotels."

"A guy has to adapt quickly to such circumstances," he said.

"That's a refreshing attitude," she said. "I'd better go find my husband. Can you handle the desk alone for a while? It doesn't look too busy at the moment."

"No problem, Mrs. Gould."

"Thanks."

She quickly departed.

Moments later, a young woman stood before the desk. She took off her knitted hat. A long flow of thick hair spilled out over her shoulders like butterscotch lava over a candy volcano. She unbuttoned her heavy coat. She brushed quite a bit of snow from her shoulders.

"Hi, Jeffrey," she smiled.

"Good morning, Dawn," he smiled back. "You're late."

"The roads are treacherous out there," she imparted. "Traffic's backed up."

"How bad is it?"

"Well, I hate driving in this stuff," she said. "It's a little slippery. But, I have to admit it could be a lot worse."

"The forecast said it should be over by noon," he said.

"I hope they're right," she said. "I don't want any trouble getting out of here tonight."

"Why?" he asked. "Do you have a hot date?"

"Me?" she laughed. "No. I don't have the energy for dating right now. By the time I get home from work, I'm too exhausted."

"Are you kidding me?" he asked. "A beautiful girl like you? It's a crime that you're not seeing anybody."

"I'd hardly say that," she said. "Frankly, I'm glad to have the break. My luck with men hasn't been too good lately."

"That's just because you haven't been with the right guy yet," he imparted. "You should let me take you to dinner."

Her expression took an uncomfortable tone.

"Thanks, Jeffrey," she said through a forced smile. "It's nice of you to offer. But, you know how the Goulds feel about employees dating."

"I won't tell if you don't."

"I don't think it's a good idea," she gently insisted. "Listen. I have to get to work. Sorry. But, thanks for the offer."

She headed for the stairs.

"If you change your mind," he called after her. "I'll be right here."

He watched her leave. But, only for a moment.

Three or four couples converged on the desk all at once. Like it or not, he had to return to work.

"So, the kid just attacked you with a baseball bat?" asked the voice on the phone.

"Do you believe it?" he said. "This six-year-old brat starts wailing me in the back of the head with this little bat! And, his parents are saying, 'Gee! Let's mollycoddle the little shit and just send him off to bed.'"

"Are you okay?"

"No!" he averred. "The back of my head hurts like hell! I got a couple of lumps on my skull the size of golf balls! I can't take crap like that anymore! I'm no spring chicken. Let's face it. I'm 52 years old! I have ulcers, diabetes, arthritis and a bad heart. I have enough problems without some preschool snot-nose thinking he's Joe DiMaggio and I'm his target for batting practice!"

"Well, I feel for you," said the voice. "But, how does that concern me?"

"Didn't you hear me?" he shouted into the phone. "He mentioned Randy Dalton! He said something about Randy Dalton being sorry! I'm telling you that kid knows something!"

"What could the kid know?" asked the voice. "Exactly what did he say?"

"Just that some imaginary friend who lives in the fireplace mentioned Dalton's name," he expounded. "But at the very least, he knew something was wrong."

"And what did you do?"

"What *could* I do?" he asserted. "I couldn't just kill the kid on the spot in front of a dozen witnesses. I freaked out for a few seconds. But, I regained my composure as quickly as possible, and then tried to play it off like it was no big deal."

"This happened at The Hillside Inn, right?" the voice asked. "You know that place has a paranormal history to it. Some legends suggest that spot has an evil presence that's existed for hundreds or even thousands of years. A lot of people believe that Mortimer Hilzak was actually a very nice person before he built a house on that property. It wasn't until after he moved there that he started going peculiar."

"You don't believe all that supernatural hogwash, do you?" he spat.

"It's hard to say," said the voice. "Normally, I wouldn't. But, who's going to tell that sort of information to a little kid? If somebody wanted to confide in someone, why choose a small boy?"

"I know," he said. "It makes no sense."

"And if the kid knows," said the voice. "Does it matter? Who's he going to tell?"

"I'm not worried about the kid so much," he said. "I'm more worried about who else knows…especially, who's running his mouth so much that he's even talking to little kindergarteners?"

"I see what you mean," said the voice. "The deal is done though, right? You made the transfer, didn't you?"

"Yes," he said. "But, it's going to take weeks to bury that money in accounts and funds so they can't find it or trace it back to us."

"That's true."

"And, I can't even start today," he said. "It's Sunday. I have to wait 'til tomorrow. I don't see any way around it. I have to talk to that kid as soon as possible. I have to find out what he knows and who he heard it from."

"How are you going to do that?"

"I don't know," he said. "I'll have to use tact. I hope I can do this nicely, though. Two people already had to die to keep this thing a secret. I'd hate to make it three."

"You swore you weren't going to be the one to kill anybody over this," the voice reminded him.

"That's right," he nodded. "And, I'd hate to have to start breaking that promise over a small child!"

"You can't just kill the kid," the voice advised. "Remember. The cops were never able to pin Dalton's murder on us. That's because it was handled with professionalism and finesse. We can't afford anything messy coming along to complicate things. Don't screw this up for me, Michael."

"I don't plan to," he said. "Believe me. I don't want to hurt the kid. But, I've worked too hard on this deal. And, nobody is going to ruin it for me! Do you hear me? Nobody!"

"Adam?" he said sternly. "I want to talk to you, son."

"What's the matter, Dad?"

"I want you to tell me what's going on," he said. "Why did you attack our friend with a baseball bat last night? Who is telling you to do things like that?"

"He's just my friend."

"Does he have a name?" he asked.

The boy shrugged.

"You don't know?" he asked. "Don't give me that! How can he be your friend if you don't even know his name?"

"He doesn't like me talking about him."

"That's ridiculous, Adam," he said. "How can he tell you to go around attacking total strangers and then figure you're not going to have to talk about him?"

"I dunno."

"That's enough, Adam!" he demanded. "What's his name?"

The boy looked down at the carpet. His whole body seemed tense. He was silent for a few moments.

Then, he looked up at his father. There was a fear in his eyes.

"He's just a man who lives in the fireplace."

"Why won't you tell me his name?" he pressed. "Does he scare you?"

"Sometimes."

"What does he do that scares you?" he asked. "Does he say he's going to hurt you?"

"No," Adam said. "I don't think he would hurt me."

"Then, what are you scared of?" he asked.

"I dunno," Adam insisted. "He's just scary."

"I don't like the idea of anybody scaring my son," he averred. "You know I'd never let anybody hurt you, right?"

"I know."

"So, who is this guy?"

"Can we please stop, Dad?"

"Are you sure you're alright?" he continued.

"Yes, Dad," Adam said with a heavy sigh. "I'm okay."

"Why is this guy telling you to hit people?" he asked.

"It's my fault, Dad," Adam defended. "I'm sorry."

"I just want to know why you're being rude to our guests," he said. "I just want to know why you're acting crazy, and why you're hitting people. I don't care if you have an imaginary friend, son. But, if he's telling you to be rude...or if he's telling you to hit people, it has to stop. Do you understand? You are not allowed to be rude. And you don't hit people."

"Yes, Dad."

"Are you going to behave?"

"Yes, Dad."

"Good," he said. "Go wash up for lunch. It's almost time to eat."

He watched the boy leave the room. Something didn't seem right.

Could something be wrong?

He didn't have time to wonder. There was too much work to do.

Donald Gorman

The sun was out. The sky was crystal clear. It was warm and breezy outside. It was about 70 degrees down by the shoreline.

The lights were low inside. It almost seemed dark. Pop music played from behind the bar. Not many customers wasted their time here on a bright, pleasant Sunday afternoon.

He sat on a barstool. He leaned heavily on the counter. A vodka on the rocks rested at his fingertips.

"It's been a long time, my friend," he said. "You're looking good."

"I wish I could say the same," his friend said. "But, you've put on a few pounds."

"I know," he acknowledged. "Life's been good in some ways. It's been harsh in others."

"I hear you're on your second marriage," his friend said.

"Yeah," he smiled. "And, I've learned a few things from the first wife. I was smart enough not to have any kids with the new one."

"That'll make life easier."

"You said it," he nodded. "That first bitch is bleeding me dry for child support."

"You're making decent money, aren't you?"

"Not that I get to keep any of it," he grunted. "Whatever Bitch Number One doesn't take goes to credit cards, mortgages, bills…"

"It's the same for everybody."

"I know," he agreed. "Life's not really that bad. I've done alright for myself. I own a few stores. A beautiful home. Los Angeles is a great place to live."

"Are you thinking about going back to Oregon this spring?" the thinner man asked.

"What?" he scoffed. "That reunion thing?"

"It's been twenty years," his friend reminded. "Don't you want to see any of your old friends?"

"If I wanted to see them," he said. "I would have stayed in touch with them."

"You lost touch with me."

"You moved to fucking San Diego, for God's sake," he pointed out. "Who's going to keep track of anybody in San Diego?"

"You have to go where life takes you," his friend said. "And, that's my point. People drift apart. There are a lot of good memories back home."

"There are a lot of bad memories, too."

There was a brief, heavy pause.

"Speaking of which," the thinner man said. "Did you hear they developed that whole wooded section of Morris Hill? There are no woods over there at all anymore. I hear they even built a small hotel directly on the spot where the Hilzak house used to stand."

"I heard about that."

"Aren't you curious?" his friend asked. "Don't you want to see how it looks?"

"You don't understand," he explained. "I was glad to get out of that town. I got out as soon as I could, and I never looked back. When you get out of a piece-of-shit town like Spruce Valley, why the hell would you ever go back?"

"It's your past," he reminded. "It's your heritage."

"Heritage?" he scoffed. "Heritage don't pay the mortgage."

Donald Gorman

"Don't you have family up there?"

"I guess," he sighed. "Of course, my parents are dead. And my sisters bailed out of that town as quickly as I did. But, I have a few people left up there."

"You're not afraid to go back, are you?" his friend suggested. "You know, because of what happened?"

"Afraid?" he scoffed. "Are you kidding me? What's there to be afraid of? That was all in the distant past. Who has time to even remember that crap? Hell! If I was to go back there, I'd probably stay in that new hotel, just for the hell of it!"

"So, why don't you?"

"Well," he said. "I guess I could think about it. Ashley's been after me to go, too. She wants to see where I grew up. It might be a laugh."

"We'll have fun," his friend coaxed. "You'll see. Who knows how much that town has grown? It might surprise you."

"Maybe," he said. "And, maybe I really will stay in that new hotel, just for the hell of it! Why not? There's nothing in Spruce Valley I need to be afraid of."

⯎

He strolled casually up to the reception desk. It was a very tall desk. He couldn't see the top of the massive structure from his vantage point. He took a few steps back until he could see a face.

"Mr. Bartlett?" he asked. "Have you seen my mom?"

"Hi, Adam," the man smiled. "Are you supposed to be out in the reception area by yourself?"

"Not really."

"Well," he said without judgment. "Your mom was in the restaurant, last I heard."

"Thanks."

The boy headed for the dining area.

He watched the child until a voice said, "Hello."

He turned to face the older gentleman. "Oh, hello," he said. "I recognize you. You're Mr. Schumacker, aren't you? The man from the bank. This is a pleasant surprise. I'm Jeffrey Bartlett. We met once before."

"Yes," he forced a smile. "Nice to see you again."

"I'm guessing you're here to see Mr. Gould," Jeffrey surmised.

"Well…yes," he nodded. "But, I'd also like to see Adam. Didn't I just see him here at the desk a moment ago?"

"Adam?" Jeffrey asked curiously. "Their son? He's over there near the restaurant."

"Thank you."

"Would you like me to find Mr. Gould for you?" Jeffrey asked.

"Uh…sure."

He turned and chased after the boy.

"Adam?" he called.

The boy stopped. He turned around. His eyes narrowed as he recognized the gray-haired gentleman who nervously approached him.

"Hi, Adam," the man said through labored breaths. "Remember me?"

"Yes."

"Can I talk to you for a minute, please?"

"I guess."

"Is there somewhere we can go to talk privately?" he asked.

"I'm not supposed to trust strangers," Adam said. He was already walking back toward the reception desk.

"You can trust me, Adam," he assured. He kept pace with the boy as he spoke. "I'm not a stranger. We've met before. I just want to talk about your friend."

"I know."

"I was hoping you could tell me his name," he said. "Where did you meet? What exactly did he tell you? Is there any chance I could meet him?"

"Sure," Adam nodded. "You can meet him. He'd like to talk to you."

"He would?"

"Yup."

"So, he's not really invisible, is he?" the old man asked.

"No."

"Where can I meet him?" he asked. "And when?"

"Right now," Adam said. "He's upstairs. On the second floor."

"Upstairs?" he asked. "Now? Where on the second floor?"

"Room 6," Adam said. "He wants to show you something. On the balcony."

"He wants to show me something on the balcony?" he asked. "What does he want to show me?"

"I dunno," Adam shrugged. "It's a secret. He says it's a surprise."

"A surprise?" he pressed. "Room 6? Right now? What's this man's name?"

"That's part of the surprise."

"It is?"

Suddenly, he felt a knot in his stomach. This was too easy. It was eerie. How was this small child involved?

Something seemed terribly wrong!

"He's waiting for you, Mr. Schumacker."

"Well, we'd better not keep him waiting," he said. "Thank you, Adam."

The boy turned and headed back toward the restaurant.

Schumacker watched the boy for a moment. Then, he turned.

He could see the fireplace from where he stood. A grand, full fire roared majestically in its stone compartment. It crackled, danced and taunted him from a distance.

There was a lump in his throat. He swallowed hard.

It was still there.

He straightened his tie. He took a breath.

Then, he marched bravely toward the elevator. The door opened as soon as he hit the button. He stepped in along with a few other people and rode to the second floor.

As he walked out into the hall, every muscle in his body grew tense. Anticipation and dread gripped his heart with increasing strength.

Who was this man in Room 6? Was it someone he knew?

Was he an insider? Was he a competitor? Someone with an axe to grind?

Perhaps it was just some greedy wise-ass who wanted to play the Blackmail card.

Was it a mistake to walk into this situation unarmed?

He hadn't even considered bringing a weapon just to talk to the young boy. But, God only knows who he'd be facing on the balcony of a hotel room!

He followed the room numbers along the wall. Room 3 was to his left. His pace quickened as he reached Room 4 to his right. His fists were clenched. His teeth were clenched. His entire body was a ball of nerves.

Finally, he found himself standing before the door to Room 6.

He stared at the brass number on the door.

He didn't like this. But, it needed to be done.

He braced himself with a good, deep breath.

Then, he raised his arm. He knocked loudly on the door.

He listened nervously for a response. There was none.

He knocked again.

"Hello?" he called through the door. "Is anyone in there?"

Dead silence was the only reply.

"Hello?" he called as he knocked again. "It's Michael Schumacker here. I believe you were expecting me."

He waited.

Suddenly, he heard the click of a lock. Then, the doorknob turned. And, the door squeaked open. It only opened to the point where it was ajar.

It went no further.

He stared at the door. He waited to see if any further invitation was forthcoming.

Everything was silent and still.

His heart was thumping loudly in his chest like a child with a baseball bat.

He took another deep breath for courage.

Then, he slowly reached out with his hand. The door squeaked as he pushed it open, like the low whine of a ghost.

He glanced around nervously from his position in the hall. It appeared to be a normal, empty hotel room. No one could be seen.

Cautiously, he ventured into the room.

"Hello?" he called in a voice that tried to mask his trepidation. "Is anyone here? I believe you're expecting me."

From inside the room, he quickly surveyed his surroundings. It was a beautiful, plush hotel suite. However, he was completely alone.

He took a few more steps into the room.

"Hello?" he called out.

Suddenly, he heard a loud slam!

He quickly spun around to see what had happened.

The door was closed. However, there was nobody in sight.

No one could have closed the door!

A frosty chill crept up his spine.

"Is anybody here?" he called out as he slowly turned to inspect the room. "I am Michael Schumacker. I was told you wanted to see me."

Not a sound could be heard.

He noticed the glass doors leading out to the balcony. He strained his eyes, but he couldn't see anyone from where he stood.

Part of him wanted to run away. But, there was too much at stake. He took a moment to brace himself against his mounting fear.

Donald Gorman

Then, he carefully made his way toward the balcony. He never took his eyes off the glass doors.

No one appeared to be out there. He didn't like this! However, he couldn't afford to take any chances. It was imperative that he pursue this issue.

He took another step toward the balcony.

"Hello?" he called again. "Please answer me! Is anyone there?"

He had three entrees cooking on the stove. Each one was perfectly timed. They would all be finishing at the same time. The side dishes were ready to go.

"Hi, Glen," she smiled from the doorway. "How are you?"

"Hey, Rita," he smiled back. "What's going on?"

"I just stopped by to let you know," she said. "Earlier today I saw Jeffrey Bartlett asking your girl Dawn to go out with him."

"So, Jeffrey Bartlett's going after Dawn, eh?" he said sarcastically. "Now there's a surprise!"

"You don't need to worry right away," she informed him. "She shot him down."

"Good for her."

"I wouldn't get too comfortable, though," she advised. "You're a good looking guy, Glen. You really are. But, so is Jeffrey. And, he has the advantage of working in a nice, cushy job wearing a nice, expensive suit."

"While I get stuck working in greasy coveralls that smell like garlic?" he asked. "Is that what you're getting at?"

Wrongful Secrets

"I didn't mean it to sound that way."

"I'm sure you didn't."

"I'm just trying to help you, Glen," she said.

"Thanks," he said. "But, I really have no interest in Dawn."

"If you say so."

"It's the truth!"

"Okay, loverboy," she said. "I just thought you should know. Could I have a seafood salad sandwich tonight at 7:30 please?"

"Seafood salad?" he said. "Sure thing, honey."

"Thanks," she said. "And, good luck with Dawn. I'm rooting for you."

"Don't you have some rooms to clean?" he asked.

She smiled as she left.

He returned to the sizzling pans on the stove. He made a face.

Jeffrey Bartlett, eh?

That's just what he didn't need to hear!

❖

"I'm glad it stopped snowing," she said from the passenger's seat.

"Yeah," he agreed. "The road's not too bad. We should be there in a few minutes. Keep an eye out for Marsh St. It should be around here somewhere. It'll take us to Armory Blvd. That's the road the hotel's on."

"Marsh St.?" she asked. "Isn't that Marsh St. up there on the left?"

"That's it," he nodded. "Good. We're almost there. What's the name of this place where we're staying?"

"The Hillside Inn."

Donald Gorman

"I could kill your sister," he said. "It's her husband who's retiring. It was her idea to have a big blow-out week long family party to celebrate. I still don't see why she couldn't find room to put up her own sister for a few days."

"Oh, come on, Tom," she said. "You know Cathy has family flying in from all over the country for this thing. She can't accommodate everybody."

"You're her sister, Margaret!"

"Be reasonable, Tom," she insisted. "Remember. You promised to be good this week."

"I can't even imagine why she's making such a big deal about Jack's retirement," he grumbled. "He's a glorified salesman, for Christ's sake!"

"He's the Managing Director of the whole west coast for the sales department of a major corporation," she corrected. "He's worked for them for nearly forty years. He started at the bottom and worked his way up. It *is* a big deal to them, and they have a lot to be proud of."

"If he's such a big shot," he poked. "Why does he live in a worthless little backwoods town like Spruce Valley, Oregon?"

"You promised to behave, Tom," she averred. "Are you going to act like this all week?"

"No," he grunted. "I'll be good."

"Thank you."

"We should be near the hotel," he said. "Watch for it, okay?"

"Sure," she said. "It's supposed to be a beautiful place. You'll see. It'll be nice staying in a hotel for a few days."

"It'll be expensive."

"Can't you just allow yourself to have a good time?" she asked.

Wrongful Secrets

"I can think of cheaper ways of having a good time that are a lot closer to home," he said.

"You're impossible," she sighed. "Oh, look! That looks like the hotel up ahead. The big white building. Doesn't it look lovely?"

"Fabulous," he grunted.

"Yes," she said while reading the stately sign in the parking lot. "'The Hillside Inn'. This is the place. This will be fun. It's so…"

She stopped talking as they pulled up to the parking lot. The sun had poked a few holes in the clouds. She squinted against the glare on the windshield.

"What's that?" she asked. "Hanging from the balcony on the second floor? Is that…?"

Suddenly, her eyes grew wide. She gasped.

Then, she screamed.

He saw the object too. His heart stopped for a moment. Then, he quickly parked his car in the first spot he could find.

His wife was still screaming. She was hysterical.

He leapt out of the car. A few people in the parking lot stopped because of the screaming. They looked around in curiosity.

Tom ran across the plowed and salted parking lot. A small crowd was gathering near the wall of the hotel. As he pushed his way through the front door, he nearly ran into a young man in a well-tailored suit.

"I need to speak to the manager," he said excitedly.

"My name is Leon Gould," he said. "I'm the owner. What can I do for you?"

"I'm Tom Prosky," he said as he led the way out the door. "My wife and I were just arriving when we noticed…"

Donald Gorman

Leon looked up to where the man was pointing. His eyes grew wide as he stared at the dead weight hanging by a noose suspended from the balcony.

"Michael Schumacker!" Leon gasped.

He turned and ran back into the hotel. He sped over to the reception desk.

"What's going on?" Carol asked.

"Michael Schumacker is hanging from a balcony on the second floor," he informed. "I think he's dead!"

"Mr. Schumacker?" she gasped. "Hanging? What do you mean 'hanging'?"

"There's a noose," he explained impatiently. "And, Michael's dangling from it! What...do I need to draw you a picture?"

"A noose?" she asked.

"Jeffrey," he instructed. "Call the cops! I'm going to get him down and see if he's still alive. At the very least, I can't let the guests see him up there. It looks like the balcony to Room 6! Were you expecting Michael today, honey?"

"No," Carol replied.

"Well, I can't just leave him there," Leon said. "I have to get him down! Call the cops, Jeffrey!"

He ran to the stairs.

"Oh, my God," Carol exclaimed. "Where's Adam?"

She glanced around nervously.

Jeffrey was still frozen behind the desk. Finally, he managed to say, "Mrs. Gould? I have to tell you something."

"Tell me later," she said. "I have to find Adam!"

"That's what I want to talk to you about," Jeffrey said.

"What?" she asked. "You have to talk to me about Adam? What about him?"

"He was just here about ten minutes or so ago," Jeffrey told her. "Schumacker was talking to him."

"He was talking to my son?" she asked curiously.

"He was asking Adam about his friend," Jeffrey explained. "Adam was telling the old guy that his friend wanted to meet him."

"His friend?" she asked shakily.

"Adam told Schumacker his friend had a surprise for him on the balcony of Room 6," Jeffrey continued.

"The balcony?" she whispered. "Room 6? Are you sure?"

"I was standing right here, Mrs. Gould," Jeffrey imparted. "I heard every word."

Carol began to tremble. Her eyes filled with tears. Still, she could see her son. He was sitting on the floor in The Den. He was right in front of the fireplace.

"Call the police, Jeffrey," she said bravely.

Adam's back was turned to her. She couldn't see his face.

Still, she knew.

Adam was smiling as he stared at the roaring fire.

Chapter 4
Purely Innocent Guilt

The clouds continued to drift away. They slowly left the sky like curious onlookers at the scene of a tragedy.

The emergency rescue team was in no hurry putting the body in the ambulance. The police were still searching for all the evidence they could find.

"Mr. and Mrs. Gould?" he said. "I'm Sgt. Agostino with the Spruce Valley P.D. This is my partner, Officer Taggerty. We'd like to ask you a few questions."

"Of course, sir," Leon said.

"No one was staying in Room 6," Agostino said. "And only you and some of your staff had access to that room. Is that correct?"

"That's right."

"We talked to Thomas Prosky and his wife," Agostino said. "They were the first ones to see the deceased hanging from the balcony. Apparently, they were coming here to check in. They have reservations to be your guests for a few days. Is that correct?"

"Yes, sir," Leon said.

Wrongful Secrets

"What is your relationship with the deceased," Agostino asked. "Was he a guest in the hotel also?"

"No," Leon answered. "He was the assistant director at The First Mercantile Bank on Emmet St. He was the man who gave us the loan to build this place. He came here yesterday as a courtesy…maybe idle curiosity. He just wanted to see what we did with the money we borrowed."

"Did he stay overnight?" Agostino asked.

"No," Leon said. "He and his wife came back last night because we offered them a free drink by the fire in The Den. But, they did not stay overnight."

"Then, why did he come back today?" Taggerty asked. "Did he have further business to discuss with you?"

"No."

"Did he talk to you while he was here?" Taggerty pursued.

"No," Leon said. "I didn't even know he was here."

He was beginning to regret this line of questioning. He was regretting his replies even more so.

"Then, why was he here?" Taggerty asked.

"Officer?" Carol interrupted nervously. "Are these questions really necessary? How are we supposed to know what happened?"

"We don't know, ma'am," Agostino said. "We're just trying to figure out what happened here. It's an interesting situation. His hands weren't tied. He wasn't restrained in any way. There are no signs of a struggle. It could be a suicide. Still, why would he want to kill himself? And, why would he come here to do it?"

"I have no idea," Leon said. "We hardly knew him. He was just our banker. Before last night, we hadn't even seen him in over a year."

"Did anything happen last night?" Agostino asked.

"No," Carol said. "Everyone had a real nice time."

"Do you mind if we question the staff?" Agostino asked. "And, maybe a few of the guests? Perhaps someone saw or heard something."

"What good would that do, Sergeant?" Leon asked.

"Is there a problem?" Taggerty asked with surprise. "I would have thought you'd be interested in finding out why this happened in your establishment."

"Well," Leon said as he searched for excuses. "It's disruptive. To both the staff and our customers. These people didn't come here to be badgered by the police."

"They didn't come here to see people getting hanged off the balcony, either," Taggerty pointed out. "If foul play is involved, we could spare your future customers from going through a similar incident."

"Are you trying to hide something, Mr. Gould?" Agostino asked suspiciously.

"Of course not!"

"Are you real policemen?" asked a small voice.

They looked down at the young boy who was suddenly standing by his mother.

"Yes we are," Agostino smiled. "What's your name?"

"Adam."

"He's our son," Carol said.

"Are you here because of that man?" Adam asked. "The one who died?"

"Uh…yes," Agostino said cautiously. "Why? Did you see something?"

Wrongful Secrets

"No."

Carol scooped her son up in her arms. "Maybe I should get him out of your way," she suggested anxiously.

"Did he kill himself because of Randy Dalton?" Adam asked.

"What?" Agostino asked. "Who's Randy Dalton?"

"We should really go," Carol insisted.

"Not so fast," Agostino averred. "Who's Randy Dalton?"

"I dunno," Adam said. "That man was talking about him last night. Then, he was saying something about him today just before he went up to the second floor."

"The old man was talking about Dalton last night?" Agostino said. "And, you saw him just before he went upstairs?"

"Yup."

"What did he say?" Agostino pressed.

"I don't remember," Adam said. "He just got upset when he mentioned Randy Dalton."

"I really have to get my son out of here," Carol said. "He hasn't had lunch yet."

"I'm real hungry, Mom."

"I know, honey," she said. "Don't worry. We'll get you some food. Pardon us, gentlemen."

She quickly carried her son out of the room. The officers watched her hasty departure.

"Does your son have some sort of involvement in this, Mr. Gould?" Agostino asked. "Is that why you and your wife seem so nervous?"

"No."

"Is that why you don't want us to talk to your staff or your guests?" Agostino pressed.

"Of course not," Leon insisted. "How could a six-year-old boy be involved in a grown man hanging himself from my balcony?"

"That's what we'd like to know," Agostino said.

"We haven't even determined if Schumacker committed suicide," Taggerty added.

"This is ridiculous!" Leon declared. "What are you implying? Do you think a little boy overpowered a grown man and hanged him over our balcony? You said yourself that Schumacker wasn't restrained in any way. How could my son have killed him?"

"We didn't say he killed him," Agostino corrected. "But, we're wondering if he's somehow connected to the incident."

"He seems to know something," Taggerty deduced. "What he said sounded awfully suspicious. Besides that, the way you and your wife are acting indicates that you're hiding something."

"What could we possibly be hiding?" Leon argued. "The boy is only six!"

"Mr. Gould," Agostino said in a tone meant to calm. "We don't really know what's going on. We haven't ruled out either suicide or foul play. We just want to get to the bottom of whatever happened here. It seems unlikely that your son had any direct involvement in the actual death. However, he does seem to know something. You seem to be aware of more than you are telling. We are going to investigate this occurrence. And, we are going to find out what's going on. The sooner you come clean, the easier it will be on you, your son and the guests of this hotel. Now, why don't you tell us what you are so afraid of? Believe me. We're going to find out eventually."

There was an anxious pause.

"Come on, Mr. Gould," Agostino gently coaxed.

"Okay," Leon acquiesced with a sigh. "Here it goes…"

Meanwhile, Carol was passing by The Den with her son. She stopped when she saw the older couple sitting in plush chairs near the fireplace.

"Are you enjoying your hot cocoa, Mrs. Prosky?" she asked.

"Yes," she said. "Thank you."

"And you, Mr. Prosky?" carol continued. "Are you comfortable? Can I get you another Scotch?"

"No, thanks," he said. "I'm fine."

"Feel free to sit here as long as you like," Carol invited. "I know that must have been a terrible ordeal for you."

"It was certainly unexpected," he agreed.

"Is there anything I can do?" Carol asked.

"I just want to sit for a while," she said. "I'm still shaking."

"I'm so sorry, Mrs. Prosky," Carol said. "Please take all the time you need."

"I imagine this must be very hard on you, Mrs. Gould," Tom said. "How are you holding up?"

"Oh," she said while considering her reply. "It's been unsettling. But, I haven't had time to dwell on it. I still have a hotel to run. Right now, I'm mostly concerned with damage control. An incident like this can cost us customers. I just have to do all I can to make sure nobody wants to leave prematurely."

"Speaking of which," he said. "Margaret has suggested that it might be best if we stayed in another hotel."

"What?" Carol asked.

"Please don't take it personally," he said. "We realize it's not your fault. And, this really is a beautiful hotel, but..."

"Please don't go," Carol begged.

"We're very sorry, Mrs. Gould," she said. "We don't blame you. We know you've done everything you can under the circumstances. And, I really love the hotel. It's a gorgeous place. But, how can we be expected to stay here after seeing such a traumatic event? How could I possibly even stay, let alone sleep in this building?"

"I understand you've been through a very unpleasant experience," Carol said. "But, it's all over now. You have nothing to worry about. Nothing like this has ever happened here before. We're coping as best we can. And, we'll make every effort to make sure the rest of your stay is as enjoyable as possible."

"I'm hungry, Mom."

"Admittedly," he began. "My wife chose this hotel on purpose. She heard about its haunted history. I thought she was crazy. But, she thought it would be exciting if there was a chance we might see a ghost or something. A ghost is one thing, but an actual dead body hanging by a noose with a purple face and bulging eyes is a bit more than we bargained for."

"Please," Carol implored. "We can offer you dinner tonight as our guest. Anything! We can't afford to lose every customer who may have been inconvenienced..."

"Inconvenienced?" she interrupted curtly. "My dear woman! I've been traumatized!"

"I'm sorry," Carol said. "I understand. But, isn't there something I can do?"

"I'm hungry, Mom!"

"We sympathize," he said. "We really do. But, I don't think…"

"Mom!" Adam asserted loudly. "I said I'm hungry!"

"I heard you, Adam!" Carol scolded. "But, Mommy is talking to these people! Please be patient!"

There was a heavy silence.

Afterward, Tom was the first to speak. "I'm sorry, Mrs. Gould," he said. "But, I think we should go. Thank you for your hospitality. Maybe we'll try this place again if we're ever back in town. My wife has family in the area. So, you may very well see us again. Come on, Margaret. Let's go."

They stood.

"Are you sure?"

"Yes," she said. "Maybe we'll try again in the future. This is a charming inn."

"May we pay you for the drinks?" he offered.

"No," Carol said. "They're on the house. It's the least we could do."

"You're very kind," he said. "Thank you. I'm sorry it had to turn out this way. I'm sure we would have enjoyed our stay."

"Okay," she sighed. "I hope to see you again. I'm sorry for everything."

She waved to them as they left.

On their way back to the car, they stopped. Neither of them could resist the urge to glance back up at the balcony.

"It's still a chilling sight," Margaret said.

"I know," he agreed. "I still expect to see that body hanging there."

"I do feel a bit guilty," she admitted. "Mrs. Gould is such a delightful woman. This really wasn't her fault. And, this is such a gorgeous hotel. I feel like I'm running out on her. But, how could I possibly stay here?"

"I'm sure she understands."

"Every time I look at this building…" she began.

She paused.

Then, she turned. She walked to the car.

Her husband followed her.

When they were both seated in the car, he put the key in the ignition. He turned the key. He heard a click. There was no other response from the car.

Just a click.

He tried the key again.

Click.

He grew aggravated. He tried a few more times with the same result.

"What the hell?" he said impatiently. "That's impossible!"

"What's wrong?" she asked.

"The battery's dead!" he exclaimed. "It can't be! This car was just inspected a month ago! I sank a fortune into this car! It's a brand new battery! Practically everything under that hood is brand new! I knew we were going to be making this long drive for your sister's pointless husband! There's no way that battery could be dead!"

"Can you get a jump start from someone in the hotel?" she suggested.

"Of course," he grumbled. "That's not the problem! It's a brand new battery! I'm going to have to replace it now! And probably the alternator, too! And, I'll have to do it right away, too! I can't go around getting a jump from everybody everywhere I go! Son of a bitch! This trip gets more expensive by the moment! We haven't even figured out where we're staying yet! And, now I have to embarrass myself by going back into the hotel that we just walked out of!"

"So, we have to go back in there?" she asked.

"What choice do we have?" he barked. "This sucks! Now I have to find a repair shop! And, how are we going to look for another hotel without a car?"

There was an uneasy silence.

"Well," she finally said. "I guess we could just stay here, if we have to. It is a nice place. And I do feel guilty for leaving these poor people at the last minute."

"Are you sure you'll be alright?"

"I'll just have to be," she said. "After all, the worst is over. The body will be gone soon. We're not in any danger. I'll just have to live with it and be strong."

"It would make things much simpler," he added.

"Yes!" she announced bravely. "Let's just stay here. It'll be easier on you when you ask for a jump. And I'll be determined to have a wonderful stay."

"Okay," he said. "Fine. We'll stay. I'm sure someone in there can take our bags up to the room. You can check in and get comfortable in the room. Maybe you can get some lunch. And once I get a jump, I'll get this piece of junk to a repair shop."

"Sounds good," she said. "And, I better call Cathy and tell her we'll be late for her party today."

"All right," he grunted. "Let's get this over with."

He opened the car door and stepped out.

Inside, two men in sharp suits were standing behind the long reception desk.

Donald Gorman

"I hate this," he said. "The cops want to talk to my son. I had to tell them about what Adam did to Schumacker last night. Thankfully, I didn't have to tell them about what you heard this morning. Do me a favor, Jeffrey. Don't tell them any more than you absolutely have to. Okay?"

"Sure, Mr. Gould," Jeffrey said. "My lips are sealed. Where are the cops now?"

"They're talking to the Ellisons from Room 7," he explained. "They want to check on if they saw anything. I convinced the cops to let my son have some lunch before they pounced on him. As if it's not bad enough having medical personnel crawling all over the place…now the cops are going to disrupt my staff and bother my customers! This is turning out to be a great day!"

A couple who appeared to be in their fifties approached the desk.

"Hello," he said. "I'm Tom Prosky. You may remember me and my wife, Margaret. We had decided to stay at another hotel after the tragedy."

"Yes," Leon nodded politely. "I remember you, sir. I'm sorry you won't be staying with us."

"Well, that's just it," he said. "We changed our minds. We decided we'd love to stay here, if you don't mind."

"That's wonderful, Mr. Prosky," Leon smiled.

"Actually," he admitted. "I must confess the main reason for our decision is that the battery died in my car. I'm going to need to find a repair shop. If someone could help my wife with our luggage, she wanted to check in and maybe grab some lunch. I'm going to need a jump start."

"Certainly," Leon said. "Jeffrey can help your wife check in. Stan can take your bags upstairs. Ring for Stan, Jeffrey. And, I'll help Mr. Prosky outside."

"I'd be delighted to help you, Mrs. Prosky," Jeffrey said.

Leon accompanied his guest to the parking lot.

"Aren't you going to need a winter coat, Mr. Gould?" the older man asked. "It's mighty cold out there."

"I'll be fine."

"It's the damnedest thing," he said. "The battery's only a month old. There's no reason why it should've died."

"These things happen, Mr. Prosky," Leon said. "Are you sure it's the battery?"

"I know what a dead battery sounds like," he said. "Here's my car. Let me show you."

He got in. He put the key in the ignition. He turned the key.

The car started. It came to life like a champ.

Tom's jaw dropped.

"It sounds wonderful to me, Mr. Prosky," Leon said. "I wish my car sounded that good. What's the problem?"

"I don't understand it!" he exclaimed. "It was dead! I couldn't get anything out of it at all two minutes ago!"

"Well, you're in good shape now."

"It makes no sense!" he stated. "It was dead! That's impossible!"

"Maybe we can go inside now, Mr. Prosky," Leon suggested. "You can join your wife for lunch."

By the time they got back inside, Mrs. Prosky was gone. Carol and her son were standing by the reception desk.

"I'm so happy you decided to stay, Mr. Prosky," she smiled.

"S-sure."

Donald Gorman

"I put you in Room 20, sir," Jeffrey informed him. "You're wife is up there now. If you'd like to go up and check out your room, we'll reserve a table for you for lunch."

"We would still like to offer you lunch on the house," Carol proposed.

"That's very kind of you."

"What's wrong, Mr. Prosky?" Jeffrey asked. "You don't look well."

"I'm fine," he said. "I'm just confused. My battery was completely dead. It's okay now. It sounds better than it did when I left California. How can that be?"

"Are you sure it was dead?" Carol asked.

"I'm certain!" he averred. "It was dead! Then, it was fine! But, how?"

"What's the matter?" Adam asked. "You said you wanted them to stay. Didn't you, Mom?"

Everyone looked down at the boy. They stared in disbelief.

There was a confident, knowing look in his steady gaze.

"Can I *please* eat now, Mom?" he asked impatiently. "I'm starving!"

"Are you busy?"

"Not really," he said. "I didn't have much of a lunch rush today. After what happened earlier, most people haven't been sticking around. I hope things pick up at dinner time."

"I can imagine it's been quiet," she said. "It's a shame about Mr. Schumacker. He seemed like a nice old guy."

"You met him?"

"I have a checking account at his bank," she explained. "That's how I got this job. I met the Goulds at the bank when I was getting a small loan."

"Do you usually talk to strangers at the bank?" he asked.

"Not generally," she said. "I overheard the Goulds talking to Schumacker, and I approached them about a job when they were done."

"You're a shrewd girl."

"I always seem to get by."

"Did you get lunch?"

"No," she said. "I'm still not hungry. Our little disaster today ruined my appetite."

"If you're not hungry," he asked. "What are you doing in the kitchen?"

"I needed a break," she said. "I've been cleaning all day."

"Did the cops talk to you?"

"More than once," she said. "I don't know why. I had no way of knowing what happened. I've been working all day. They wanted me to tell them about Adam. There wasn't much I could tell them. I hardly know him. I did mention the kid's been acting a little creepy the last month or so. Do you think he was involved, Glen?"

"He's not even seven yet."

"I know," she nodded. "It doesn't make sense. The cops seem awfully interested in him, though."

"That's odd."

"Jeffrey tells me Adam was talking to the old guy just before he was hanged," she imparted. "He was a little freaked out. He said it almost looked like Adam set the whole thing up."

"Do you believe him?"

"I'm not sure," she said. "He sounded serious."

"Come on, Dawn," he said. "How can you believe that little kid had anything to do with the old man's death?"

"Have you seen that kid lately?" she asked. "He's been getting a little freaky. It's hard to think he actually killed anybody. But, what I've heard is enough to make me a bit nervous."

"Adam?" he asked. "Are you kidding, Dawn?"

"You should hear what people say about him," she defended. "Jeffrey tells me some couple was getting ready to check in when they saw the body. They didn't want to stay here after that. But when they tried to leave, their car wouldn't work. So they checked in out of desperation. As soon as they did, their car worked like a dream. Jeffrey says Adam practically admitted that he was responsible."

"You've been talking to Jeffrey a lot lately, have you?" he asked.

"Not if I can avoid it."

"You seem to be quoting him quite often," he observed.

"Only about Adam."

"Rita Giardano tells me he asked you out this morning," he said.

"Yes," she said while rolling her eyes. "I let him down easy. I used Mr. Gould's policy on employee dating as an excuse. I didn't even bother telling him that I'm sort of seeing someone."

"You're seeing someone?"

"Kind of," she admitted. "It's nothing serious. He's a nice guy, but I don't know if it's going to play out in the long term."

"How come you never said anything?"

"Like I said," she reminded. "It's not that serious. Besides, I didn't want to scare you off before you kept your promise to cook for me."

"Cook for you?" he poked. "What about Jeffrey?"

"I have no interest in him."

"What about your boyfriend?"

"He doesn't cook."

"What about Mr. Gould's employee dating policy?" he persisted.

"Well, as long as he doesn't date any employees," she quipped. "He's got nothing to complain about."

They shared a warm smile.

"Can I have my usual tuna sandwich at 7:30 tonight, please?" she asked.

"If you come over to my place," he offered. "I can come up with something that's a lot more exciting than tuna."

"I'm sorry," she said. "I'm going out tonight."

"Your boyfriend?"

She nodded with a guilty downward glance.

"Then, why am I making you a sandwich?"

"I told you," she reminded. "He doesn't cook. Plus, we won't get around to dinner 'til much later."

"Why not?"

"Listen, Glen," she said. "Can I please just get a sandwich?"

"Okay."

"Believe me," she said. "I'm sorry, Glen. I promise we'll do something soon. I mean it. Alright?"

He stayed silent.

"Have you talked to the cops yet?" she asked.

"Not yet," he said. "I guess they'll probably catch up with me this afternoon."

"Please don't tell them what I heard about Adam," she said. "Okay?"

"Don't worry," he said. "I don't think he killed anybody. And, I certainly don't believe he has the power to make cars break down and then come back to life. You shouldn't believe it either, Dawn."

"I'll try not to," she said. "But, that kid is really starting to scare me."

That look in her beautiful brown eyes was genuine.

"See you later, Glen."

He couldn't read her expression. But somehow, he wasn't in the mood to cook.

"Are you sure there's nothing else you'd like to tell us, Mr. Bartlett?" he asked.

"Absolutely, Sergeant."

"According to a few of your guests," he continued. "You were present when Adam talked to the deceased this morning. Concealing information from the police is a crime, Mr. Bartlett."

"I'm well aware of that, Sergeant."

"Then, why don't you tell us what we already know?" he asked. "What did Adam say to Mr. Schumacker just ten minutes before he died?"

"I have no idea," Jeffrey said. "If Adam talked to Mr. Schumacker, I didn't notice. I was at the reception desk all morning. This is a hotel. And, it's been busy all day."

"Are you telling your staff to lie, Mr. Gould?" he asked.

"I wouldn't do that," Leon said. "Why would I? Do you really think my son has something to hide?"

"I wouldn't have thought so," he said. "But, you people are acting mighty suspicious."

"We obviously don't think Adam is guilty of murder, Mr. Gould," Taggerty explained. "But, we need to know if he had some sort of connection to what happened. If Adam told Schumacker to go to Room 6 to meet someone, and ten minutes later the man is found dead, we need to know who he met in that room."

"We told you," Leon reiterated. "Adam's friend is imaginary. Isn't that right, Adam?"

"Yup."

"Adam?" he asked. "Did you tell Mr. Schumacker that your friend wanted to meet him in Room 6?"

"No."

"Do you know how very important it is to always tell the truth?" he asked. "Especially when you're talking to the police?"

"Yes."

"And, you didn't talk to Mr. Schumacker at all today?" he pressed.

"No sir."

"Why would people say you talked to him if you didn't?" Taggerty asked.

"I dunno," Adam said. "People like to tell stories."

Donald Gorman

"But, you did talk to him last night?" he asked. "You hit him with your baseball bat?"

"Yes. I'm sorry."

"Why did you hit him?" he asked.

"Mom says it's 'cause I was tired," Adam said. "It was way past my bedtime."

"Where did you hear the name Randy Dalton?" he asked.

"I dunno," Adam shrugged. "I don't remember."

"Was it from your imaginary friend?" Taggerty asked.

"Could be."

"This is a confusing scenario," he said. "For all we know, this could have been a suicide. There was no sign of struggle, and Schumacker was not tied up when he was hanged. We'll have to check on the name Randy Dalton. If there's a connection, we will probably be back to talk to your son. It seems strange that a name like that would be at the heart of this commotion. Adam couldn't have killed Schumacker. But at the same time, it seems unlikely that he is purely innocent. Your behavior and cover-ups seem to imply that you believe Adam is involved in this case. However, his level of guilt has yet to be determined. Believe me, Mr. Gould. If your son is involved, we will find out. Your best option is to come clean as soon as possible."

"I'm sorry, Sgt. Agostino," Leon said. "There's just nothing to tell you. And, I resent your implication that my son has 'a level of guilt' in any of this."

"Well, I'm sorry you feel that way, sir," he said.

Wrongful Secrets

"May I recommend you help your son with his memory, Mr. Gould?" Taggerty suggested. "We need to know who's really telling him things."

"He's only six," Leon reminded.

"That doesn't make Schumacker any less dead," Taggerty said.

There was a heavy, unnerving pause.

"We'll leave you alone for the time being, sir," he said. "But, I have a feeling we'll be back. This incident just isn't sitting right for me."

"Have a good day, gentlemen," Leon said with a bit of a tone.

Taggerty waited until they were outside before saying, "I don't like this."

"I know how you feel."

"That kid was lying," Taggerty said. "He talked to Schumacker today. Those guests had no reason to say he did if it wasn't true."

"But, why is the kid lying?" he posed. "The father's just being overprotective. That's understandable. But, what is the kid hiding?"

"Do you think the father knows what's going on?" Taggerty asked.

"It's hard to tell," he said. "He knows more than he's admitting, but it's hard to say how much. I don't think the kid really knows what's going on, either. But, he knows that he's covering for a friend. He just doesn't realize the magnitude of the crime."

Back inside, Carol had rejoined her family.

"Dad?" Adam asked. "Are those cops going to arrest me?"

"No," he said. "They have no reason to do that, son. But, I want you to know that I didn't like lying for you. And, I didn't like seeing you lie, either. Lying is a very bad thing. It's just that in this case, we don't want the police to bother you any more than is necessary. Do you understand?"

"Yes, Dad."

"You didn't know what your friend was going to do, did you?" he asked.

"No," Adam said. "I don't even know what he did. Did he kill that man?"

"That's what the police are trying to find out," he said. "That's why we let you lie about talking to him today. If your friend did kill him, we don't want it to look like you were involved."

"What did the cops say, honey?" Carol asked.

"I'll tell you later," he replied. "Right now, I have to get Adam to see this is a very serious matter."

"Am I in trouble?" Adam asked.

"Not if you tell me the truth, son," he said. "When exactly did you talk to your friend? And, what exactly did he tell you to do?"

"He talked to me just before breakfast," Adam said. "Over by the fireplace. He told me that man was coming back here because of what I told him last night. My friend said he doesn't like that man because he keeps bad secrets. He wanted me to tell the man he had a surprise for him on the balcony of Room 6."

"Is that all he told you?" he asked.

"He told me not to tell anybody," Adam added.

"Is that all?"

"Yes."

"Okay, Adam," he said. "Now I want you to listen to me. This is not a game anymore. It's very, very serious. I want you to tell me the truth. Who is the friend you keep talking about?"

"I told you," Adam reminded. "He's the man who lives in the fireplace."

"Nobody can live in the fireplace, Adam!" he said sharply.

"My friend does."

Leon and Carol shared a nervous glance.

"Let me try," she said. "Come with me, Adam. We're going to the fireplace."

"Yes, Mom."

"Do you see the fire?" she asked. "It's a big fire. And, it's very hot."

"I know, Mom," Adam said. "But he lives there."

"Is he there now?" she asked.

"Yes."

"Can you see him?"

"No. But, I know he's there."

"How can you tell?" she asked.

"I just know."

"Can you talk to him?" she asked.

"Yes."

"Show me," she instructed.

"Hi," Adam said, seemingly to the fireplace. "It's me. Can I ask you a question? Did you kill that man the cops were talking about today?"

The fire continued to burn and crackle in its stone cage.

"Well?" Adam asked. "Did you?"

The fire whipped and lashed upward into the chimney. It kept grinding and churning like the exotic dance of a pagan ritual.

"I know," Adam said. "You already told me he had wrongful secrets. But, that's not answering my question."

He just stared into the bright, hyperactive flame…the mesmerizing fire that flailed playfully before him.

"But, I…" Adam began. "Hello? Hello?"

He stopped. He turned toward his parents.

"He's gone," he explained. "He does that sometimes. But, he always comes back when he's ready. I don't think he wanted to talk in front of you two."

"Did he kill Mr. Schumacker, honey?" Carol asked.

"He didn't say," Adam told her. "He just said he didn't like the man because he had 'wrongful secrets'. Do you know what those are?"

"Yes," Carol nodded. "You told me about those yesterday. Did your friend tell you about them?"

"Yup," Adam said. "But, he didn't want to talk right now, though. He just told me I did a good job today. Then, he said he'd talk to me later. I'm not worried, because he always comes back when he's ready."

"You still haven't told us your friend's name, Adam," Carol said.

The boy looked down at the carpet. He was silent for a long time.

"Adam?" she insisted. "What's your friend's name?"

Finally, he looked up at his mother. There was almost a flash of fear in his eyes.

"His name," he muttered slowly. "Is Mr. Fuego."

"Mr. Fuego?"

She shuddered as she glanced at her husband.

"Yes," he said. "Can I go play now, Mom?"

"Okay, honey," she said softly. "But, don't wander off too far. It'll be dinner time soon."

She watched him walk away. She turned to her husband.

"What do you think, Leon?" she asked.

"I didn't see or hear anything," he said. "He was just talking to himself while looking at the fireplace."

"That didn't scare you?"

"Why should it?" he asked. "He's a boy with an imaginary friend. That's not an uncommon thing, Carol."

"What about Mr. Schumacker?"

"Whatever happened to him had nothing to do with our son or our fireplace," he stated with certainty.

"If you believe that," she questioned. "Then why were you lying to the cops?"

"To keep them away from our son, of course," he said. "Do you think they would've sat through this sad display we just witnessed? As entertaining as it was, the cops would have had no patience for it. They'd be hounding Adam for more tangible clues."

"You're right about the cops," she admitted.

"Of course I am."

"But, Leon?"

"Yes?"

"How can you say that what Adam just showed us is entertaining?" she asked.

"What would you call it?" he asked.

"You didn't find it just a little scary?" she asked.

"A boy talking to a fireplace?" he scoffed. "Scary? If the fireplace was talking back to him, *that* would be scary."

"You didn't get the sense that something very real was going on there?" she asked.

"Carol," he said. "Kids have imaginary friends. It happens all the time."

"Imaginary friends don't tell kids to hit people," she insisted. "Or ask people to go up to Room 6 ten minutes before they're found dead hanging from the balcony."

"It was all a coincidence."

"What about that name?" she asked. "Dalton, was it? Where did Adam get that name? You know the cops are going to come back to ask about it. Michael turned white as a sheet when Adam mentioned that name. Dalton is why he came back to the hotel to talk to Adam. You realize that, don't you?"

"What are you implying, Carol?"

"We bought this property because of its reputation for being haunted," she said. "What if it's true?"

"Are you out of your mind?" he asked. "You believe in ghosts now?"

"I don't know," she stammered. "I didn't believe it when we moved here. I still don't know what I believe, as far as ghosts are concerned. The only thing I'm certain I believe in is protecting my son!"

"So, what does that mean?"

"I'm not sure," she said. "But, I'd feel a whole lot better if I knew you were on my side."

"Of course I'm on your side, Carol," he protested. "Adam is my son, too. I just think you're making too much of this."

"My six-year-old son is connected to a murder in my hotel," she pointed out. "How could I possibly make too much of that?"

"For one thing," he argued. "No one has established that a murder has been committed. For another thing, your son is not connected to anything!"

"How do you know?"

"He's only six!" he snipped. "And he talks to the fireplace!"

"Are you so sure there's nothing supernatural going on here?" she asked. "Are you so sure that you're willing to bet your son's life on it?"

"We're not betting anything!" he argued. "There's no such thing as ghosts! Adam is not connected to Michael's death!"

"I wish I could be as certain as you are," she said.

"From now on," he said. "Let me do the thinking."

"You still didn't explain where Adam heard the name Dalton," she persisted.

"Who knows?" he shrugged impatiently. "Thousands of people pass through this hotel every month. Other representatives from the bank have stayed here. He could've heard the name anywhere."

"But, why would anyone talk to Adam?" she asked. "Why would they tell Adam to send Michael up to Room 6?"

"If it'll make you feel any better," he offered. "I'll talk to Adam again. I know I probably should. But, I'm sure there's a simple explanation. Believe me. You have nothing to worry about. Now, let's drop this. I have work to do."

He turned and left. She watched him walk out of the room.

She still felt jittery. Things weren't right.

There were too many unanswered questions. There were still too many missing pieces in the puzzle.

And, Adam was still in the middle of it all!

She made a point of walking by The Den about an hour later. As she suspected, her son was sitting on the carpet in front of the fireplace.

Her heart skipped a beat. Every muscle in her body grew tense.

She stayed out of sight. She moved stealthily. She didn't want Adam to know she was watching.

She took cover behind the nearest wall. She strained to hear what her son was saying.

He was speaking. However, she couldn't make out the words.

She was hoping to hear a second voice.

There was none.

Still, she struggled to listen.

Suddenly, she saw Adam standing right in front of her. She was startled. There was anger in her son's eyes.

He glared at her without reservation.

"Mom!" he declared sharply. "My friend doesn't like it when you spy on me!"

Chapter 5
When Something is Wrong

She glanced casually around the diner.

Everything looked so predictable. The uniforms on the waitresses. The hunter's coats on the burly, hefty losers at every table. The old men seated at the counter who couldn't help looking homeless as they sipped their muddy coffee.

She glanced around again. She stirred her iced tea with a sigh.

"Is something wrong, honey?"

"No."

"Come on, Dawn," he said. "You've been kind of distant all evening."

"Have I?"

"Yes," he said. "You hardly let me touch you when I picked you up at your place. I couldn't even get a kiss out of you."

"Where are we going after dinner?"

"Dawn?" he persisted. "Did you hear me? What's wrong?"

"I'm sorry, Spencer," she said. "It's not your fault. It's been a hard day."

"That guy who killed himself," he deduced. "That really hit you hard, huh? I didn't think you knew him."

"I didn't," she said. "But, it's still hard to think that it happened where I work. I'm still going to have to clean up in that room. A room where somebody died. And, the cops were crawling all over the place. They were even asking me questions."

"I can see where that could seem a bit brutal," he said. "I'm sorry. Maybe I should've been a little more sensitive."

"No, Spencer," she said. "It's my fault. I shouldn't dwell on it. People die every day. And as you say, I didn't even know the man."

"I would've thought you're not so easily spooked," he said. "Working in that hotel. Doesn't it have a certain reputation? Haven't people claimed to see ghosts in there?"

"Yes," she admitted. "A few sightings have been reported to the owners. Nobody who works there has actually seen anything, though. I certainly haven't. But then again, I work during the day. Most of the sightings happen at night."

"Do you believe in ghosts?" he asked.

"I don't know," she shrugged. "As far as that goes, I'm not sure what to believe. I think our souls still exist after we die. But, I'm not expecting to see any ghosts at work, if that's what you mean."

"I like to think some places might be haunted," he imparted. "Of course, it's not common, like you might see in movies. But, I do think certain places are prone to having a presence that persists. For instance, I hear that at the site of The Battle of Gettysburg, strange and unexplained events happen on a regular basis. It's not hard to picture that one of the bloodiest battlefields of its day would leave behind many souls with unfinished business…from people who aren't ready to leave this earthly plane yet."

She looked at him as she toyed with her food.

"Perhaps The Hillside Inn is one of those places," he continued. "That site does have a violent past, doesn't it?"

"I guess," she admitted. "But, how do you believe ghosts are just going to pop up out of thin air? Besides, the cops seem to think the owners' son is involved. And he's only six! If the cops arrest a small boy for hooking up with ghosts and committing a murder, I will know for sure I'm living in the wrong town. I'd probably have to move."

"The cops are blaming a small boy and a ghost?" he asked.

"Not really," she muttered impatiently. "Can we change the subject please?"

"Sure," he said. "I'm sorry. A few minutes ago, you asked where we were going after dinner. We've already been bowling. Did you still want to do something after we eat?"

"God!" she griped. "Bowling! This is like the fifth time we've gone bowling, Spencer. Since when is bowling considered a date?"

"I thought you liked bowling."

"It's okay every once in a while," she said. "But, not every time we go out. I should be able to go out one night without having to change into a pair of shoes that have been worn by hundreds of people before me."

"I'm sorry, Dawn," he said. "I just thought…"

His voice trailed off.

She couldn't avoid the hurt look in his eyes.

"No," she sighed. "*I'm* sorry, Spencer. It's all my fault. It's been a nasty day for me. I shouldn't take it out on you."

"If you like," he said. "I'll never take you bowling again. Would you like to go somewhere after dinner? I wanted you to have a good time tonight."

"I don't think so," she muttered. "Thank you, Spencer. But, I just want to go home. I'm not feeling well. I think I'm getting a headache."

"You don't look well," he observed. "And, you've hardly touched your food."

"Can we just go, please?"

"If you wish," he said. He signaled to the waitress. "Let me get the check. And then, we can get out of here."

She hardly spoke on the way home. She gazed out into the dark streets.

The sky was such a deep, morose black. It was so silent…

Not in the mood for stars.

The mounds of snow looked as though they were a dusky bluish gray. The snowy streets were torn and marred by dirty tire tracks and anonymous footprints.

Cars were few and far between. They drove by with deliberate speed. They seemed to be in a hurry to go somewhere else.

Occasionally, a pair of pedestrians could be seen on the shoveled sidewalks. They were all bundled up in heavy winter coats, hats and gloves. Some shivered against the cold. Certainly, they all wished they were inside.

Wrongful Secrets

No one wanted to be out here on a night like this.

He parked the car in front of her home. It was a two-story house that at one time had been a beautiful single-family dwelling.

Her apartment was on the second floor.

"Are you sure you're alright, honey?" he asked.

"I'll be okay."

"Would you like me to go upstairs with you?" he asked.

"I don't think so."

"I can't even go up with you?" he persisted.

"No," she feigned a smile. "I'll be fine. I just want to take a Tylenol and go to sleep. I'm sure I'll feel better in the morning."

"I hope so."

He leaned over to kiss her. It was an empty kiss. It was hollow and indifferent.

"Dawn?" he asked. "Are you sure there isn't something you want to tell me?"

"If I had something to tell you," she replied. "I would just say it."

"I wish you would," he said. "I really like you. And, I thought we were having a good time. But, I'm not a fool. I can tell when something is wrong."

"Nothing's wrong, Spencer," she insisted. "Honestly. I just have a headache."

"Fine. A headache."

There was no disguising the doubt in his voice.

"Good night, Spencer," she said as she opened the car door. "Thank you for everything. I had a nice time."

"Sure," he muttered. "Good night. I hope you feel better. And, don't worry. I promise. No more bowling."

She didn't respond. She just slammed the car door shut.

He watched her enter the building where she lived. Then, he drove off.

The sky was still a deep, morose black. It was so silent…

No mood for stars.

They were in bed. He reached over to turn out the light.

"Leon?" she asked.

"Yes?"

"Please tell me the truth," she asked. "Why are you downplaying what's happening with Adam?"

"You know the answer to that," he said. "I don't want the cops bothering our son or messing around in our hotel any more than is absolutely necessary."

"That's not what I mean," she asserted. "And you know it. Why are you refusing to accept the possibility that Adam's friend may be some supernatural being?"

"Not this again!"

"How can you deny the proof that's been mounting right in front of us?" she asked.

"There are no such things as ghosts, Carol," he insisted.

"Something is definitely going on here, Leon," she argued. "Something is definitely wrong. And, I think I know why you're glossing over it. You're afraid to face the same thing I'm thinking. I know, because we're both thinking the same thing."

"And, what's that?"

"We're both thinking," she explained. "That it might be in Adam's best interest if we got him away from this hotel."

"Are you kidding?" he replied in shock. "Get him away from the hotel? Why? Just because someone died here?"

"Whether it was murder or suicide," she pressed. "Michael's death was no accident. There is no doubt Adam was connected. He didn't pull the name Dalton out of thin air. No matter where he heard that name, the trouble started in this hotel. And for Adam's sake, it may be best to move him out of harm's way."

"I knew it!" he snapped. "I knew you were going to overreact to this!"

"Overreact?" she said. "How can I possibly overreact about a matter concerning the well-being of my son?"

"A man died, alright?" he observed. "That's all that happened! Somebody died! It happens every day! It's ludicrous to think Adam had anything to do with it! It doesn't matter if it was murder or suicide! It doesn't matter whether Dalton was involved or not! It was a fluke! A one-time incident! It had nothing to do with Adam! Our son is not talking to ghosts! There is no reason to throw away the massive investment we spent our whole lives building… the investment that we would be homeless and penniless without! Everything we have is sunk into this hotel! Do you really want to throw away everything we've worked for because Adam's been in a mood lately?"

"Been in a mood?" she averred. "Is that what you call it? Adam has not just 'been in a mood!' Strange things have been happening since he started talking to his new friend! One man is dead, Leon! That is not 'been in a mood!' I knew that was the reason you've been trivializing what's going on with Adam! You knew that I would be the first to put our son's safety before this damned hotel!"

"I'm not trivializing our son's safety!" he argued. "I knew you would be the first to get all emotional, irrational and fly off the handle! I knew you'd be the first to blow things out of proportion! That's why I've been trying to keep a proper perspective on things! Sure, things are a bit odd right now…"

"A bit odd?" she interrupted angrily.

"Alright. Listen," he sighed. "Let's not fight. I know you want to protect Adam. I'm concerned, too. But, all we have here is a few coincidences fueled by a fear of the history of this place. Deep down, you know Adam has no connection to what happened."

"How do you explain that he told Michael to go to that room?" she asked.

"For all we know," he ventured. "Dalton could be the guy who is behind this."

"How would he have known Michael was coming back here today?" she continued. "Why was the door to Room 6 unlocked even though the key wasn't missing?"

"The police explained that," he reminded. "Rita had already cleaned that room this morning. She must have left the door unlocked."

"But, how did the killer know she was going to do that?" she asked. "How did Adam know? What about the fact that Rita swears she locked the room when she left?"

"Who knows?" he shrugged. "Maybe Rita's the killer."

"Rita Giardano is not a murderer!" she proclaimed.

"I'm not making specific accusations," he pointed out. "I'm just saying that nobody knows what really happened. And, it doesn't make any sense to blame ghosts or Adam. There's no reason to run away from the business we've staked our whole lives on just because of a few coincidences and irrational fears."

She was silent for a minute.

"Maybe you're right," she finally admitted.

"Of course I am," he coaxed. "Can we put this behind us now, please?"

"I guess."

"Thank you."

He kissed her. He looked in her eyes. They were green, beautiful and filled with doubt and vulnerability.

"You know I love you, Carol."

"I love you, too."

"Everything will be fine," he whispered. "I promise you."

They kissed again. There was reassurance and comfort.

The next kiss was longer. It was a reminder of a passion that had been too easily forgotten.

She turned out the light.

It was time to remember again.

She could feel the warmth of the fireplace. It was so soothing.

It was so comforting.

No one else was there, aside from her husband…

And that boy!

She didn't like him. She didn't know why. It was so unlike her to dislike a child. He couldn't have been more than six or seven.

How could she dislike him so?

It was difficult to tell. But, she felt a disturbing, tingling sensation whenever the boy was near.

You know…the way a person feels when something is wrong.

The boy's face was stern. His expression was nearly angry. He pointed toward the fireplace.

The flames sprang up and leapt into the air. They hurled dangerous, intimidating slashes of red and yellow into the room.

Suddenly, a rope was hanging from the ceiling. She gasped as she recognized the man whose neck was in the noose. His face was discolored. His eyes were lifeless and bulging. He was suspended about five feet above the carpet.

The entire spectacle seemed far too familiar.

Then, those bulging eyes came alive! They looked right at her!

"Thou shall not have wrongful secrets," the hanging man demanded.

She screamed.

She grabbed her husband's arm. "Let's get out of here, Tom!" she shouted.

He just sat there.

"Why?" he asked.

She stared at him in shock.

"What do you mean, 'why?'" she asked while tugging at his arm. "Let's go!"

He didn't move.

"But, I'm happy right here," he said.

"Tom!" she begged. "Please! We have to get out of here!"

The hanging man began to laugh. It was a maniacal, evil laugh.

"You have nowhere to go," the boy imparted. "My mom wants you to stay here. So, you're not allowed to leave!"

"Tom!" she implored. "We have to leave now! Please! Come with me, Tom!"

"But, the fire is so cozy," he gently insisted.

Flames were shooting out of the fireplace. They soared across the room in fiery arches with wispy tails of smoke.

The hanging man was still laughing.

"The fire is dangerous, Tom!" she raved. "Someone's going to get hurt! Can't you see that?"

"Everything's fine, Margaret."

She pulled on his arm. He wouldn't budge.

"You're not going anywhere," the boy averred.

Her eyes were flooded with tears of fright. Flames rode haphazardly across the room, splashing against the carpet like tiny explosions.

The fire reflected in the boy's angry eyes.

"Mom wants you to stay!"

"Everything's just fine, Margaret."

The entire room seemed to be closing in on her. She glanced around in panic.

The hanging man wouldn't stop laughing.

"Stop pulling at me, Margaret," her husband said calmly. "Sit down. Relax."

She let go of his arm. A few flames shot by just in front of her face.

She cried as she ran hysterically toward the exit. She didn't want to leave her husband behind. However, she could not stay in that place any longer!

She raced out of the front door. Snow covered the parking lot outside the hotel. It must have been cold. But, she didn't notice. She just dashed as quickly as possible to her car.

But as she approached the vehicle, she stopped short. She stared in disbelief.

He was there! He was just standing there in front of the car!

How could that be?

Sure, he was much younger than she. Still, he was just a little boy! When she left him, he'd been standing in front of the fireplace.

How did he get out here so quickly? She didn't see him run past her or anything!

How did he do it?

He was scowling...much like he'd done in The Den. His angry expression scared her.

"Mom wants you to stay!" he scornfully reminded.

Suddenly, she was startled by a loud explosion. Her car blew up behind the young boy. It was a large, combustible explosion that heaved tall flames and a thick blanket of black smoke up into the air.

The car was entirely consumed by fire. Yet, the boy never even flinched.

She shrieked in horror.

She spun around and sped back into the hotel. She could see The Den from the lobby. Flames were still shooting across the room from the fireplace. Still, nobody seemed to notice. People were casually walking by as if nothing were wrong.

She walked slowly toward The Den.

There were two nooses hanging from the ceiling at this point. The same man was still hanging in the first noose.

He was still laughing.

The second noose was around the neck of someone who was much more familiar.

"Tom!" she gasped in fright.

Her husband looked down at her from his position at the end of the rope. He was suspended at least five feet off the ground. His face was growing a deep shade of red.

He smiled down at his wife.

"You should hang out with us, Margaret," he said. "This is fun!"

She screeched in absolute terror.

She sat up in her bed. Her breathing was heavy. Her face was drenched with sweat.

All was quiet. Her room was as black as the heart of Death.

The stillness enveloped the room. She struggled to regain her composure.

She glanced over at her husband. He was sleeping soundly beside her in the bed.

She breathed a sigh of relief.

Suddenly, there was a booming crash. The curtains by the window caught fire with a rumbling burst of spontaneous combustion. Brilliant long ribbons of red and yellow flames ran up the drapes. They flung themselves carelessly up toward the ceiling.

She stared in horrified disbelief as the fire roared by the window. She couldn't move. She couldn't speak.

Then, a form appeared amid the flames. It looked as though three teenage girls were trapped in the fire.

Fear shadowed their faces as their expressions absorbed the orange hues of the taunting fires. They reached out to the terrified woman in the bed.

She could hear their voices. They sounded faint and far away.

"Help! Please! Help us! Please…!"

She screamed with fright.

Her husband rolled over in bed. A genuine concern could be heard in his groggy voice. "Margaret?" he mumbled. "What's the matter?"

"Look!" she exclaimed as she pointed. "Over by the window!"

He rolled over. He squinted as he looked over by the curtains.

"So, what's the problem?" he muttered. "You don't like the drapes?"

"No!" she stammered. "You don't understand!"

"It's 2:00 in the morning, Margaret," he grumbled. "It's a little early to overreact to these people's taste in interior design. Don't you think?"

"No, Tom!" she frantically insisted. "The curtains were on fire just a minute ago! I swear!"

He turned his sleepy eyes to the window again.

"They seem fine now," he said. He allowed his head to drop back into the pillow.

"I mean it, Tom!" she pressed. "The curtains were on fire! There were three girls trapped in the flames! They were calling to me for help!"

"I don't hear anything," he muttered as he closed his eyes. "They must've worked it out."

"I'm serious, Thomas!" she proclaimed with a tone he knew not to trivialize. "The fire looked real! So did those girls! It scared me half to death!"

He rolled over on his back. He opened his eyes again.

"Three girls, huh?" he sighed impatiently. "Like the girls who died in that fire on this site twenty years ago?"

"Don't make light of this, Thomas!"

"I wouldn't dream of it."

"It looked so real," she said. "The fire. The girls. I heard them screaming."

"Are you okay now?"

"I'm calming down," she said. "But, I was already terrified. I was just waking up from an awful nightmare."

"You had a bad dream?"

He sat up while listening to her account of the dream. Like it or not, sleep was becoming an unlikely prospect.

When she was finished, he advised, "It was just a dream, sweetheart. It wasn't real. You just had a bad reaction to seeing that dead guy when we arrived. It's perfectly natural for you to flip out a little. But, it's just a harmless dream."

"It's not just the dead guy, Tom," she said. "It's everything! It's that boy! You saw him! You saw that evil look in his eyes! He wouldn't let us leave! A brand new car battery wouldn't work when we wanted to leave! Then as soon as we agreed to stay, the battery worked fine!"

"That had nothing to do with…"

"You saw the boy," she anxiously interrupted. "When he said, 'You didn't want them to leave…did you, Mom?' That was no accident! That was no coincidence!"

"Oh, for God's sake, Margaret…"

"I'm telling you, Tom," she persisted. "That boy is evil! This *place* is evil! That was no dream! It was an omen! If we stay here, something bad will happen to you! I just know it!"

"What are you saying?" he asked. "Do you want to move to a different hotel?"

"Well, I'm not staying here!"

"Will you cut it out?" he grunted. "I already drove all the way up here. I have to put up with your whacko sister and her crazy family all week. Now you want to go on a mad hunt for another hotel? Why do you always take these things so seriously? I'm sorry your bad dream scared you. I thought you'd be happy that you saw some ghosts. Isn't that why you chose this place?"

"Things are different now, Tom," she imparted. "It's not a game anymore. This place is dangerous!"

"If I agree to change hotels in the morning," he sighed. "Will you let me get some sleep?"

"Yes."

"Fine!" he declared. "We'll check out first thing in the morning! Okay?"

"Thank you," she said. "I love you, honey."

"Yeah, yeah, yeah," he grumbled as he rolled over in bed. "Now, good night!"

She laid back down. However, she couldn't even close her eyes.

She felt a consuming need to watch the window in the eerie darkness.

"Mr. and Mrs. Gould?" he said. "We need to have a serious talk with you and your son."

"We'd be happy to talk to you, Sgt. Agostino," Leon said. "But, it's Monday morning. Our son is back in school."

"Things have taken a critical turn in our investigation, sir," he said. "It's imperative that we find out exactly where your son heard the name Randy Dalton."

"Why?"

"We've discovered that Dalton was murdered a few months ago," he explained. "He was strangled with the chord from a curtain. It was a very professional job. People who were connected to Schumacker's bank were suspected at the time. But, they were cleared for lack of evidence. Certain bank records were acquired and investigated, but nothing concrete could be proven."

The young couple just stared in disbelief.

"It turns out," he continued. "That Schumacker was involved in a scheme to skim funds during certain transactions…especially transfers of moneys where it was easy to hide large amounts in foreign accounts and phony accounts, usually during money laundering schemes made by unscrupulous clients. Most of these clients were rich, and it was easy to convince them their money was safe until it was completely inaccessible. These people are so rich, they never even find out they've been robbed."

"That's terrible," Carol said.

"But, Schumacker and his friends got greedy," Taggerty said. "They got sick of settling for small amounts that their clients wouldn't miss. They decided to go for a big score against a Canadian drug lord who was running over 40 million through some trumped up European bank accounts in Stockholm, Oslo and Madrid. It's hard to be careful when you get cocky. And for a deal this big, they needed to enlist some outside help. Two men, including a Randall Dalton, threatened to pull out for some reason or other. Both men paid with their lives."

"That's a fascinating story," Carol admitted. "But, what does it have to do with my son?"

"Of course, much of this story is still speculation," Agostino said. "An investigation was triggered by Schumacker's death. It seems unlikely that he would kill himself less than a day after he personally transferred many of the funds that would have initiated this scam. We need to know where your son heard the name Randy Dalton."

"I can answer that," Leon said.

"You can?" Agostino asked.

"Yes," Leon nodded. "I'm sorry neither Adam nor I remembered yesterday. I think the shock of the tragedy followed by a police interrogation made us both nervous. We're not used to this kind of thing. I hope you can understand."

"Of course, Mr. Gould."

"We gave Michael a tour of our hotel Saturday," Leon explained. "I conducted part of the tour. My wife took over when I got busy. Adam was around off and on during that time. I forgot that Michael took a call on his cell phone while I was showing him around. He tried to keep it private, and it wasn't a long call. But, the discussion got a little heated. Michael threw a few names around. And as I grew to think of it, Dalton was one of the names he mentioned during that call."

The policemen looked suspicious.

"Are you sure?" Agostino asked.

"Relatively sure," Leon said. "At the time, the call seemed insignificant to me. But after what's happened, the incident came back to me."

"That's nice," Agostino said. "But, it still doesn't explain who lured him up to that hotel room and killed him."

"Maybe we should question all the guests who have been staying here the past few days," Taggerty suggested. "Sure, we've already talked to some of them. But, perhaps a detailed investigation of each and every one of them is in order."

"I must protest against that," Leon said. "These are our customers."

"This is a murder investigation, Mr. Gould!" Taggerty impatiently reminded.

"A *possible* murder investigation," Leon corrected. "There's no proof that this wasn't a suicide."

"As I said," Agostino reiterated. "Suicide seems improbable in this situation."

"I don't want to stop you from doing your job, gentlemen," Leon said. "But, I'm trying to run a business here. This hotel is my livelihood."

"We'll be as discreet and considerate as we can, sir," Agostino assured him.

"I'd appreciate that."

"And, we'll want to talk to Miss Giardano again, too," Taggerty added. "The maid who was cleaning Room 6 yesterday. Among other things, we want to double-check her account of whether she may have left that room unlocked when she was done."

"Rita?" Carol said. "I think she's starting in Room 3 today."

"Okay," Agostino nodded. "We'll start there. Then we'll talk to some of your guests. Please be available in case we need you."

"Sure thing, gentlemen," Leon said.

He watched the cops walk to the elevator. Then he turned to his wife.

"I don't like this," he muttered.

"Neither do I," she agreed. "But, what can we do?"

"Not much."

"Was it true what you told them?" she asked. "Did Adam really hear the name Dalton during a phone call?"

"The phone call was real enough," he said. "Michael got a little upset. He spouted off a few names. I don't specifically recall Dalton, but it's possible. I can't even swear it was a business call. I just mentioned it to the cops to get them off Adam's back."

"Thank you."

At that moment, an older couple approached the reception desk.

"Mr. and Mrs. Prosky," Carol smiled. "How are you this morning?"

"We're checking out, I'm afraid," Tom said.

"Why?" Carol asked as her smile vanished. "Is something wrong?"

"I just can't stay here anymore," Margaret imparted shakily.

"She had a bad dream last night," Tom explained.

"Oh," Carol said. "I'm sorry."

"A horrible nightmare," Margaret corrected. "Followed by ghosts! I saw those girls who burned to death in the fire! It was more than I could handle! Especially after seeing my husband's corpse in that nightmare!"

"That sounds dreadful, Mrs. Prosky," Carol said. "Is there anything we can do?"

"No," she stated with finality. "You are very nice people, and I'm deeply sorry. But, I just can't stay here anymore."

Then, she saw the small boy standing not ten feet away from her.

She jumped with a start. She began to tremble as she stared at him.

"How long have you been standing there?" she asked fearfully. "Never mind! It doesn't matter! I just want to leave!"

"I'm really sorry, Gould," Tom said. "It's not your fault. This is a beautiful little hotel you've got here. But, my wife gets a bit skittish about these things."

"I understand."

"Let's just settle up the bill," Tom said. "And, we'll be on our way."

"Are they leaving, Mom?"

"Yes. They're leaving, Adam."

"Yes!" Margaret added nervously. "We're leaving! It's okay to leave, right? Tell him that it's okay for us to leave!"

"Of course it's okay for you to leave, Mrs. Prosky," Carol said. "Adam knows that."

"Tell him anyway, please!"

"He's just a boy, Mrs. Prosky," Carol gently assured her. "He's perfectly harmless."

"Please!"

"Adam?" Carol acquiesced with a sigh. "It's okay for the Proskys to leave."

"I know, Mom."

"Thank you," Margaret sighed. "I'm sorry to be so silly, Mrs. Gould. I know I may be going a bit overboard. But, that dream last night scared the Dickens out of me!"

"There's no need to apologize, Mrs. Prosky," Carol said.

"Are we all set, Tom?" she asked her husband. "Let's go."

They all said their final good-byes. Then, Margaret quickly dragged her husband out of the hotel.

As they neared their car, Tom said, "Will you let go of my arm already? I can walk on my own! What's your hurry? We're out of there, aren't we? You should feel safe now."

"You haven't started the car yet," she reminded.

"For God's sake, Margaret," he complained. "Whatever happened yesterday was a fluke. Everything will be fine. Will you please calm down?"

"I'll calm down when we get away from this place," she said.

They got in the car. He turned the key in the ignition.

"See that?" he smiled. "You had nothing to worry about. It started right up on the first try."

"Yeah," she scoffed. "It started because I made that woman tell her devil-child to leave us alone!"

"You're a nut, Margaret," he said. "Now, where should we look for another hotel?"

"Just drive around," she said. "I'm sure we'll come across something."

"Well," he said as he pulled the car out of its parking space. "At least *your* nightmare is over. I still have to spend a week with your family."

He drove away from The Hillside Inn.

"Thanks for your time, Miss Giardano."

"Anytime, Sergeant," she said. "I just wish I could've been more help."

"Not at all," he said. "You've been a big help. Have a good day."

The two men walked out of Room 3.

"Well, that was a waste of time," Taggerty said.

"I guess," he muttered impatiently. "We needed to double-check her story, though."

"So, now what?"

"We return our focus on that kid."

"That's what I was thinking," Taggerty agreed. "This case still smells awful fishy. And that spooky kid and his friend are the reason why."

"Right," he nodded. "I don't think this was suicide. That boy knows something. Or at least, his friend does. The father is covering for his son. I get that. But, I doubt that boy's friend is imaginary! I think he's very real. We've got to find out who the friend is! Because whoever it is, he's not just dangerous. He has access to information. He's smart! And 'smart and dangerous' is a real scary combination!"

Chapter 6
You've Been Very Bad!

There had been a cold spell. There was even a storm that had dropped two feet of snow on the area a week before.

However, the temperatures had begun to rise. Snow was melting during the day. Still, large, dirty white mounds lined parking lots and roadways throughout that section of Oregon. Thin patches of refrozen ice reflected sunlight off the streets like a thousand shards from so many broken mirrors.

Winter was in no hurry to disappear.

They sat in their room. Usually, they couldn't afford the luxury of taking a half hour to watch TV with a cup of coffee. Their time was not their own.

But, this was a special day.

"Good morning," the news anchor said. "It is now 6:15 AM on Friday, March 26, 2004. Our top story this morning: In the town of Spruce Valley, Police Chief Edward M. Farley announced yesterday that he has officially ruled the death of banker Michael D. Schumacker to be a suicide. If you'll recall, Schumacker was found..."

"Do you believe it?" she smiled. "After over two months of constant police harassment, they finally ruled it as a suicide. It's actually over!"

"It's about time," he said. "Hearing it on the news makes it sound official. Maybe we can get our business back to normal."

"This has been a rough few months," she admitted.

"And you thought we were going to have to leave this hotel," he reminded. "Did you really think Adam had anything to do with that mess?"

"I didn't know what to think, Leon," she said. "The only thing I was sure of was that protecting my son is my top priority."

"I told you there was nothing to worry about," he boasted. "Adam's been fine these past two months. Sure, he's a kid. He's had his aggravating moments. He's had his moods. He's even made a couple of rude comments to our customers that I wish he hadn't. But overall, he's been a good kid."

"I guess."

"Is there a problem?"

"I don't know," she said. "I still haven't been convinced that there *isn't* a problem."

"What do you mean?"

"That whole thing blew over rather quickly," she observed. "Don't you think? I mean, our son was behaving very strangely for a while. Michael turns up dead in a very bizarre set of circumstances that were never properly explained. The police call it a suicide, because they have nothing to go on. And all during the investigation, Adam goes from scaring everyone around him, to being the perfect angel. Doesn't that seem odd?"

"Honestly, Carol," he said. "Why can't you just be happy for a minute? This whole escapade is over. Why can't you just enjoy it?"

"Do you really believe this is over?" she asked.

"Yes," he stated confidently. "It was a single, solitary, unfortunate incident that we can all put behind us. I have a hotel to run. I don't have time to create unnecessary anxieties for myself."

"I envy your optimism."

"Good morning, Dawn," he beamed.

"Hi, Glen."

"What's the matter?" he asked with genuine concern. "You look a little down."

"It's Spencer."

"Is he your boyfriend?"

"Yes," she said. "I've been seeing him for about three months. I don't know what's wrong. It's not that he's a bad guy or anything. I'm just not that into him."

"Why don't you just end it?"

"I keep trying," she explained. "But, I can never go through with it. I don't want to hurt him. I don't have the heart."

"You're not doing him any favors by stringing him along," he imparted.

"I know," she said. "I've kept him around because he's a convenient Saturday night date. But, the thing is…I think he's getting serious."

"After only three months?" he asked. "He doesn't sound too emotionally stable. Plus, why do you need a convenient Saturday night date? I'd love to take you out."

"So would Jeffrey Bartlett," she said. "He's always on my case. I've been thinking of talking to Mr. Gould about him."

"Would you like me to have a word with him?" he offered.

"No, thanks," she smiled. "Let Mr. Gould handle it. That way, I know I went through official channels."

"Okay," he said. "What about your boyfriend?"

"I'm not sure what to do."

"Today is Friday," he pointed out. "Why don't you let me take you out tonight? That would show him."

"It sure would," she admitted with a coy grin.

"So, what do you say?" he asked. "I never did get to cook for you. Or I could take you somewhere nice. Nobody knows the best restaurants in town as well as a chef does."

"You may have a point."

"Of course I do."

"What would I tell Spencer?" she asked. "He's expecting me to go with him tonight."

"You want to dump him, right?" he suggested. "This gives you some incentive, as well as an excuse."

"Well…" She paused to consider the offer.

"Come on," he gently coaxed. "I promise we'll have dinner right away. That way, I won't have to make you a sandwich before you leave. Besides, I'm running low on chicken salad. And, I don't feel like making more."

"You make a compelling case."

"I'm a compelling guy."

"Can I think about it?" she asked. "I'm not sure what I'd tell Spencer."

"Tell him you're sick of bowling," he suggested.

"I already did," she said. "We haven't been bowling in months. His new thing is basketball."

"He makes you play basketball?"

"He makes me *watch* basketball," she said. "It's the college playoffs this month. I'm so sick of concession stand candy, franks and fries! I don't know how I've kept from gaining a ton."

"You poor girl!" he sympathized. "See? I'm doing you a favor!"

"Let me think about it."

"Take all the time you need," he said. "Just remember what I told you about chicken salad."

"I'll let you know by the end of the day," she said.

"Fair enough."

"By the way," she said. "Something smells great in here."

"Today's lunch special is coconut shrimp," he informed her. "You see? There are advantages to dating a chef."

"I could believe that if you slipped me a few of those shrimp under the table at lunchtime," she suggested.

"I'd be happy to do that," he offered. "For a girl who was going out with me tonight."

"I'll keep that in mind."

"By the way," he said. "Did you hear the news this morning? The cops labeled that banker's death as a suicide."

"I heard," she said. "I was so glad to hear it! At last, this place won't be crawling with cops anymore. What a relief! I'll bet Mr. and Mrs. Gould are ecstatic."

"I haven't seen them yet today," he said. "But, I'm sure you're right."

"In a way," she admitted. "It still kind of scares me, though. I still think something's wrong with Adam. He still gives me the creeps."

"Why?" he asked. "Nothing has happened since the hanging."

"That kid still frightens me," she said. "It's the way he looks at you. It's just not natural coming from a boy his age."

"Don't let it bother you, Dawn," he said. "Just be thankful that the cops are gone for good."

"Maybe you're right," she shrugged. "Oh well. I'd better get to cleaning. Have a good day, Glen. And, save me a few of those shrimp for lunch."

"You know my stipulations," he reminded playfully.

She winked with a smile before she left.

"How was everything, sir?" asked the waitress.

"Good, thanks."

"Can I get you anything else?"

"No," he said. "Just give us the check. As soon as we finish our coffee, we'll be on our way."

"Yes, sir."

She quickly added up the bill. Then, she placed it face down on the table.

"I'll be back in a minute to take that for you," she smiled. Then, she scurried off.

He looked at the girl who was sitting across from him.

"Nobody makes greasy eggs and bacon like these little local diners," he commented.

"I don't know how you eat that shit," she said.

"Are you kidding?" he said. "This is the best breakfast food there is. How do you come to a diner and order Raisin Bran? They have people who will cook for you here."

"Raisin Bran is better for you than this garbage," she said. "Raisin Bran won't clog your arteries and give you a heart attack before you're forty."

"Oh, bull!" he scoffed. "You think just because you pour milk on your food instead of catsup, you think it's healthier for you."

"No," she disagreed. "I think my food is healthier, 'cause it doesn't leave a large puddle of grease on your plate when you're done."

"Oh, just finish your coffee," he said. "It's time to go."

"Chris?" she asked. "Do you think anybody's ever going to catch us? You know, with that baby scam thing? We've got to be making some enemies."

"How's anybody going to catch us, Jennifer?" he assured her. "We do all our business on the internet. We don't go looking for clients. They come looking for us."

"I still feel a little guilty," she admitted. "After all, these people come to us looking to adopt babies. They're all real desperate 'cause they can't have kids on their own."

"Don't you get it, honey?" he said. "That's what makes them such an easy target. That's why they're willing to pay so much. That's why it's so easy to jerk them around for months and make them spend extra for 'added expenditures'. That's how we get the big pay-offs. When our webpage disappears, how are they going to find us?"

"But, doesn't it bother you when we don't deliver?" she asked.

"Why should it?" he said. "I didn't make these people impotent. I offer a service."

"What service?"

"We give these people months of optimism," he justified. "We give these people hope. Isn't that worth a few thousand dollars?"

"We give them *false* hope."

"Hope is hope," he argued. "It's months of relief from the agony of knowing they'll never have children. That's got to be worth something. You're not going to complain when the McLeods' money pays for your Raisin Bran, are you?"

"No."

"Alright then," he said. "Listen, Jennifer. What we're doing is a victimless crime. It's completely harmless. Nobody ever really gets hurt."

"Nobody except Jim."

"That was an accident," he reasoned. "We wouldn't have fought if he wasn't going to turn us in. It was none of his business. He was my brother, for Christ's sake! He should've been on my side!"

"You didn't have to kill him, Chris!"

"How many times do I have to say it was an accident?" he asked impatiently. "It's okay, though. They'll never find out what happened. Luckily, when I put him in his truck and pushed him over that cliff, the whole thing caught fire when it hit bottom. By the time they find it, all the evidence will be destroyed. For all they know, he could have just drove off the cliff! Don't you see? We're in the clear!"

"Now that Jim's gone," she asked. "Who's going to start up our new websites?"

"That's why I've been taking that computer class, Jennifer," he replied. "Now, I don't want to hear any more about this. Finish your coffee, so we can leave. Did you say we're going to be stuck in Oregon another night?"

"Yeah," she nodded. "I figured we'll never make it back to Seattle today. So, I got us a room reserved for tonight a few miles north of here."

"Where abouts?"

"It's in a small town called Spruce Valley," she explained. "Everything's booked up because of the State college basketball finals. But, I got us a room in some place called The Hillside Inn."

"How far is it from here?" he asked.

"It's about sixty miles north of here," she said. "Not far off the coast."

"Okay," he said. "We'll kick around here for an hour or two. Then, we'll head north. Where's that damned waitress?"

"Relax, Chris," she said. "We're not in any hurry."

"That's easy for you to say," he grunted. "You're not the one that has to face my mother when she finds out about Jim. Hopefully, she won't find out what we did."

"What *you* did!" she corrected. "Leave me out of this!"

"Alright then!" he grumbled. "So, don't tell me to relax!"

Wrongful Secrets

⊷✥⊶

She finished making the bed. She stood silently for a moment. Then, she sat on the bed with a sigh.

She took out her cell phone and hit the speed-dial.

"Spencer?" she said into the phone. "It's me."

"What's up, honey?"

"I won't be able to go out with you tonight," she said sympathetically. "I'm sorry."

"Why?" he asked. "What's going on?"

"My cousin's in from out of town," she said. "He's only in town for one day. I promised to take him out tonight."

"That's okay," he suggested. "We can take him to the basketball game. He'd love it. We're into the finals. The winner of tonight's game goes on to…"

"I don't think so, Spencer," she interrupted. "We haven't seen each other in a long time. We have a lot of catching up to do. We have family stuff to talk about. It would bore you silly. You understand, don't you?"

"But, Dawn," he complained. "I've been looking forward to tonight's game all week! You can't just walk out on me now!"

"It's family, Spencer," she insisted. "Please be adult about this. I'll clear some time so we can have lunch tomorrow. We need to talk anyway."

"What does that mean?" he asked.

"It just means that we need to talk," she said.

"That sounds scary," he said. "I know what it means when a girl says 'we need to talk.' Is there a problem?"

"No."

"Does this have something to do with this 'cousin' you're blowing me off for tonight?" he pressed.

"Of course not."

"First, you give me some half-assed story about a cousin coming in from out of town," he argued. "And now, we need to talk? I don't like this! What the hell, Dawn? If you have something to say, tell me already!"

"Don't be like that, Spencer," she said in a placating tone. "I really do have to see my cousin tonight. You and I can have a nice lunch tomorrow, and we'll talk. That's all I meant. Please don't make a federal case out of this."

"Is it the basketball?" he said desperately. "The finals are almost over. After next week, we never have to go to another game."

"Please stop, Spencer."

"I know you got sick of bowling before," he said. "Sometimes, I get a one-track mind and I get carried away."

"Spencer!" she said curtly. "I am seeing my cousin tonight! I will have lunch with you tomorrow! You can pick me up at the inn at noon! Okay?"

"Okay."

The sound in his voice made her feel guilty.

"Sorry about tonight," she said sweetly. "I'll see you tomorrow at noon. 'Bye."

"'Bye."

He still had that sound in his voice. Her eyes felt a bit moist. She didn't know why.

It was only Spencer. Oh well.

She stood up. She plugged in the vacuum.

Work took her mind off her troubles. And the sound of the vacuum drowned out the lingering guilt.

"Hello," he smiled. "Welcome to The Hillside Inn. My name is Jeffrey Bartlett. How may I help you?"

"I'm Christopher Hurd," he introduced. "This is my wife, Jennifer. I believe you have reservations for us to stay here tonight."

"Yes we do, Mr. Hurd," he said after spotting the name in his book. "Could you sign in, please?"

"Sure."

Chris took the pen from the counter. He looked over what he had to sign.

"Ah, Mrs. Gould," Jeffrey said. "It's nice to see you. This is Mr. and Mrs. Christopher Hurd. They have reservations for tonight."

Carol politely introduced herself.

"I was just telling this lovely young couple," Jeffrey explained. "That I've reserved Room 26 for them on the third floor tonight."

"Wonderful," Carol said. "That's a beautiful room. I'm sure you'll love it."

"I'm sure we will," Chris said.

"That's a gorgeous fireplace, Mrs. Gould," Jennifer said. "Do you ever use it?"

"Oh yes," she said. "During the coldest part of winter, we have a roaring fire going in there all the time. But now that it's March and the days are getting warmer, we give it a rest some days. We still have a fire in there every night until the middle of spring."

"It must be wonderful," Jennifer commented. "So peaceful and calming."

Donald Gorman

"It is," she said. "Sometimes, we invite some of our guests to have a free cup of hot cocoa or glass of wine at night when the fire is going. You seem like a nice young couple. Would you like to stop down here for wine or cocoa this evening?"

"That would be great," Jennifer beamed. "Could we, Chris?"

"I don't see why not," Chris said. "Thank you, Mrs. Gould. That's very kind of you."

"Think nothing of it."

"I think we'll settle into our room now, if you don't mind," Chris said. "It's nearly time for dinner."

"Do you need help with your luggage?" Jeffrey offered.

"No thanks," Chris said. "We only have a few cases. We can manage. Can you recommend a good restaurant around here?"

"We have a fine restaurant right through those doors," she said while pointing.

"Oh," Chris said with surprise. "I think we were expecting to see a little of this nice town tonight. I'm sure you have a fine restaurant here. But, we don't get to this area very often, and we…"

"Don't apologize," Carol said. "I understand. There's a great little Italian place on Livingston called Vincienzo's. It's about a block after you turn right off Armory Blvd."

"Sounds lovely," Jennifer said.

"Thanks, Mrs. Gould," Chris said. "We'll see you later tonight. And, maybe we'll try your restaurant for breakfast in the morning before we leave."

"We look forward to seeing you," she said.

Chris took the key from Jeffrey. He took one suitcase. His wife took another. They walked to the elevator.

They only waited for a minute. The elevator door opened.

No one got out.

However, a boy who appeared to be about seven years old stood in the corner. He stood perfectly still. He just stared at the young couple.

They waited for the boy to move.

He stood eerily still. He just stared at the young couple.

"Are you getting off the elevator, kid?" Chris asked.

The boy didn't move. He just shook his head while staring at the young couple.

Chris and Jennifer stepped into the elevator. The door closed.

The elevator started to rise slowly. Nobody else was there. Chris and Jennifer stood in the front. The boy stayed in the back. He didn't move.

Jennifer leaned toward her husband. "Is it me?" she whispered. "Or does this elevator seem awful slow?"

"It does move kind of slow," he quietly agreed.

"Who's that kid?" she whispered. "He keeps staring at us. He's making me nervous."

"I don't know who he is," Chris whispered. "But, he is kind of creepy."

"Can't you make him stop staring?" she whispered. "He's starting to scare me."

"He's just a kid," Chris whispered. "What could he possibly do? Besides, we're just about up to our floor."

Just then, the elevator stopped. The bell rang. The door opened.

Donald Gorman

They stared out into the hall.

"Hey, kid," Chris asked. "Do you know where Room 26 is?"

In a low, solemn voice, the boy replied, "It's like the third or fourth door on the left. Right down the hall."

"Thanks, kid."

He stepped off the elevator with his wife.

"You've been bad!" the boy declared.

The young couple stopped dead in their tracks. A chill ran up Chris' spine.

He spun around to face the boy. "What did you say?" he asked.

"I know what you've done!" the boy sharply accused. "You've been very bad!"

The young couple shared a guilty, frightened glance.

The elevator doors started to close.

Chris returned to his senses. "Wait!" he cried. "Hey, kid! Wait!"

It was too late. The doors were closed.

Chris and Jennifer froze. They looked at each other with fear in their eyes.

"What the hell was that?" Chris asked.

"I don't know," Jennifer replied shakily. "Whose kid was that? What do you think he meant? You don't think…"

"It couldn't be!" Chris exclaimed. "There's no way that kid could know! I've never seen him before. Have you?"

"No," she stammered. "I never saw him before in my life!"

"This can't be for real," he scoffed. "That kid doesn't know anything. He's a kid. He's probably just playing a game or something."

"Do you think we should chase him down?" she asked. "Should we ask Mrs. Gould whose kid that is?"

"I don't think it's necessary," he said. "The boy has to be playing some kind of war game or spy game or something."

"Do you really think so?"

"Sure," he grinned. "Me and Jim used to do stuff like that all the time when we were that age. We've got nothing to worry about."

"If you say so."

"Sure," he reiterated. "Don't worry about it. Come on. Let's get to our room."

They carried their luggage to Room 26. Chris unlocked the door. They went in.

As they set their cases on the bed, his cell phone rang.

"Hello?" he answered.

"Hi, Chris," said the caller. "It's your mother."

"Hi, Mom," he said. "What's up?"

"Have you heard from Jimmy?" Mom asked. "He was supposed to call me. I haven't heard from him in over a week."

"Sorry, Mom," he said. "I haven't heard from Jimmy in nearly a month."

"It's not like him not to call me," Mom said. "He's usually such a good boy."

"He's probably busy," he said. "It happens to everybody once in a while. I'm sure he's fine. Listen, Mom. I have to go. If I hear from Jim, I'll have him call you."

"Well, where are you, Chris?"

"I'm down in Oregon on business," he said.

"Oregon?" Mom asked with curiosity. "What kind of business could you have down in Oregon?"

"I'll explain it to you later, Mom," he said. "Really. I have to go. And, don't worry about Jimmy. I'm sure he's fine. I'll have him call you if I hear from him. 'Bye, Mom. I love you."

"I love you too, Chris," Mom said. "'Bye."

He hung up.

"Well," he sighed. "Mom hasn't found out about Jim yet. I guess they haven't even found the body. That's good news for us."

"It is?" Jennifer asked.

"Sure," he explained. "The longer he goes undiscovered, the harder it will be for the cops to pin down an exact time of death. That will hamper their investigation. Plus, the natural elements will have to contaminate any existing evidence. I'm telling you. We're definitely in the clear."

"Will you stop saying 'we'?" she insisted. "I had nothing to do with this."

"You can't say that anymore, sweetheart," he argued. "Now you're an accessory after the fact."

"If that's true," she said with a sudden chill of realization. "Then I'm even more scared about that kid in the elevator."

"Yeah," he admitted. "That kid was a bit creepy. And, that little incident was kind of suspicious. It's hard to believe that kid really knows anything, though."

"I know, Chris," she reluctantly agreed. "But, I think we should keep an eye out for that boy. Seriously! I don't care how young he is. That kid scares me!"

The sun was setting over the ocean. Waves crashed against the shore. They ran up against the beach then retreated like children playing Tag. The water reflected the bold orange shade of the sun, which slowly sank into the horizon as if going for a dip.

A warm, gentle breeze eased past beachcombers on blankets and kids in bathing suits. A young couple walked past a tall, vacant lifeguard chair.

It was a shame to walk out of this setting and into a bar.

He recognized its seedy décor from his last trip to this town. He walked up to the bar and took a seat beside his friend.

"Hi, Frank."

"Hi, Logan."

"Been here long?"

"No," Frank said. "Maybe half an hour. You're right on time."

"How've you been?"

"The same," Frank said. "And you?"

"I just made a deal with a company up here in L.A.," he said. "It's worth a lot of money, too. I'm on Cloud 9. You might be seeing me a bit more often."

"Hurray for me."

"What's the matter, Frank?"

"What's always the matter?" he grunted. "The second wife's a bigger bitch than the first. No matter how much money I rake in, the two of them divide it up between them and I'm left with nothing! Alimony, child support, bills…"

Logan signaled to the bartender.

"Ashley just decided she needs a bigger car," Frank said. "I guess it's supposed to go along with her ever-growing ass."

"Bartender?" Logan said. "Can I have a Scotch and water please?"

"And I just refurnished the whole house," Frank continued. "At her insistence. She's great at finding ways to spend my money."

"Good luck finding a woman who isn't," Logan said.

The bartender placed a glass on the bar. He poured the Scotch. Then, he filled it with water.

"I'll get this round," Frank said. "Get me another, Marty."

"Thanks, Frank," Logan said.

"Don't mention it," he said. "How are things with you and Vanessa?"

"Alright," Logan said. "She's a good girl, for the most part."

"Lucky you."

"You're so cynical, Frank," Logan said. "So jaded. Do you ever enjoy anything?"

"Occasionally," he said. "I love vodka. Thanks, Marty."

He took a big gulp from his glass.

"Oh," he continued. "That's another thing. You might be interested to know I actually decided to go to our high school reunion in June."

"You did?"

"Yeah," he said. "Ashley talked me into it. I'm starting to look forward to it, too. And just like I told you, I reserved a room at that hotel they built over the ruins of the old Hilzak place. I couldn't resist."

"You're a piece of work, Frank."

"It's called The Hillside Inn now," he explained. "Do you believe it? I wonder if they did that on purpose. 'Hillside' sounds kind of like 'Hilzak'. Just like the way we used to call the place Hell Shack."

"Maybe it's called 'Hillside'," Logan said. "Because it's on the side of Morris Hill."

"Maybe," he said. "But, it still seemed like such a coincidence."

"So, past memories don't bother you?" Logan asked.

"Why should they?" he said. "That was twenty years ago. We already got away with it. The cops can't touch me now. Besides, we've got some good memories of that place. That was a much simpler time."

"Not all the memories were so great," Logan reminded.

"I know," he sighed. "That night still haunts me sometimes. But, facing my demons is supposed to be therapeutic, isn't it?"

"I guess."

"Damn!" he muttered. "I know what happened to those girls wasn't right. And I do feel guilty. I really thought I loved Trixie at the time. Teenage love. It's amazing how screwed up your head gets at that age."

"It's all hormones."

"Right!" he scoffed. "Something else takes over when you get a little older. I'm not sure what it is, but it certainly ain't brains!"

"You got that right," Logan agreed. "So, you don't mind staying in that place?"

"No," he said. "I already told you it's good to face your demons."

"I hear Rich will be staying there too," Logan said. "I think you're both nuts. Speaking of demons, I hear the place is still haunted."

"Jesus!" he laughed. "You don't believe in that shit, do you?"

"Not usually," Logan said. "But, that place creeps me out. Especially after what happened. Didn't you tell me you saw the ghost of Old Man Hilzak just before the fire?"

"I thought so at the time," he said. "But, I've sobered up more than once since then. Let's face it. It couldn't be. I was seventeen, drunk and that whole thing with Trixie got me mixed up. I wasn't thinking straight."

"I still think you're taking a chance," Logan advised.

"Whatever," he said. "Why? Where are you and Vanessa staying?"

"We found a place near the high school," Logan said. "It's called The Black Falcon Hotel."

"I remember that place."

"I hear they remodeled it," Logan explained. "It's bigger and fancier now. Bill Ambrose told me. He'll be staying there too."

"We'll all have to get together," he grinned. "Maybe this trip won't be so bad after all. What's Ambrose doing nowadays?"

"I hear he's got some high-paying job with some major airline," Logan replied.

"Good for him," he said. "That little bastard! I always figured he'd put the rest of us to shame. He can buy the drinks!"

Wrongful Secrets

"Sounds good," Logan nodded. "In fact, right now I'll buy the next round as soon as I get back from the men's room."

"You heard him, Marty," he said to the bartender.

He watched Logan walk to the bathroom.

He felt a sudden chill.

He could still picture the vivid image of three terrified girls in a window framed by fire. Had he really seen the face of Old Man Hilzak as the vicious flames closed off the window? Had he heard that voice?

"Some people never die! Some things never end!"

No. It couldn't be!

He was just a kid. He was drunk.

Plus, everything else…

The night was clear, black and stringent. There was a depth to the darkness that unnerved even the barren tree branches that lined the hill. It seemed to eat away at the sallow half moon. The scattered stars were bright but fearful.

Inside, a small group of people enjoyed the comfort of a warm, cozy fire.

"Thanks for inviting us, Mrs. Gould."

"You're quite welcome, Mrs. Hurd," she said. "And, please call me Carol."

"Then, call me Jennifer."

"Would you care for more wine, Jennifer?" she offered.

"That would be nice," Jennifer smiled. "Thank you."

"And how about you, Mr. Hurd?" she asked.

"Yes, please," he said. "And you can call me Chris."

"Fine."

She smiled as she poured.

"This is a great wine, Carol," he said. "You have excellent taste."

"We do our best."

"And, the fireplace is absolutely charming," Jennifer added. "I couldn't think of a better way to spend a chilly March evening."

"I'm glad you're having a good time," Carol said. "We can't possibly invite everyone who stays here down to do this with us. Leon and I only ask the guests we really like to join us here in The Den at night. And you seem like such a pleasant young couple."

"Thank you for saying so," he smiled. "We feel honored."

"I know it's hardly a presidential citation," Leon said. "But, we do try to be selective. And my wife usually makes good choices."

"I'd like to propose a toast, if I may," he offered while raising his glass. "Here's to Love, Luck and Good Choices."

"Love, Luck and Good Choices," they chorused.

They raised their glasses. They drank.

"So, what brings you to town, Chris?" Leon asked.

"We were visiting family downstate," he said. "Actually, we're from Seattle. That's a long drive from here. So, we decided to take our time and spend the night."

"What line of work are you in?" Leon asked.

"I'm an entrepreneur," he said. "I'm in the…"

He stopped. There was a distressed look on his face.

"Oh my God!" he gasped. "Do you see? It's him!"

"Oh no!" Jennifer exclaimed. "It's that kid!"

Leon and Carol exchanged a worried glance.

They spun around and surveyed the room.

"What kid?" Carol asked steadily.

"He's gone now," Jennifer sputtered. "I could've sworn he was just here! Then, he just vanished!"

"When we first checked in," he explained. "There was a young kid on the elevator. I don't know whose kid it was. He just stared at us for the longest time. Then, he yelled at us. He yelled something like, 'I know what you've done! You've been very bad!'"

The Goulds looked at each other with growing concern.

"What did the kid look like?" Leon asked.

"I don't know," he shrugged. "Six or seven years old. Three, maybe three and a half feet tall. He had dark hair and very intense brown eyes."

"That sounds like our Adam," Carol stated. "Are you saying you just saw him?"

"That's your son?" Jennifer asked. "Does he usually go around threatening people?"

"Not very often," Carol said.

"Perhaps I'd better go check on him," Leon suggested.

"Perhaps we'd *both* better go," Carol advised. "Would you excuse us please?"

"Sure," Chris nodded with a curious expression.

The Goulds hurried over to the elevator.

"Damn it!" Carol muttered. "Do you think Adam is up to his old tricks again?"

"Let's not jump to conclusions," Leon said. "Let's get the whole story first. Frankly, we don't know for sure that he ever had any 'old tricks.' Michael's death was ruled a suicide. Remember?"

The elevator door opened. They got in. Leon pushed the button for the second floor.

"The cops don't really believe that was a suicide," Carol sharply reminded. "And neither do you. I'm worried, Leon. Maybe it's not a good idea for the Hurds to stay here tonight!"

"Don't get ahead of yourself," he averred. "We'll check on Adam first. Then, we can make whatever decisions we need to make after that!"

They rushed to their room. Leon unlocked their door. Then, they quickly made their way to their son's bedroom.

Carol opened the bedroom door. It was dark inside. The sliver of light afforded by the open door revealed a boy in bed who was well tucked under the covers.

"He's sound asleep," Carol whispered. "Should we wake him?"

"Under the circumstances," Leon said. "I think we'd better."

"I'll do it," Carol sighed.

She walked over to the bed. She leaned over and gently shook her son's shoulder.

"Adam?" she said softly.

He moved a little. But, he didn't reply.

She spoke a little louder this time. "Adam?" she said.

"Hmmm?" he muttered as he rolled over.

"Adam?" she repeated. "Mommy needs to talk to you."

"I'm sleeping, Mom!"

Wrongful Secrets

"So, you weren't downstairs a few minutes ago?" she asked gently.

"No, Mom! I'm sleeping!"

"Did you yell at one of our guests today?" she inquired softly. "Did you tell somebody that you know what they did and they were very bad?"

"No, Mom," he mumbled. "You told me to never talk to the guests. Remember?"

"Are you sure you didn't talk to anybody?" she asked.

"Yes, Mom!" he whined. "Let me sleep!"

"Okay," she whispered. "Good night, sweetheart."

He mumbled as he moved a little.

Carol and Leon left the room. She closed the door silently behind her. They each took a seat in the living room.

"Well," she sighed with consternation. "He was fast asleep. He didn't even open his eyes the whole time I was speaking to him."

"So, we know he wasn't downstairs just now," Leon surmised. "But, what about before? Do you think he accused the Hurds in the elevator earlier today?"

"He said he didn't," she reminded. "Can we believe him? Can we dare to believe him? Our guests' lives could be at stake."

"For one thing," Leon stated. "We can't just throw that nice, young couple out on the street now. It's nearly 11:00 at night. Where are they going to go? And, what are we going to say to them? 'I'm sorry. You have to leave because our seven-year-old son just might be possessed by spooks, and if he accuses you of something, you just might possibly die…maybe?' Do you know how we would look?"

"What if something happens to those people, Leon?" she asked.

"What could happen?" he reasoned. "There is still no proof that Adam had any connection to Michael Schumacker's death. And, there's no proof that Adam even talked to the Hurds. It could have been anybody. The Chisholms in Room 14 have a seven-year-old, don't they?"

"She's a girl," she reminded. "And, she's blonde."

"I still say we have nothing to worry about," he insisted.

"You were as worried as I was when the Hurds first mentioned it," she pointed out.

"It was a knee-jerk reaction," he justified. "Luckily, I had time to come to my senses."

"Are you sure?"

"We can't throw guests out every time we think Adam may have talked to them," he averred. "Especially at 11:00 in the evening! I'll admit it may be a good idea to be a bit more vigilant tonight."

"What are you going to do?" she asked. "Patrol the halls all night until dawn?"

"Don't get smart!" he argued. "I don't know what I'll do yet. I'll probably sleep with one eye open. I doubt I'll get much sleep, anyway."

Meanwhile down in The Den, the young couple was concerned.

"What do you think that was all about?" Chris asked.

"I don't know," Jennifer said. "But, that was awfully suspicious. Do you think they know something about their son that we should be scared of?"

Wrongful Secrets

"How can you be scared of a little kid?" Chris scoffed. "Sure, he's a bit weird. But, he's just a kid. If he comes near me, I'll strangle him with my bare hands."

Just then, there was a rumble in the fireplace. A large, angry spike of flames shot loudly up into the flue.

The couple jumped with a start.

"Did you see that?" Jennifer gasped. "As soon as you mentioned the kid, the fire shot up as if it was mad! It's almost like the fire was protesting your threatening the kid!"

"Don't be ridiculous!" Chris said. "Sometimes fires just do that."

"I can't help it," Jennifer said. "That kid freaked me out before. There's just something about him. He makes me nervous."

"Listen," Chris assured her. "You're worried over nothing. It's not like this place is crawling with spooks or demons or anything. It's just a kid. Don't give it another thought."

"But, I swear I just saw him here not two minutes ago," she insisted. "Then, he just disappeared!"

"Yeah," he grumbled. "I saw him, too. There's got to be some explanation. I guess we're both still upset about Jimmy. Your mind can play tricks on you at a time like this. Just the same, I might keep an eye out for that little brat, though. He does seem to be a little creepy."

Chapter 7
Chilling Coincidence

Earlier that evening, the darkness seemed crisp...

...And, not so intimidating.

It was cold. It was quiet. Not many people roamed the streets. Maybe everyone had something better to do inside.

Perhaps, everyone just knew something.

Another young couple sat in a back booth of a tasteful little eatery uptown.

The clock on the wall of the restaurant said it was nearly 8:00. The lighting was delicate. Music played softly in the background.

"This is a nice place," she commented.

"So, are you glad I didn't cook for you on our first night together?" he asked.

"So far," she said. "But, this doesn't get you completely off the hook. I'm going to get you to cook for me eventually."

"I'll be happy to," he said. "Someday."

Wrongful Secrets

"How did you choose this restaurant?" she asked. "It's classy, but not too elegant. Discreet, but not too intimate. Pleasant ambiance, without being too brazen…"

"It sounds like you're giving a review for The Times," he said. "Do you have a second job that I don't know about, Dawn?"

"No," she said. "But, I like to size up the places where guys take you on dates. It's a good way to get a feel for their intentions."

"Is that important?"

"Sure," she said. "Too expensive or romantic right away means a guy's too anxious. Burgers and fries means the guy's just a loser."

"That's quite a system," he said. "Sounds like you put a lot of thought into this."

"Well," she said. "A girl's got to look out for herself."

"I see," he said. "Well, I hope I'm not coming off as a loser, but I'm not that anxious for you to tell me."

"Now you're just toying with me."

"So," he inquired. "What does it mean if I tell you I chose this place because I know the chef?"

"Is that supposed to impress me?" she asked playfully.

"Not really," he said. "It just increases our chances that the chef will wash his hands before he prepares our food. Plus, we'll probably get better cuts of meat, and vegetables that don't come in cans."

"Wow!" she poked. "The royal treatment, huh? A girl could get used to this."

"Wait 'til I tell you the movie we're going to see afterward," he said.

"Which movie?"

"*The Princess and the Pea*."

"Isn't that a kids' story?" she asked.

"Yes," he said. "But, it's filled with royalty and fresh vegetables."

"You're quick on your feet," she giggled. "That's nice to see. Are we really going to the movies tonight?"

"That's my secret," he said. "You'll have to wait and see."

"No gore movies, Glen," she asserted. "Okay?"

"Well...if you insist."

"By the way," she said. "If you know the chef, do you get a discount at this place?"

"He's just the chef," he said. "He's not the owner. He's not empowered to give discounts. Just like I don't have the authority to give you discounts on your sandwiches at the inn. Why do you ask?"

"I don't want to think your choices of restaurants are limited to places where you know the chef," she explained. "That would make you cheap."

"Wow!" he smiled. "You're brutal with your system. Anyway, I know a lot of chefs. But, I don't get any discounts anywhere."

"So, what's the point of knowing so many chefs, then?" she asked.

"It's got nothing to do with having a point," he said.

"Then, how do you know them?"

"Culinary school."

"That would explain it," she smiled.

"Speaking of your sandwiches," he asked. "What did you say to your boyfriend when you broke the date?"

"I told him a cousin was visiting from out of town," she said. "I don't think he believed me."

Wrongful Secrets

"Why wouldn't he believe you?" he asked.

"Who knows?" she shrugged indifferently. "Of course, he was all upset about me not going to his basketball game. I promised I'd have lunch with him tomorrow so we could talk. I still haven't asked Mr. Gould if I could take a long lunch."

"What are you going to talk to him about?" he asked.

"I'm just going to end it with him, I think," she said. "At first, I was going to wait and see how things went with you tonight. But now, I think I'm going to tell him we're done regardless of how it goes."

"Are you implying things aren't going well tonight?" he asked.

"Not at all," she said. "But it's still too early in the evening to tell."

"Don't worry," he said. "I remember all the rules: no discounts, no bowling, no basketball and no gore movies."

"Very good," she laughed. "I'm proud of you."

"I'm a quick study," he said. "I'm sorry things didn't work out for you with that guy. But I must admit, I'm not *too* sorry. It worked out to my benefit."

"Yeah," she sighed. "His name is Spencer Robinson. He's not a bad guy overall. But, he's not too sharp. Definitely not very imaginative when it comes to dating."

"All bowling and basketball?"

She nodded.

"Sounds like you're going to keep me on my toes," he teased. "You'd better be worth it."

"I *am* worth it," she stated with confidence.

"I can believe that," he said. "You look beautiful tonight, Dawn. I've never seen you in anything other than your maid's uniform. Street clothes are much better for you. You look absolutely stunning."

"Thank you," she said. "It's hard to believe any of us have a life outside of the inn sometimes. I must admit you look nice when you're not hiding behind that greasy apron, too. And I never knew it before, but you've got great hair! It's a shame you have to hide it underneath that chef's hat all day long."

"Thanks," he said. "I go to a European stylist uptown."

"How can you afford that?" she asked.

"It's not easy," he said. "But, I manage. Actually, *he's* the only person who gives me discounts. He used to be a chef."

Her sweet brown eyes lit up when she laughed. He couldn't help but notice. He could already tell that she really was 'worth it.'

Hours later, he drove her back to her apartment. He parked in front of her building.

"That was wonderful, Glen," she said. "How did you get tickets to a Russian circus on such short notice? Especially so far up north?"

"I have a friend at the box office," he explained. "I called him this morning and asked him to hold on to a couple of tickets for me just in case."

"I thought all your friends are chefs," she said. "Or at least, they used to be chefs."

"Not all of them," he said. "I'm a popular guy with many friends in various vocations all over the state of Oregon. It's part of what makes me such a good man to know."

"I'll have to remember that."

"Please do."

"The drive up the coast was very pleasant too," she commented. "The sky was so dark and clear. The stars were so bright."

"Even this time of the year," he added. "The shore looks beautiful in the moonlight."

They shared a warm and gentle gaze. Her eyes lit up like ocean waves beneath a full moon.

"It's getting late," she finally said. "I'd better get in. I have a long day of cleaning ahead of me tomorrow. And, I'm having lunch with Spencer as well. If I don't get some sleep, I'll be completely useless all day."

"Will I be part of the inspiration for what you'll be discussing with Spencer at lunch?" he asked.

She didn't answer right away. She intentionally teased him with a coy smile.

"Maybe."

"I'll take it," he said. "And, don't forget. We can't mention this at work tomorrow. Mr. Gould would fire both of us."

"I know."

"Good night, Dawn," he said. "And, thanks for tonight."

"No," she said. "Thank *you*. It was a great night, Glen. I had a good time."

Their kiss was not too long. It was not too telling. It was not too intent. It was just a prolonged hint...a taste, but not a promise.

It was a wish, but not an affirmation.

Afterward, she leapt out of the car without another word. When she was safely in the building, he drove off into the clear, dark night.

Donald Gorman

❧

It was a bright, clear morning. A few chunky clouds hurried by. They seemed as if they were trying to escape the frosty air outside. Clumps of muddy snow clung to the ice-streaked pavement. If the weatherman was wrong, they could hold out hope for another day's survival.

A smartly dressed young man was attending the reception counter. The woman entered the lobby. She removed her hat. Again her butterscotch hair spilled over those delicate shoulders in that way that he found so delightful.

"Good morning, Dawn," he beamed.

"Hello, Jeffrey," she said. .

"You look kind of tired today," he observed. "Long night last night?"

"You could say that."

"I know it was Friday yesterday," he said. "But, you have to be careful when you're working the following day. If you were going out with me, I'd make sure you got in nice and early, so your Saturday wouldn't be so much of a struggle."

"Don't start, Jeffrey," she sighed impatiently. "I'm not in the mood. You know Mr. Gould's policy about employee dating. Besides, I'm already seeing somebody."

"That figures," he said. "I hope this guy realizes what a lucky man he is."

"I'm sure he does," she said. "But, thank you for saying so."

"Not at all."

"Speaking of Mr. Gould," she said. "Do you know where he is? I need to talk to him before I start working."

"I think he's over in the kitchen or the restaurant," he said. "Something to do with the breakfast rush, I believe."

"Thanks," she said.

She rushed out of the lobby. She found her boss in the restaurant. He was talking to a small family at Table 4. She waited for him to finish before she approached.

"Mr. Gould?" she asked.

"Hi, Dawn," he said. "What can I do for you?"

"Do you mind if I leave the premises for lunch at noon?" she asked. "I have some important business to discuss with someone. I may be gone for a little over an hour."

"A long lunch?" he asked. "How long will you be?"

"I'm not certain."

"Well," he considered. "As long as you get all your work done before you leave tonight, I guess it will be okay."

"Thanks, Mr. Gould."

Meanwhile, another maid was unbuttoning her winter coat in the lobby to reveal her uniform underneath.

"Good morning, Rita."

"Hi, Jeffrey."

"I'm glad you're here," he said. "I'm supposed to speak to you."

"What's up?" she asked curiously. She walked gingerly up to the counter.

Jeffrey's eyes scanned his surroundings. Then, he leaned over and whispered, "Mrs. Gould wanted me to ask if you'd start up in Room 26 this morning. But, she doesn't want her husband to know."

"Why?" she asked. "What's with all the secrecy?"

Donald Gorman

"I don't know," he said. "A young couple named the Hurds is staying there. I think Mrs. Gould is concerned about them. But, she doesn't want her husband to know she's checking on them. Knock once or twice. If they don't answer, let yourself in with the key. Alright?"

"Sure."

She took her time getting ready. There was no reason to hurry. The work would still be waiting for her when she got to it.

She walked the cart with her cleaning supplies casually over to the elevator. When the door opened, she allowed four people to step out. Then, she pushed her cart in. She pushed the button for the third floor.

When the door opened again, she pushed her cart out into the hall. She walked leisurely down to Room 26.

She knocked on the door.

"Hello?" she called. "I'm the maid."

There was no reply.

She knocked again.

"It's the maid," she called. "I've come to clean your room."

There was still no answer.

She knocked a third time.

"Hello?" she called. "Mr. Hurd?"

There was still no reply.

She took her key. She unlocked the door. She opened it slowly. She cautiously stuck her head in.

"Hello?" she repeated politely. "I'm the maid."

She looked inside. She glanced around. The bed caught her eye.

She froze. The door swung open. Her eyes grew wide. Her face turned pale.

She screamed in unrestrained terror.

"Adam?" he said sternly. "We need to talk, son."

"What's up, Dad?"

"This is very important," he said. "I need you to tell me the truth."

"Okay."

"A young couple stayed here last night," he explained. "They were in their twenties. Their names were Mr. and Mrs. Hurd. They said they saw you in the elevator yesterday. They claimed you yelled at them and said they were very bad. Did you do that?"

"No."

"Listen carefully to me, son," he averred. "This is very, very important. The police are coming. They will be here in a few minutes. I need to know the truth. You won't be in trouble if you tell me the real truth. We won't punish you. I promise. Not if you tell me the truth. Did you talk to a man and a woman in the elevator yesterday?"

"Why are the police coming?" Adam asked.

"Something bad happened."

"Did those people get hurt?" Adam asked. "Are they dead?"

Leon and Carol looked at each other.

Then, he looked back down at his son. "Yes," he said. "They're dead."

"I knew it!" Adam declared. "I knew they were bad!"

"So, you did talk to them in the elevator?" he asked.

Adam glanced down at the floor. "Yes," he admitted reluctantly.

165

"Did this have something to do with your friend?" he asked. "Did that Mr. Fuego tell you to do that to those people?"

"Yes."

"Why?" he asked. "Did he tell you anything about those people?"

"How did they die?" Adam asked. "What happened?"

"Adam!" he growled.

"Let me talk to him," Carol intervened. She knelt down and brushed the hair out of her son's face. "Sweetheart?" she continued. "Mommy needs you to be strong right now. I need you to concentrate. What did Mr. Fuego tell you about those people?"

The boy glanced back down at the floor.

"He doesn't like me to talk about this stuff," he muttered timidly.

"Please, sweetie?" Carol coaxed. "This is very important. I promise you won't be in trouble. But, we need to know before the police show up, so we can protect you. Now, what did your friend say about those people?"

"The man was worse than his wife," Adam explained. "He killed his brother Jimmy."

Carol looked up at her husband. Then, she turned back to her son.

"Why did he do that?" she asked calmly.

"They were running a phony business on the internet," Adam said.

"They were?" Carol asked. "What kind of business?"

"I dunno," Adam shrugged. "But, Jimmy was going to turn them in, so his brother killed him."

Carol stood. She faced her husband.

"Do you think it's true?" she asked.

"I haven't the slightest idea," Leon muttered. "And, I don't really care. We can't mention any of this to the cops."

"Do you still think this place isn't really haunted?" she pressed. "Do you still think some sort of dangerous spirit isn't messing with your son?"

"We still don't know what happened," he insisted. "It could have been an accident."

"An accident?" she argued. "Are you kidding me?"

"We won't know what really happened until the police get here," he stated.

"Two people are dead, Leon," she sharply reminded. "And, it's not the first time something like this took place in our hotel!"

"Mom?"

She turned to her son. "Yes, dear?" she asked.

"Are you and Dad mad at each other?" Adam asked. "Is it my fault?"

She knelt down to his level again. "No, sweetie," she said soothingly. "We're not mad at each other. We're just having a talk. And, don't blame yourself for anything. I'm proud of you for telling the truth."

"So, I'm not in trouble?"

"No, baby," she assured him. "You're not in trouble. We love you very much. We both do. Don't worry. Everything will be okay."

She took the boy in her arms. She glared up at her husband as she held her son.

"Here you go, dear," he said in a calming tone. "A little bit of honey and a little bit of lemon. Just the way you like it."

He set the steaming cup on the table before her.

She didn't move. She didn't make a sound.

"Are you all right, Rita?" he asked. "Can I get you anything else?"

She didn't move. She didn't make a sound.

"Well," he said. "I have to go back to the kitchen now. You just take it easy, love. And if you need anything, just call. Okay?"

She didn't move. She didn't make a sound.

He watched her for a minute. Then, he returned to the kitchen.

There was a woman in a waitress uniform standing by the sink. She toyed with the graying hair she had held up in a butterfly clip.

"How is she, Glen?" she asked.

"Not good," he said. "She hasn't moved or spoken since she sat down. And, she's looking pale too. I'm a little worried, Pearl. I brought her some tea, and she didn't even flinch. She's probably in shock."

"Poor girl," she commented. "You can't blame her. It must have been a grizzly sight. Mr. Gould is keeping everyone out of the room until the cops arrive. He's even thinking about letting Rita go home for the day. He asked if I could clean her rooms for the day instead of waiting tables. I certainly wouldn't mind today."

"At least you won't have to clean Room 26," he joked.

"Stop it!" she said while slapping his arm. "That's terrible!"

Wrongful Secrets

"Sorry," he smiled. "Listen. I heard some guests in the lobby before. They said there was talk in The Den last night. A couple in their twenties claimed that a little boy yelled at them last night."

"Really?"

"Apparently," he continued. "The Goulds got nervous and ran off to check on their son. Then in the morning, this happens. Do you think Adam could be involved?"

"It wouldn't surprise me," she said. "That boy still scares me. There's something about him that just ain't right."

"Do you really think so?"

"Nobody believes that banker committed suicide back in January," she declared. "The boy made that happen! I tell you! That boy is linked to the devil!"

"Isn't that a bit extreme, Pearl?" he asked.

"You believe what you want to believe," she said. "Just keep that boy away from me! If I doubted it before, I don't doubt it now! Keep that boy away from me!"

"I was hoping we'd seen the last of you, Mr. Gould," he said.

"Believe me, Sgt. Agostino," Leon said. "This little reunion is no thrill ride for me either."

"I'm sure it isn't," he said. "So, you've kept everyone out of the room since the bodies were discovered? We'd like to keep all the evidence in tact."

"Yes," Leon said. "No one's been in the room. But, I have to warn you to brace yourself. This is one of the weirdest sights I've ever seen in my life."

"Thanks for the warning."

Leon put the key in the lock. He opened the door to Room 26. He and his wife led the officers inside.

They took a moment to survey the tragedy.

"Holy smokes!" Taggerty exclaimed. "I've never seen anything like this!"

"Both bodies are flat on their backs in bed," he observed. "They must have burned in their sleep. And that fire must have gone up rather quickly, if they burned without either of them waking up."

"What gets to me," Taggerty added. "Is that the bed is the only thing that caught fire. If the fire got this ugly so quickly that it fried these two people so completely without waking them up, how did the fire stay contained to the bed? That's physically impossible, isn't it? I mean, look at those bodies. They're practically chunks of charcoal with heads!"

"It does seem kind of odd," he agreed. "The sprinkler system obviously went off. But it seems unlikely it would work so quickly on the kind of fire this must have been. Didn't the fire alarm wake you up, Mr. Gould?"

"No," Leon said. "The alarm never went off."

"That's extremely dangerous, Mr. Gould," Taggerty pointed out. "You're very lucky nobody else got hurt."

"I realize that."

"You should have your system checked as soon as possible," Taggerty recommended.

"I will."

"I still want to know the cause," Agostino said as he circled the bed. "There are three cigarette butts in the ashtray on the nightstand. Smoking in bed can certainly result in a fire. Still, neither of them woke up. That seems odd. Were they drinking last night?"

"Yes," Carol said. "A little, anyway. They each had a few glasses of wine down in our den. They seemed sober enough when we all sat down together."

"We'll have to look into this further," he said. "You say they registered under the names Christopher and Jennifer Hurd from Seattle, Washington?"

"That's right," Carol nodded. "They were a nice young couple in their mid-twentes."

"And, you're sure this is them?" he asked.

"Not absolutely," Leon said. "It's not like you can tell by their faces."

"No," he grimaced. "I guess you couldn't."

"Who found the body?" Taggerty asked.

"One of our maids," Carol said. "Rita Giardano. She went in to clean the room."

"Is it your policy," he questioned. "That you enter occupied suites this early in the morning? What if a guest is sleeping?"

"She must not have checked the registry," Carol said. "Which is strange. She's usually good about things like that."

"So, you didn't send her in there on purpose?" he pressed.

"What's that supposed to mean?" Leon asked.

"I don't know," he said with a tone. "Why don't you tell me?"

"We never send the maids in any order, Sgt. Agostino," Carol intervened. "As long as they get their work done, we don't push them to do the rooms in any specific order."

"Where is Miss Giardano now?" he asked.

"Last time I saw," Leon said. "She was sitting in our restaurant downstairs. The poor girl seemed to be in a state of shock. I can't blame her. We told her she could go home after the ambulance crew checks her out."

"We've asked one of our waitresses to do her rooms today," Carol added. "A woman named Pearl Stewart. I'll be covering her tables during the lunch rush."

"Well," he said. "I think we've taken up enough of your time. Thanks for everything. If you'll excuse us, we'd like to look around here a bit longer."

"Of course," Leon nodded. "Just call if you need anything."

"We will."

Leon quickly ushered his wife out of Room 26. She said nothing as he whisked her off onto the elevator.

He waited until they were alone downstairs in the lobby. Then, he grumbled, "Did you see that? Those cops are awfully suspicious. They know something's up!"

"How could they?"

"What do you mean?" he asked. "They know something's wrong the same way we do. That whole scene looks incredibly suspicious. The bed was burned to a crisp. Both occupants didn't move a muscle. They died in their sleep and their bodies look like two oversized used matchsticks. The fire got real big and hot real fast, yet nothing outside of the bed got burned."

"The sprinklers went off," she reminded. "Just like they were supposed to."

"But, the fire alarm didn't," he added. "The whole thing reeks to high heaven!"

"So, you think our son was involved?" she asked.

"I didn't say that!"

"No," she pressed. "But, you were thinking it! You've been thinking it all along! That invisible friend of his that you don't like to talk about! You asked him about Mr. Fuego before the cops arrived. You think he's back. Don't you?"

He stayed silent.

"You think he's back," she insisted. "And, so do I! It's becoming more obvious and undeniable that it's time to get Adam away from this death trap once and for all!"

"I'm not going to discuss this with you now, Carol," he stated.

"This is the second suspicious death incident in this hotel in three months," she reminded. "The cops are upstairs at this very moment…"

"Which is exactly why we're not going to have this conversation now," he interrupted. "But when we do get a chance to talk, the first thing I want to know is why Rita went to that room first thing in the morning!"

Her sudden silence hung heavy with guilt.

A well-dressed man with a gray goatee approached the reception counter.

Leon leaned over to his wife. "We have a lot to discuss later," he grumbled discreetly.

"We certainly do," she agreed.

Then, they flashed their most professional smiles.

"Can we help you?" she asked.

"My name is Dr. Vincent Tseung," he announced. "I booked a room for two nights. I phoned in my reservation last week."

"Yes," she said. "I remember taking the call."

"And, I must confess," he said. "I chose this hotel on purpose."

"What do you mean, Dr. Tseung?" she asked.

"I'm here on business," he explained. "Or, what I mean to say is…I'm a psychiatrist by trade. But, that's not why I'm here."

"Then, why are you here?" Leon asked.

"I'm sure you're aware that this site has a certain history to it," he expounded. "And a certain reputation. I'm here because of my secondary vocation. I'm here to study this hotel."

"Study it?" Leon asked.

"My secondary vocation, sir," he said. "I study paranormal phenomenon."

"Mack Stein's Deli?" she asked. "That's where you're taking me to lunch? If I order a bagel, will they Super-Size it for me?"

"It's not McStein's Deli," he corrected. "It's Mack Stein's Deli. This is a great place. Trust me. Honest to God, Dawn! Nothing I do is good enough for you, is it?"

"I'm sorry, Spencer," she sighed. "You're right. This does look like a very nice place. I apologize. It's been a crazy morning."

"I can tell," he said. "I was shocked when I saw those police cars at the inn. I thought that whole matter with the banker who hanged himself had been cleared up. And now you have a new mess where two people died in a fire in one of the rooms?"

"That's right," she said. "Can you believe it? We just got things back to normal. We finally had one full day where we didn't have any cops crawling all over the inn, and then this happens! I don't know if I can go through this again."

"How bad could it be?" he asked. "Was the fire set on purpose?"

"They're looking into the possibility," she said. "I don't think it's too likely. But, everyone is still freaking out about these two tragedies happening so close together. And of course with the inn's reputation, a lot of people want to blame spooks, ghosts and demons. It's all turning into a big circus."

"Why do you stay there, Dawn?" he asked. "That place is driving you crazy. It's bad for you. Get out. Get a job somewhere else."

"It's not always that easy," she said. "Jobs are hard to come by in this town. And, I'm not really trained to do anything. Besides, the Goulds are nice people. They try to be good bosses, as much as they can. They didn't ask for this disaster. They're just trying to cope with the cards they were dealt."

A waitress came by and took their order. They each quickly chose a soup, sandwich and coffee combination.

Afterward, Dawn asked, "Where was I?"

"It's not always that easy," he reminded. "I have a feeling you were leading somewhere."

"Right," she said. "Thank you. Sometimes, it's not easy to just walk away. If you have bills and responsibilities, you need to have money coming in. There are other aspects of your life that are easier to control. You get to know people, and you try to get along. You experiment. It's a bit of a gamble."

"What are you trying to say?" he asked.

Donald Gorman

She hesitated. She could see the pained anticipation in his eyes.

He obviously knew. Still, that didn't make this any easier.

"I'm sorry, Spencer," she finally said. "I don't think we should see each other anymore."

"Why?"

"I don't know, Spencer," she said. "It's just not working out. Sometimes people just aren't meant to be together."

"This has something to do with your 'cousin' from last night, doesn't it?" he accused.

"No."

"I knew that wasn't a cousin you were seeing last night," he grumbled. "I knew you were cheating on me! I could hear it in your voice."

"This has nothing to do with last night," she insisted. "This has been building up for a long time. Practically right from the beginning."

"Why?" he asked. "What's the matter?"

"We have nothing in common," she pointed out. "You're a nice guy, Spencer. You really are. But, we just don't match up. You need someone who likes bowling and basketball and monster truck rallies and all the things you're into. And, I'm sorry, but that's just not me."

"But," he said with an agonized expression. "I love you, Dawn."

"I'm sorry, Spencer."

"I'll change," he offered desperately. "Basketball ends next week anyway. We don't have to go to any more games."

"Stop, Spencer," she said impatiently. "Listen. I'm not trying to hurt you, but it's over. Okay? It's just over."

Wrongful Secrets

"This *is* about last night, isn't it?" he demanded. "Who is he? I'll kill him!"

"Cut it out, Spencer," she said. "I already told you this has nothing to do with last night. And after this morning, I'm really not in the mood for this. Just relax and eat your soup."

"I can't lose you, Dawn," he averred. "I just can't."

"You have no choice," she said. "Please don't make a scene. I'm already getting a headache. Please don't make this day any worse."

"Well, what am I supposed to do?" he argued. "Yesterday, everything was fine. I knew what was going on. I knew what was mine! Today, you're bailing on me for no good reason…except your 'cousin' from last night!"

"How many times do I have to tell you," she insisted. "This has nothing to do with last night! This has been building up for the whole two months or so that we've been dating! Please stop shouting and eat your soup!"

"I'm not shouting!"

Neither of them spoke for a few moments.

She watched him. He didn't know what to do with his hands. He was clearly masking his pain with anger. He was nearly pouting.

She felt guilty.

"What are you thinking?" she asked quietly.

"I was just thinking," he muttered. "That I could be having lunch with *my* cousin right now. She's not such a slut."

She jumped to her feet.

"What are you doing?" he asked.

"I'm not a slut, Spencer!" she proclaimed. "And, you have no right to talk to me that way!"

"You're right," he sighed. "I'm sorry. I don't know what came over me. Please sit down. Finish your lunch. I'll be good. I promise."

She considered her options. Then, she sat down.

She wasn't sure why. Her headache was getting progressively worse.

This was going to be a very long lunch.

"Hello again, Mr. Gould."

"Hello, Sergeant," he said. "Back so soon?"

"We've only just begun our investigation, sir," Agostino said. "The second suspicious death case in your hotel in the last three months. And, I already have some interesting questions and observations for you. Can we go somewhere private?"

"I'm intrigued," he said.

He led them to his ground floor office. He closed the door behind them for privacy.

"First of all," Agostino began. "One of your guests, a Mr. Daniel Thariff claims he was sitting by your fireplace last night when Mr. Hurd mentioned that a small boy yelled some accusations at him earlier that day. According to Mr. Thariff, you and your wife got nervous and immediately ran off to check on your son. Then of course, this morning the Hurds were found in bed…burnt to a crisp."

"Let me tell you something else about our friend Mr. Thariff," he imparted. "Yesterday he claimed that he saw the ghost of Mortimer Hilzak carrying an axe up our staircase."

"Are you saying his account of last night is untrue?" Agostino asked.

"That's right," he said. "Mr. Thariff is a nice man. But, his grip on reality is not as tight as it should be."

"Then, let me add this to the equation," Agostino said. "I did some checking on our friend, the late Christopher Hurd. Apparently, the Seattle Police Department just found the body of his brother James yesterday. He was in his pick-up truck at the bottom of a cliff. The truck evidently exploded when it crashed. The fire was out by the time anyone found him, but the body was burned almost beyond recognition."

"That's a lovely story, Sergeant," he said. "But, what's your point?"

"Your son made specific accusations against Schumacker in January," Agostino observed. "That banker was connected to a murder where a man was strangled with a curtain cord. Your son's accusations were right. Then, Schumacker is found the next day hanging from your balcony."

"Your department ruled his death to be a suicide," he reminded.

"Then, your son is reputed as having made accusations about Mr. Hurd," Agostino continued. "The Hurds are found charbroiled in your hotel room right after the Seattle Police discover Christopher's brother burned to death in a truck at the bottom of a cliff."

"That would be one hell of a coincidence..." he began.

"That *is* one hell of a coincidence, Mr. Gould," Agostino interrupted. "I think it's a rather chilling coincidence. Don't you?"

"It would be," he admitted. "If it were true. But, I have no reason to think my son talked to the Hurds yesterday."

"We have a witness," Taggerty reminded.

"I already told you about your witness," he countered. "Besides, even if it *were* true, what does it mean? Are we back to blaming my son's imaginary friend?"

"I'm not sure what it means, sir," Agostino replied. "But nonetheless, I'd like to talk to your son."

"Why bother?" he said. "We already know his imaginary friend lives in the fireplace. Let's just go talk to the fireplace. Let's go. I'll take you there now."

"This isn't a joke, Mr. Gould!" Agostino barked.

"This is the second time you have tried to implicate my seven-year-old son in a murder!" he growled. "This is the second time you don't even have any evidence that a murder has been committed! You have no reason in the world to think any of the Hurds have been murdered! You have offered no proof that even Christopher's brother was murdered in Seattle! You're flying off half-cocked, and you're blaming my little boy for crimes that aren't even crimes! This very much *is* a joke, Sergeant! And, don't you deny it!"

A very tense pause hung heavily in the air.

"Listen, Mr. Gould," Agostino finally said. He kept a calm tone in his voice. "We're doing our best to solve a case of some very suspicious deaths. And we're trying to do it in a way that disrupts your business as little as possible. But, I'm going to find out what happened here, even if I have to close this damned deathtrap hotel down. Do you understand me?"

"You can't do that!" he demanded. "This is my livelihood!"

"Then, let's work together to put an end to these mysterious, suspicious deaths," Agostino suggested. "Okay?"

"That's fine with me," he agreed. "But, it's still a complete waste of your time to talk to Adam."

"Have it your way," Agostino said with an even temper. "At least, for the time being. But, I'll promise you this, Mr. Gould. With or without your help, I'm going to find out what's going on in this nasty little pit of death, if it's the last thing I do!"

Meanwhile, a young boy sat in front of the fireplace. He stared intently at the lavish, gorging flames.

Chapter 8
Separating Good From Evil

It was a magnificent marble staircase. Obviously, a lot of work and money had been invested in it. He stood at the top. He took a minute to admire its beauty.

He wore a camera on a strap around his neck. He had some electronic device in his hand. He adjusted a dial. He glanced around.

It was warm. The atmosphere was very comfortable and inviting.

And, you just had to love that staircase!

Suddenly, he felt a chill. He shivered against the abrupt brush of cold air. He looked down at the device in his hand. The needle began to jump and dance up the meter. It was measuring something...

...Some sort of presence.

He could see his breath curl up in a cloud before his face.

God, it was cold all of a sudden!

The needle in his machine kept bouncing up and down the meter.

It was spectacular! Someone…or something was here!

Then, he saw it on the staircase. It looked like a man. But, his appearance was not right. It was a little foggy. It was almost a shadow composed of bright light.

How was it possible?

The man's face was angry. He wore an old tattered hat. His clothes were outdated. His coat, his pants…nobody dresses like that anymore.

The man was carrying an axe.

The man at the top of the stairs couldn't take his eyes off this sublime vision that slowly climbed up toward him.

Finally, he came to his senses. He placed his mechanical device on the ornate railing by the stairs. He fumbled with his camera. He lifted it up to his face.

But the vision vanished. That wondrous apparition with the axe was gone!

"Damn!" he muttered under his breath.

He put down his camera. He picked up his device. The needle still danced in the meter that measured abnormal activity.

His breath still puffed up in little clouds before his face.

He looked around. An old couple walked down the hall to their room. They had come from the elevator.

However, nothing out of the ordinary could be seen.

It was still cold. The needle on his device kept dancing its erratic jig.

"Marvelous," he muttered. "Fascinating!"

He turned off the device. He put it in his pocket.

Then, he walked down the stairs. He took his time. He admired the beauty of the staircase. He stopped where the specter had disappeared.

It was especially cold on that marble step. It made him shiver.

There was definitely a trace left behind of what he had seen.

He smiled.

Then, he continued his journey down the stairs.

When he reached the bottom, he turned to the main room. The lobby was busy. Two people stood behind the reception counter. Both of them were attending to hotel guests. There were a few couples waiting in line. People of various ages walked across the lobby. Four people stepped into the elevator.

There were five or six people sitting in The Den. They were enjoying the warmth of the fireplace.

One person caught his eye.

It was a young boy. He couldn't have been more than six or seven years old. He just sat on the floor staring at the fire.

The man stood by the staircase. He watched the boy. He could sense an interaction.

He pulled the mechanical device out of his pocket. He turned it on. It took a few moments for it to begin operating.

Finally, he aimed it at the fireplace.

The needle on the meter didn't move. It was completely dead.

The man stared at it with curiosity. He hit the side of the device a few times with the palm of his hand.

The needle didn't move.

Wrongful Secrets

"That's odd," he whispered to himself. "Even without spectral activity, there should be some movement in a room with this many people."

He stared at the device. He didn't know what to do.

"I just put fresh batteries in it," he muttered. "What the hell?"

Suddenly, the young boy rose to his feet. He left the room.

The man gazed back down at his device. The needle began to move. It wasn't a hectic movement which would indicate spectral activity. It was the subtle, gentle movement that would be caused by the motions of the surrounding people.

He glanced around the room. Then, he returned his attention to the device.

The needle continued its gentle swaying within expected parameters.

"Extraordinary!" he gasped.

He turned off the device. He put it back in his pocket. He followed the young boy's path. It led him to the lobby.

Everything was beautiful in the lobby, he noticed. The furniture, the carpeting…

Everything.

The last couple left from the reception counter. They walked slowly toward the exit.

As the man crossed the lobby, one person left the reception counter.

"Hello," the man at the counter said with a practiced smile. "My name is Jeffrey Bartlett. How may I help you?"

"I'm Dr. Vincent Tseung," he said. "I checked in this morning. I'm sorry to bother you, but I have to ask. Did you see that small boy who was just sitting by the fireplace? He must've been six or seven."

"Sure," Jeffrey said. "That was the owners' son Adam."

"That's the owners' son?" he asked. "You mean that boy lives here?"

"Yes."

"Excellent," he said. "Just as I expected."

"Excuse me?"

"Do you know where the boy went?"

"No," Jeffrey said. "His father was just here a moment ago. You just missed him. I think he went to the kitchen. Would you like me to contact him for you?"

"No, thank you," he said. "That won't be necessary."

"Is there anything else I can do for you?" Jeffrey asked.

"No," he said. "That's fine. It can wait. You've been most helpful. Thank you."

"Have a nice evening, Dr. Tseung."

"Actually," he said. "Now that you mention it. There is one thing you can do for me, young man."

"And what's that?"

"I only booked my room for two nights," he explained. "Is there any way I can extend my stay for another two nights?"

"Of course, Doctor," Jeffrey smiled. "I'm sure we can arrange something."

He grabbed a pen while looking down at the book of reservations.

"Good," Tseung muttered. "I've suddenly found a reason or two to stick around a few days longer."

She sighed. She wiped her forehead with a clean rag.

She had just about finished cleaning the room when her cell phone rang.

"Hello?" she answered.

"Hi, Dawn," the caller said. "It's me."

"Spencer!" she snipped. "Why are you calling? I already told you. We're through."

"I was hoping you'd changed your mind."

"Well, I haven't!"

"Will you at least have dinner with me?" he asked. "Can we at least talk about it?"

"I have plans!"

"Plans?" he pressed. "Is it your 'cousin' again?"

"Whatever I'm doing," she stated. "It's no concern of yours. I told you, Spencer! We're through!"

"You keep saying that."

"Then, stop calling me!"

"Please, Dawn," he said. "I just want…"

"I don't care what you want, Spencer!" she interrupted. "I tried to be as nice as I can during lunch. But, I'm done being nice! It's over, Spencer! Don't call me anymore!"

"Just give me one more chance."

"No, Spencer," she insisted. "You tried, and it just didn't work. There's no chemistry between us. It just isn't there! Now, please grow up and leave me alone!"

"I don't have to leave you alone," he argued. "I invested almost three months in you! I've done everything for you! I fell in love with you, Dawn!"

"I'm sorry to hear that," she said. "I didn't mean to hurt you."

"The hell you didn't!" he snapped. "I tried everything! What did you want from me?"

"I'm sorry things didn't work out," she said. "Sometimes these things just happen. Please don't make this any worse than it has to be."

"You can't just walk away from me," he warned. "Not after all I've done for you!"

"Please just stop, Spencer."

"I'll get you back," he said. "You're at least going to give me another chance! I love you, Dawn! I love you!"

"Harassing me won't serve any purpose," she said nervously. "I don't need any more psychotic crazy people in my life! I already have enough of those!"

"I'm not crazy," he argued. "I just love you. And, all I'm asking for is another chance."

"Good-bye, Spencer," she bravely persisted. "It's over! Believe me! You'll get over this a lot easier if you just please leave me alone!"

She hung up the phone.

She stood there for a minute. She was trembling. Her heart was beating like a cave full of slam-dancing dinosaurs. She hadn't counted on this.

All she could do was hope that Spencer wasn't going to cause any problems.

But at that moment, it was difficult to believe she would be so lucky.

Wrongful Secrets

❖⊷❖

There was yellow crime scene tape across the door to Room 26.

"I wish you would let us take that stuff down," he said. "Our customers find it very unsettling. I'm trying to run a business here."

"I'm sorry, Mr. Gould," the officer said. "We're in the middle of an investigation."

"You seem to be using a lot of equipment and personnel," he observed. "You still have no reason to believe a crime has been committed."

"Two people died, sir," the officer reminded. "Under very mysterious circumstances. We take that quite seriously."

He sighed in lieu of a response.

The elevator door opened. The man who stepped out presented a definite image.

Leon rolled his eyes. "Not another cop," he complained. "Isn't there any crime going on in this town? Can't one of you guys find something better to do?"

"I'm sorry to disturb you, sir," the man said as he approached. "Are you the owner of this hotel?"

"Yes," he said impatiently. "I'm Leon Gould."

"It's nice to meet you, sir," he said. "My name is Edward Farley. I'm the Chief of The Spruce Valley Police Dept."

"The Chief of Police?" he asked. "I'm surprised you make house calls."

"I usually don't," Farley said. "In fact, this is the first time I have stepped into an ongoing investigation since I took this position."

"So, to what do I owe the honor?"

"Can we talk privately, Mr. Gould?" Farley asked.

"Okay."

"Could you gentlemen excuse us please?" Farley asked the attending officers.

Both policemen nodded and walked away.

Farley and Gould ducked under the yellow crime scene tape and entered Room 26.

"Good luck finding a seat," Gould said. "Everything's been doused by the sprinklers. It's going to be quite an ordeal getting this room operational again."

"I don't need a seat," Farley said. "It's just as well we don't touch anything that might prove to be evidence, anyway."

"Why do you insist on treating this like a crime?" he asked. "It was a fire. It was an accident. Why are you making mountains out of molehills?"

"First, Mr. Gould," Farley began. "Let me tell you that I'm no fool. You don't become Chief of Police by being an idiot. That being said, I have to tell you that I hate this place."

Gould's jaw dropped.

"I don't mean this hotel per se," Farley explained. "It's nothing personal, I assure you. It's this site. This piece of land."

"Why?"

"As I said," Farley continued. "I'm no fool. If you were to ask me if I believe in ghosts, I would have to answer with a definitive 'no.' I don't cotton to the boogeyman or anything like that. And, I don't scare easily. But, there has always been something wrong with this spot on Morris Hill."

"What makes you say that?"

"I've been on The Spruce Valley Police Force for a long time, Mr. Gould," Farley informed him. "I was just a beat cop when the old Hilzak house burned down."

"You were?"

"Yes," Farley nodded. "I was in charge of that investigation along with my senior partner at the time, Joseph Woods. It was the saddest case either of us ever worked on. I don't think Joe ever forgave himself for what happened."

"Why would your partner blame himself for anything?" Gould asked.

"We knew those kids were partying in that house," Farley explained. "We knew the place was a fire hazard. We knew it was in danger of collapsing. We knew the kids were underage and shouldn't be drinking. We ignored it because it was just a small group of kids that really weren't bad kids. We figured that if we knew where they were, we could keep an eye on them and make sure they didn't get into any real trouble. Plus, we wanted to avoid dealing with parents and paperwork, etc. We figured nothing would happen."

Gould watched the police chief as he spoke. There was a sadness in the old man's eyes.

"I'll never forget those three girls who died in that fire," Farley continued. "They were all beautiful, young girls. Trixie Sinclair, Kimberly Johnson and Cheyenne McCall. All three of them were high school seniors with their whole lives ahead of them. You can't imagine how it tore Joe's heart out at the end…having to tell the parents of each and every girl, 'Sorry your daughter died. Sorry we chose not to stop those kids when we had the chance. And now, even though we're pretty sure who was responsible for the fire, we can't even convict anyone for the wrongful death of your precious child.' It really broke Joe's heart. It shook me up pretty good too. The worst part is, it could've been prevented."

"So, you did know who started the fire?" Gould asked. "Why couldn't you convict him?"

"He had an alibi," Farley grumbled. "His cousin gave him and his friends an alibi for the evening. We had no way of placing him at the scene. Frances Bentworth. He was the ringleader. He was Trixie Sinclair's boyfriend, too. That's how we know it was him. He didn't set the fire on purpose. Or at least, we never thought so. It was probably an accident. But it always struck us as kind of funny that the fire started downstairs, while all three girls were upstairs. At a party like that, why would all the girls be upstairs together while all the boys were downstairs where they could easily escape? It just seemed kind of strange. We figured there was a reason for it."

"What do you think the reason was?" Gould asked.

"We had our suspicions," Farley said. "Even at the time. But a few years later, I got a call that really struck home for me. You see, all those boys left this town as soon as they could. I don't blame them. A lot of people do that when they graduate. This town doesn't have much to hold young kids to it. And those boys were mighty unpopular in this town right after the fire."

"I can see why."

"Like I said," Farley reiterated. "I got a call a few years later. I have a friend in the LAPD. He was familiar with our ordeal with the Hilzak house. It turns out Bentworth moved to Los Angeles when he moved out of this town. He's had a couple of scrapes with the law."

"What kind of trouble did he have?" Gould asked.

"As it turns out," Farley expounded. "Bentworth is an alcoholic. He also likes the ladies. Unfortunately, when he's drinking, he doesn't like to take no for an answer. The problem gets much worse if he's been seeing the girl. He got in trouble a few times for getting a little too frisky and grabby after a girl has told him to stop. No one ever pressed charges on him, but my friend tells me a problem has been noted. This links up with our suspicions over what happened with the Hilzak fire. We suspected there was a reason why the girls were separated from the boys. If Bentworth got a bit overzealous with Trixie, that would explain why the girls were upstairs consoling her while the boys were all downstairs where the fire started."

"It might also make you wonder if the fire was intentionally set," Gould suggested.

"That thought occurred to us as well," Farley admitted. "We didn't want to push that issue too strongly, because we already had an uphill battle just proving the boys were even at the house."

"I see."

"Of course," Farley reminded while rolling his eyes. "We lost that battle too. We figured their alibi was a lie, but there was no way to prove it. I can't tell you how much guilt Joe Woods and I felt over losing that case. We looked at other suspects. None of them panned out. We knew it was those boys, but without proof, we couldn't make it stick! I still get sick over it!"

"Well, I'm sorry about that, Chief," Gould said. "But, why does that bring you back here now?"

"When the Hilzak place burned down," Farley informed him. "Part of the surrounding wooded area burned with it. Luckily, the fire department got up here quickly. This hillside was not so remote that they couldn't get water. And, it was snowing. The fire could have been a lot worse, considering it was in the middle of a forest. Most of the trees up here survived the fire."

"What's your point?"

"In the nearly twenty years after the fire," Farley said. "Nothing grew on this section of the hill. Nothing grew over the places where the trees burned. But, that's not all. After the fire, everything on this part of the hill started to die. Trees that survived the fire started to wither away years after the tragedy."

"Are you serious?"

"Yes," Farley nodded. "Didn't you see how much of this hill was dead when you started building here?"

"Sure," Gould said. "But, we just figured that was damage from the fire."

"The fire didn't do all that," Farley explained. ""It never reached that many trees. The actual fire damage was much smaller. Most of the decay happened gradually years after the fire."

Gould didn't respond.

"Think about it," Farley reasoned. "Even if the fire had destroyed that much of the hill, why wouldn't something else have grown there since then? It's been twenty years! There has been plenty of time for something to start growing again."

"Now that you mention it," Gould said. "It does seem a bit strange."

Wrongful Secrets

"I'm telling you," Farley averred. "There's something wrong with this spot of land. It's almost as if this area somehow wants to take care of its unfinished business."

"What are you suggesting?"

"I don't really know," Farley said. "It's like I told you. I'm no fool. I don't believe in ghosts and goblins. But, something's not right here. I've heard the legends of how Mortimer Hilzak was a good man before he moved here. I heard the stories of this hill being haunted by his spirit after his death. I laughed at those fairytales just like everyone else. But, something had been wrong with this hill ever since that house burned down. I was a bit nervous when I heard you were going to build this hotel. But, how could I find a logical reason to complain? And then after Schumacker's death a few months ago, a familiar churning returned to my stomach. It was a queasy feeling that I haven't felt in years. You and I both know Schumacker didn't commit suicide."

"How can you be so sure?" Gould asked.

"Don't play games with me, Gould!" he grumbled. "Don't waste my time! That's not why I'm here!"

"Then why are you here?"

"I'm here because of *that*!" he proclaimed while pointing at the bed. "Look at that bed, Gould! That mattress went up so quickly that it killed two people before they could even wake up! Still, nothing else in this room burned! How do you think that happened?"

"The sprinklers turned on," Gould suggested.

"Oh yes," Farley scoffed. "The sprinklers turned on! The fire alarm failed! Absolutely nothing in the room burned except the two people who were meant to die! It was all one big, grand coincidence! How convenient!"

"Why are you implying those people were meant to die?" Gould questioned.

"The husband's brother was found dead," Farley said. "He was found just yesterday, burnt to a crisp. Both brothers were burned beyond recognition. Your son reputedly scolded Hurd shortly before he died. Just like how your son confronted Schumacker just before he 'hanged himself'. The coincidences keep mounting, don't they?"

"With all due respect, Chief Farley," he asked. "What are you going to do? Are you planning on closing down my hotel for suspicion of ghosties and ghoulies?"

"Of course not!"

"Then, what are you trying to say?"

"I'm here as a courtesy," Farley said. "I want to talk to you man to man. We both know this investigation is going to waste an incredible amount of manpower for the next few days, and it's going to turn up nothing!"

"It was an accidental fire," he pointed out. "Maybe there's nothing to turn up."

"You and I both know that's bullshit!" Farley barked. "All I want from you is the truth! I just want you to tell me what's really going on!"

"What makes you think I know?" he replied impatiently. "Do you think I asked for this? Do you think I sank every dollar I could dig up to start a hotel just so people could die here?"

"I'm sure you didn't."

"Then, what do you want from me?"

"You must have some idea of what's going on here," Farley said. "This is your hotel."

"I'm sorry," he said. "I have no idea."

"Then, for God's sake," Farley said. "Let me talk to your son."

"My son?" he asked. "He's only seven! Do you really think he knows anything?"

"I don't know, Mr. Gould," Farley sighed. "I just want these deaths to stop. Look at that bed, Gould. Look at it! That has to stop! That's one thing we can both agree on, isn't it? It's time for these suspicious deaths to stop!"

He chose the perfect place. It was elegant without being romantic. It was delicate without being intimate… or something like that. He did his best to remember the criteria she had outlined the previous evening.

He did his best. After all, he was only a chef.

"What's the matter, Dawn?" he asked. "You seem a little distracted."

"I'm sorry," she said. "It's not you. It's Spencer."

"Spencer?" he asked. "Your ex-boyfriend? Or am I being presumptuous calling him an ex? I thought you were going to break up with him."

"I did," she said. "I had lunch with him today. I told him it was over. But, he's not taking it well. He called me in the middle of the afternoon. Then, he called me again just before you picked me up. I told him to let it go and leave me alone. He doesn't like the idea. He wants me back. I think he's going to be a problem."

"Is there anything I can do?" he asked.

"No," she sighed. "It's too early to tell what's going to happen at this point. We were only going out for a few months. How could he get so carried away so quickly?"

"I don't know," he said. "I hate to ask, but did you…"

There was an uncomfortable pause.

"What?" she asked. "Sleep with him? Yes. We were intimate a few times. I had hoped in the beginning that he had some promise. I wanted to believe it could turn into something. That hope didn't last long, though."

"That could be part of the problem," he said. "Guys can…"

He was interrupted by the ringing of a cell phone.

She took the phone out of her purse. She answered, "Hello?"

"Hi, Dawn," said the caller. "Where are you?"

"Spencer!" she snapped. "You have to stop calling me! I told you! It's over! It's none of your business where I am!"

"Are you with your 'cousin' from last night?" Spencer asked.

"I'm not going to play this game with you, Spencer!" she demanded. "We're through! Stop calling me!"

She hung up.

"Sorry about that," she said with an embarrassed smile. "Let me turn my ringer off. I have a feeling he's going to keep doing that all night."

"That's alright," he said. "I'm just sorry you have to go through this."

"It's okay," she sighed as she put the phone back in her purse. "I'll deal with it. I blame myself, really. I should've known better than to date a carpet cleaning specialist."

"A carpet cleaning specialist?" he asked. "Is that what he does? How did you two meet?"

Wrongful Secrets

"Can we not talk about this, please?" she asked impatiently. "I'd rather forget everything I know about Spencer Robinson tonight."

"Of course," he said. "I'm sorry."

"That's okay," she said. "This is another nice restaurant. How do you do it?"

"It's one of the advantages to being a chef," he said. "I know where all the best places are in the whole state of Oregon."

"That's not what I meant," she said. "I think we already had that conversation. I want to know how you can afford two beautiful evenings in two fancy restaurants in one weekend on a chef's salary."

"I'm a magician when it comes to money," he said playfully. "The trick is…you just have to know *how* to spend more money than you take in. Plus, it helps to have a job where you can take your work home with you."

"Glen!" she pretended to gasp. "Are you saying you take food home from the inn?"

"I didn't say that," he defended playfully. "That would be dishonest. Besides, even if it was true, I would never admit it."

"Glen Cummings!" she said with feigned shock. "You little scamp! I'm surprised at you! I can't imagine the Goulds would allow such a personal misuse of their hospitality! Not to mention their resources!"

"That's why I would never betray their trust in me," he said.

"I should hope not!"

"My real secret is," he explained. "It's all just a matter of creative, inventive financial control. You just have to know how to manage your money."

"I wish you could show me how to do it," she said. "I'm terrible with money. I'm always broke."

"I could give you lessons, if you want," he offered.

"You could?"

"Sure," he said. "If things work out between us, I can show you all my tricks. I can be your financial adviser. It'll have to wait 'til I get to know you better, though. My secrets could be dangerous if they fell into the wrong hands. They're not for public use."

"Okay," she smiled. "I'll have to keep that in mind."

It was a smile that invited him to share all his secrets.

Later that evening, they drove through the cold, dark streets of Spruce Valley. They approached her house.

"Do you have to work tomorrow?" he asked.

"Yes," she said. "I usually have Sundays off. But, I traded days with Maya. She has family obligations tomorrow, so she offered to cover Monday for me."

"That's nice," he said. "I'm off tomorrow. I plan on catching up with some sleep."

"I can't wait to get a chance to do that," she said while pulling her cell phone out of her purse. "Oh, look at that! I have twelve calls on my phone! And it looks like almost all of them are from Spencer! Damn it! I think he's going to be a problem!"

"I wish I could do something to help," he said.

"There's nothing you can do," she said. "I'll have to talk to him tomorrow. I hope I don't have to take any drastic measures."

"Like what?"

"I don't know," she said. "An Order of Protection, maybe. I hope it doesn't come to that. Oh well. I'm not going to worry about it 'til the morning."

"That's probably best," he said. "It's getting late."

It was very cold for that time in March. The darkness was sullied by a gray, murky cloudiness. No stars came out to play. Even the moon was hidden away.

He pulled the car over to the curb in front of her building. He shifted the car into Park. He walked her to her front door.

The cold knew how to find its way past her coat. She shivered as her mouth blew little cloudy remnants of her breath into the chill of night.

He put an arm around her for warmth as they walked.

At her front door, she turned to face him with a smile.

"Thanks for a wonderful evening, Glen," she said. "I wish I knew how you keep coming up with tickets to these great shows."

"I know people."

"I guess you do."

"Hey," he said. "I remember the rules: No bowling, basketball or gore movies."

"Very good," she smiled. "You're easy to train. You just might be worth keeping."

"I'm glad to hear you say that," he grinned. "It somehow makes the whole evening seem even more worthwhile."

Their kiss verified her declaration even further. It lingered long enough to extend an aspiration toward the future.

There were more kisses. The aspiration expanded.

Like the delicate construction of a dream.

Afterward, she whispered, "Good night, Glen. Thanks for everything."

"Good night, Dawn," he said. "It was my pleasure."

She unlocked her door. She sweetly smiled before she disappeared inside.

Somehow, the walk back to his car didn't seem quite as cold.

And, the ride home didn't seem as dark.

Earlier that evening, a small number of people found it to be cozy inside.

"I'm surprised it's as cold as it is outside this late in March," he observed.

"Sometimes, that happens around here this time of year," Leon said. "It doesn't usually last long. I think it's supposed to warm up later this week."

"It's supposed to snow tomorrow," Carol imparted. "I hear we may get half a foot or more."

"Is it always like that around here in late March?" he asked.

"Not often," Leon said. "But, I wouldn't call it rare."

"But, we have ways to cope," Carol smiled.

"You certainly do," he said. "This fire is delightful. And, you have an exquisite taste in wines, Mrs. Gould."

"Thank you."

"So, what brings you to Spruce Valley, Dr. Tseung?" Leon asked. "I remember you mentioned something about being a paranormalist."

"That's true," he said. "I began studying paranormal activity as an extension of my studies of psychiatry and psychology. Of course, most of my travels have led me either to hoaxes and other false claims. But, I have had a few sites that have turned up some thought-provoking evidence which supports the notion that the study of existence beyond our perception is a legitimate pursuit."

"You have?" Leon asked.

"Take this hotel, for example," he said. "I was drawn here by its reputation. I'm sure you're familiar with the story of Mortimer Hilzak."

"Yes," Carol nodded. "And we know about the three girls who died when the house burned down twenty years ago."

"Those stories are fascinating even by themselves," he said. "But when I heard about the man who supposedly hanged himself back in January, I couldn't resist coming here. I knew they were going to rule it a suicide even before I heard it on the news. Somehow, I could just tell that was bound to happen. But, I think the chances of that banker's death being a suicide are about as likely as Mortimer Hilzak's death being a suicide."

"You don't think Hilzak hanged himself?" Leon asked with shock.

"Of course he didn't!" he imparted. "And, neither did your banker friend. The forces that caused their deaths are the same forces that caused Hilzak to violate his daughters and kill his family. This is a hotbed of psychically-charged activity."

"What do you mean?" Carol asked.

"I've already been monitoring some of the energy in this hotel," he said. "I have all sorts of equipment I brought with me. There are forces running through this building that do not come from living beings...or at least, things that are not living now."

"Are you kidding me?" Leon asked skeptically. "You're telling me that you have a machine that proves that we have ghosts?"

"Yes," he said. "Well…it offers proof to those who are properly trained, anyway."

"How does it work?" Leon asked.

"It measures energy, heat, light…" he began. "It measures a number of forces that can't be seen with the naked eye. There are places in this building that give off very dramatic readings."

"Really?" Carol asked with fascination.

"Not to mention," he added. "I think I saw the spirit of Mortimer Hilzak on the stairs. With the accompanying read-outs on my monitoring system, I am led to believe that his presence here is very real indeed."

"You saw Mortimer's ghost on the stairs?" Carol asked. "We've had guests report various sightings since we opened this place. But, neither Leon nor I have seen anything. I always waved off any claims as being the overactive imagination of tourists."

"It's a grave mistake to underestimate what's happening in this hotel," he cautioned. "These unexplained deaths should be proof of that. Strange and tragic events will continue to haunt this place as long as people trespass on this spot."

"Are you suggesting," Leon asked skeptically. "That if we stay here, I'm going to kill my family and then hang myself like Hilzak did?'"

"It's possible," he nodded. "I really have no way of guessing what will occur. At any rate, these strange deaths will continue. Let me explain. In some religions, Good and Evil are personified as beings like God and Satan. In other religions, opposing forces travel and coexist throughout the universe like Yin and Yang. Both concepts are very similar in that they both acknowledge that God is everywhere. As with many others, I believe the two opposing forces run on parallel plains and coexist as one force that we know as Free Will, and everything happens by choice."

"If everything happens by choice," Carol asked. "Who does the choosing?"

"It's the interaction of the opposing forces," he replied. "The choice of compassion for others is what we tend to label as Good, whereas Evil comes purely from selfishness. When Compassion is the dominant force, good things are the result. When Selfishness is the chosen force, bad things happen. The two supposedly run along parallel plains and rarely clash, unless acted upon by an object or individual. But when there's a glitch and the two forces run into each other, watch out!"

"Why?" Carol asked. "What happens?"

"Depending on your viewpoint," he explained. "Some say the glitch causes the two forces to run into each other resulting in friction, like the friction between geographic plates causes earthquakes. Others believe the glitch drives the forces apart, separating Compassion and Selfishness and causing an explosive reaction like splitting the atom. Either way, the glitch seems to gather those who were left here due to bad choices."

"Are you saying that we're the center for supernatural earthquakes?" Leon asked.

"Something like that," he nodded. "And during certain times, either force can dominate. And when the opposing force takes over, that's when a place becomes most volatile. I think this hotel is due for a monumental clash. I think a major combustion or grand explosion is preparing to happen. I don't know when. I think something will cause it. Perhaps the return of someone who has affected this place before. But make no mistake: Something serious will happen soon!"

"You'll forgive me," Leon said politely. "If I have a difficult time believing you."

"I understand," he said. "You must make your own choices. The grand combustion won't happen right away. Hopefully, you'll learn before it's too late! I'd like to stay a few more days, if I may. This hotel fascinates me. And with your permission, I would like to speak with your son."

"Adam?" Carol asked. "What do you want with Adam?"

"Given the opportunity," he expounded. "The forces like to communicate through a vessel. Young children are often chosen, because children are the least likely to have been contaminated by either force."

"And you think the forces already chose Adam?" Leon asked.

"When I was taking readings before," he replied. "My system went dead when Adam was sitting in front of the fireplace. The system never goes completely blank around so many people. There's too much energy and motion. I believe something was intentionally blocking my transmission. Besides, didn't Adam admonish all the victims shortly before they died?"

Carol and Leon looked at each other with discomfort.

"I don't want my son to be involved in this any more than he already has been," Leon declared. "The cops keep talking to him every time something happens. In fact, The Chief of Police talked to him earlier today."

"And, what did your son say?" he asked.

"Not much," Leon said. "He never does. I always advise him to keep quiet. I think his friend does too."

"His friend?" he asked. "Does his friend have something to do with the fireplace?"

"Yes."

"I thought so," he smiled knowingly. "That seems to be the source of the glitch."

"So, Dr. Tseung," Carol asked. "Do you think that it's Good or Evil that is trying to speak through my son?"

"Both forces are trying," he said. "Whichever force has been successful seems to depend on whether or not the victims are evil...or should I say selfish."

"According to both the cops and Adam," Leon said. "The victims all seem to be evil so far."

"Then, it's even more imperative that you let me talk to your son," he warned. "So far, Good has been in control...I think. And when the impending clash between forces occurs, there's a good chance that the opposite force may take over. Let me talk to your son, Mr. and Mrs. Gould! As both a psychiatrist and a paranormalist, I may be able to get some answers. I might be able to help him. I need to talk to that boy. Believe me. I may be able to save countless lives...not to mention your hotel!"

Chapter 9
Entanglements

The morning was still cold. A thick, stoic blanket of gray clouds kept the sun from warming the ice-stiffened lawns. That certain feeling was in the air.

It was going to snow.

Still, life must continue for everyone in Spruce Valley.

It was Sunday morning. However, she had to go to work. She showered and dressed. She sat at the kitchen table with coffee and a half-eaten doughnut.

Her maid uniform was clean, crisp and pressed. Her eyes were still a bit foggy.

Yet, she was surprisingly happy. She hadn't felt this good in a long time.

She took a sip of hot coffee. It felt good going down. Just the right amount of cream and sugar. She considered having a second doughnut before she left.

Then, her cell phone rang. She could hear its muffled, sad cry for attention coming from her purse.

She took out her phone and answered, "Hello?"

"Hi, Sweetie."

"For God's sake, Spencer!" she replied with exasperation. "Stop calling me! I'm sick of telling you it's over!"

"Come on, Dawn," he said. "At least talk to me about this. Tell me what's wrong before you leave me. I can change, honey. I can change!"

"I don't have time for this," she grumbled. "I have to go to work!"

"I thought you didn't work on Sundays," he said.

"I switched shifts with someone who couldn't work today," she told him curtly. "Anyway, it's none of your business. Leave me alone, Spencer!"

"Let me at least take you out to lunch," he suggested. "I'll pick you up at the inn. You can tell me what's wrong and…"

"No, Spencer!" she demanded. "It's over! We're through! Stop calling me!"

She hung up. She turned off the ringer. She threw the phone back in her purse.

Suddenly, her head was throbbing. She rubbed her temples with trembling fingers. She wondered if she still had any aspirin in her medicine cabinet.

All of a sudden, the day didn't seem so cheery. Still, she knew she had to go to work.

She ate the rest of her doughnut. She discarded the notion of having another. Then, she took a big sip from her cup.

She made a face. This just wasn't her day!

Even her coffee was getting cold!

He was dressed in a sharp suit. She wore a bright but sophisticated dress. They were preparing to start their day.

He idly watched the news in a cozy chair. The cup in his hand was still steaming.

She busied herself with a little light housework.

"Thanks for breakfast, sweetheart," he said. "The eggs were delightful."

"I'm glad you liked them," she said. "Are you almost ready to go downstairs?"

"Just another minute or two," he said. "Where's Adam?"

"He's down in the restaurant already," she informed him. "He likes Reggie's cooking. It saves me work in the kitchen."

"He likes Reggie's cooking better than yours?" he asked. "That's hard to believe."

"Glen's too, I hear," she said. "It's fine by me. They are both trained chefs, after all. I just learned from my mother."

"Don't sell yourself short," he assured her. "You do a wonderful job in the kitchen."

"Thanks."

There was a momentary pause.

Finally, she said, "Leon? Do you think it's wise to let Dr. Tseung talk to Adam?"

"I'm not really sure," he said. "I haven't quite convinced myself it's a good idea."

"I'm not so sure either."

"Do you believe that story he told us last night?" he asked.

"I don't know what to believe," she said. "I would have thought all his supernatural hype was all a bunch of baloney before we bought this hotel. But after what I've seen these past few months, it's hard to dismiss his theories."

"Personally, I think he's full of shit," he said.

"You don't really believe that, Leon," she said. "I know you don't. You've been just as curious as I am about what's happening in this hotel."

"All I know," he said. "Is that one man committed suicide, and the Hurds died by accident."

"That was no accident, and you know it!" she argued.

"Listen, Carol," he said. "I'll admit things have looked a little strange lately."

"*Strange?*" she interrupted with a confrontational tone. "*Strange?*"

"But, that's hardly an excuse to call the ghost patrol," he continued. "I'm trying to run a hotel. And I'm trying to deal with reality here!"

"The reality is," she reminded. "That people are dying! Some kind of force that we don't understand is at work, and whatever this thing is, it has involved your son! *I* know it! *You* know it! Even The Chief of Police knows it! You want to face reality? Let Dr. Tseung talk to Adam! If nothing else matters to you, think about how these deaths will affect our business! People don't go to hotels because they want to die!"

"All right," he said. "Calm down! I guess it can't hurt to have the old guy talk to Adam. I don't know what he'll get out of him. But, we'll give it a shot."

"That's all I ask," she said.

"And I resent the implication that I care more about business than I do my own son," he added with indignation.

"You're right," she said. "I'm sorry. I was upset."

"I understand."

―✢―

After leaving a message for her mother to call her, she had to turn her ringer back on. She didn't want to. But, she had no choice.

Her drive to work was filled with anxiety. It hadn't begun to snow yet. Still, she was running late.

As the morning progressed, the sky seemed to grow darker.

She dreaded the thought of driving home in a snow storm.

She parked her car in the employees' section of the lot. She quickly crossed the cold expanse to the inn. Once inside, she removed her hat and unbuttoned her coat.

Jeffrey greeted her with his usual unwelcomed flirtations.

She escaped to The Den as quickly as she could. Luckily, there was a warm, brilliant fire burning in the fireplace.

She enjoyed the warmth for just a moment. Then, her cell phone rang.

"Hello?" she answered. "Mom?"

"No," said the caller. "It's me."

"Damn it, Spencer!" she snapped. "I'm sick of this! Leave me alone!"

"Just have lunch with me, Dawn," he offered. "I'll pick you up at the inn, and we can grab a quick bite somewhere and talk."

"No, Spencer!" she demanded. "I don't want to see or hear from you ever again!"

"Just one quick lunch, Dawn," he begged. "You can tell me what you want, and I'll fix it. We can fix anything, sweetheart. You'll see."

"We agreed in the beginning," she reminded. "That this was just a casual thing. No strings and no entanglements. Why are you doing this?"

"Well," he said. "I suppose I got tangled. I fell in love with you."

"I'm sorry," she said. "But, that's not my problem."

"Just have one quick…"

"I said no!"

She hung up. She turned the ringer off again. Mom would just have to wait.

That's all.

"Hi, Dawn," said a shy voice.

She spun around to see who was speaking. She smiled awkwardly down at the young boy.

"Hi, Adam," she said. "How are you, sweetie?"

"Okay, I guess," he said. "Who were you just talking to?"

"On the phone?" she asked. "Oh, it was just an old ex-boyfriend."

"It was Spencer Robinson, wasn't it?" he asked.

"How did you know his full…" she gasped.

"You don't like him very much, do you?"

"No," she said. "I guess I don't."

"He's been mean to you," he said. "He won't leave you alone."

"Yes. That's true."

"You want him to go away, don't you?"

"That would certainly make my life easier," she agreed.

"Oh."

There was a brief, unsettling pause.

"Well, Adam," she finally said. "I have to go to work now. Okay? Have a good day, sweetie. It was nice to see you."

"Nice to see you, too."

He turned and left the room.

She watched him walk away. She felt a bit jumpy.

Had he been there long enough to hear her entire phone conversation? Why did he ask so many questions? How did he know so much?

There was something about that boy that still made her nervous.

⁍✠⁌

"This is a nice office you have here, Mrs. Gould," he said.

He made himself comfortable in the leather chair.

"Thank you," she said. "Leon and I use it for hotel business and paperwork. It's small, but it's functional. It seemed like a good place for you to talk to Adam. My husband is trying to find him now. Small boys have a way of disappearing."

"This is a fine place for our meeting," he said. "And, I'm in no hurry."

Wrongful Secrets

"Dr. Tseung?" Carol asked. "Before we introduce you to Adam, there are a few questions I'd like to ask you."

"Of course."

"Assuming your theory about these parallel forces is correct," she asked. "What causes these glitches that you mentioned?"

"Who knows?" he shrugged. "Obviously, we can only speculate. But, you have to figure that with two forces running rampant together throughout the entire universe, they are bound to come across a snag here and there for some reason. Some people postulate that these snags or conflicts are the very cause of the creation of everything that has ever existed."

"But, where do these forces come from?" she asked. "How did they originate?"

"There again," he said. "Who knows? Where did God come from? It's the same question. Who has the answer?"

"So," she reiterated. "There's a glitch on this site, it has probably always been here, and it will never leave?"

"As I told you," he said. "This is all pure speculation. But, all indications lead me to conclude that those assertions are correct."

"Is our hotel doomed to suffer these occurrences forever?" she asked.

"That's very possible."

She was silent for a moment. That was not the answer she wanted to hear.

"So, you're saying," she asked. "There is no Good or Evil? There is only Free Will? And what we perceive as Good and Evil depends on whether someone chooses Compassion or Selfishness?"

"That is a fair assessment of the basic concept," he nodded. "And some people who we consider good, such as Gandhi or Mother Teresa seem to be more susceptible to the compassionate force…while those who we consider evil, such as Hitler, Al Capone or Rasputin seem to be more susceptible to the force of Selfishness."

"I see," she said. "And, do you really think we are about to endure some grand supernatural explosion of some sort?"

"I'm sorry," he said. "It's difficult to give you a definite answer, or any details for that matter. But, I think something dramatic will happen here before winter falls again on this town."

"Do you think we should leave this hotel all together?" she said.

"All I can say is," he answered. "It might be wise."

"Oh, great!" she said. "My husband is going to love to hear that! I do have one more question, Doctor. Did you say that this place collects the souls of those who died here?"

"A spirit can remain and dwell anywhere," he explained. "Especially, if a person dies wrongfully or has unfinished business in life."

"I've heard that before."

"But, if a person dies near or around a glitch in the parallel forces," he continued. "There seems to be an even greater compulsion to stay close to where he died. And if the glitch is somehow responsible for one's death, it's nearly impossible for a spirit to escape. That's why a building like this is such a great place to look for unearthly manifestations."

Just then, the door to the office opened. Carol's husband entered the room.

"Leon," she said. "Where's Adam?"

"I couldn't find him," Leon said. "I've been all over this hotel. He seems to have vanished."

"Vanished?" she asked with concern.

"I wouldn't worry about it," Tseung said. "If the forces have bonded with him, they will protect him from any potential danger."

"Really, honey," Leon said. "Adam does this all the time. You know that. This is a big hotel. He could be anywhere."

"But what about that grand explosion you keep talking about?" she asked.

"Oh, that won't be for at least a few months," Tseung explained. "Besides, when it happens…you'll know it!"

"I'm sure Adam's fine," Leon agreed. "But, I'm afraid you'll have to wait to meet him, Doctor."

"Oh well," he said. "That's okay. I'll be in town for a few days. I have plenty of time. There's no hurry."

"In that case," Leon said. "If you'll excuse us, we have a hotel to run."

"Of course," he said while rising to his feet. "I have things I should do as well. I'll call you later, if that's alright."

"Sure," Leon said. "We're always somewhere in the building."

"Good day, then," he said. "It was nice talking to you, Mrs. Gould."

"You too, Doctor."

Then, he left the room.

After a few seconds, Leon turned to his wife.

"You know, as I was looking for Adam," he imparted. "A strange thought occurred to me. What if that guy's a cop?"

"I don't think that's possible," she said. "When you hear him talk about spirits and the occult, he seems too passionate. And he's very knowledgeable. He answered a bunch of questions for me while you were gone. He seriously believes that some sort of major supernatural event is coming soon. It's starting to worry me. He thinks we should get away from this hotel. I'm not so sure we should doubt him."

"You don't really think," he scoffed. "We should throw our whole lives away on the whim of a complete stranger, do you? Do you really believe just any little ghost-chaser who says he has a machine that registers spooks? Are you really that gullible?"

"What he says makes a lot of sense, Leon," she argued. "And given what we've seen these past few months, how can you be so flippant?"

"I just think the guy's full of crap," he maintained.

"Is that why you couldn't find Adam?" she asked. "You think he's either full of crap or he's a cop?"

"No," he said. "I couldn't find Adam because this is a very big hotel, and he's a little boy who never stops running around."

"Well, never mind," she said. "I'll go find my son. You sit here and think about how many lives will be lost if you're wrong about the Doctor."

She marched out of the room with an attitude. She even slammed the door behind her to punctuate her anger.

Wrongful Secrets

※

The snow was just starting to fall. He wasn't worried. He was driving a dark green '98 Cherokee. It could get him through anything.

He checked the digital clock on the dashboard. It was nearly 1:00 in the afternoon.

It was the perfect time for lunch.

He parked in the lot. He hurried into the inn. He stood in the lobby.

It caught him by surprise. No one was there!

The lobby was completely empty.

There wasn't even anybody standing behind the reception counter. Who ever heard of such a thing? It was the middle of the day!

He looked over toward The Den. There was a roaring fire in the fireplace.

He walked over and stared at the fire. He wondered what he should do.

A small, shy voice startled him from behind.

"Hi."

He turned around to face the young boy.

"Hi, kid," he said. "Who are you?"

"Adam."

"Hi, Adam," he said. "Do you know where everybody is? This whole place looks deserted."

"I dunno."

"I need to find somebody who works here," he said. "I came to get somebody."

"You're Spencer Robinson, aren't you?"

"H-how did you know?" he stammered in disbelief.

"Why are you here?"

"I'm the boyfriend of one of the maids who works here," he said. "I came to pick her up. I'm taking her to lunch."

"Dawn doesn't want you to take her to lunch," the boy said as his eyes narrowed.

"H-how did you know I was here to see...?" he began.

"Dawn wants you to leave her alone," the boy asserted. "Dawn told you to leave her alone a bunch of times."

"Listen, kid," he said. "I don't know who told you what, but Dawn knows we're having lunch together."

"I don't think so."

"What?" he said with impatience and shock. "What are you talking about, kid? You don't know anything about me and Dawn!"

"I know Dawn doesn't want to have lunch with you," the boy said with a simmering anger. "I know she told you so."

There was a loud clanking sound.

Spencer turned to see that the grating had fallen away from the opening to the fireplace. It made him uncomfortable to realize that it had done so on its own without any apparent cause.

"Uh...listen, kid," he pointed out awkwardly. "The grating fell off the fireplace. Maybe you should go tell somebody before the entire hotel burns down. I have to go find Dawn. Do you have any idea where she might be?"

"She doesn't want to see you!"

"It's none of your business, kid!" he snapped. "If you're not going to tell me where she is, I'll just have to go find her on my own...even if I have to tear this hotel apart!"

Suddenly, four lashes of fire stretched out from the fireplace. They wrapped themselves around Spencer almost like tentacles. Then, they quickly pulled him across the room and into the fireplace.

When Spencer was inside, the grating raised up on its own and put itself back into its proper position.

The boy stood there. He watched the man screaming for help as the flames engulfed him.

The man cried out in agony. The boy just watched with no expression on his face.

"Help me!" Spencer shrieked. "Oh, God! Please! Help me! Please! Help!"

He pounded against the steadfast grating with red, blistering hands.

The flames hungrily devoured his clothes. They lapped and whipped at his burning flesh. They encircled and swallowed him up in their wrath.

"Please! It burns! Help!"

The boy watched him disappear in the growing, merciless fire. With absolutely no sign of emotion, Adam watched as the fireplace reduced its victim to a motionless lump of charcoal.

Eventually, nothing moved in the fireplace. The flames resumed their normal height.

The boy turned and slowly walked out of the room.

Moments later, Leon entered the lobby from his office in the back. He was amazed that he was alone in the large room. He looked around for any other sign of life.

Jeffrey hurried into the room from another direction.

"Jeffrey!" Leon scolded. "Where were you? You know you're not to leave the reception counter unattended!"

"I'm sorry, Mr. Gould," Jeffrey said. "I had to step out for a moment. I swear I was only gone for a minute or two. I'm sure I didn't miss anybody."

"You better not have," Leon admonished. "Please don't do that again!"

"Yes sir."

Suddenly, Leon began to sniff at the air.

"Do you smell bacon?" he asked. "I wonder what the lunch special is today."

Meanwhile, no one was in the parking lot either.

Curiously enough, nobody was there to notice a dark green Cherokee sinking slowly…slowly down into the asphalt parking lot as if it were quicksand.

The Cherokee just kept sinking until it had completely disappeared underground.

Additionally, a heavy snowfall coated everything in a fresh, clean blanket of white.

.

Chapter 10
Unique, Indelicate Hunger

It was the middle of the afternoon. They stepped off the elevator on the second floor. They walked down the hall to her apartment.

"By the way, Mrs. Gould," he asked. "Are you sure you found your son this time?"

"Yes, Dr. Tseung," she said. "He's in our apartment. I told him to stay in the main room. Last time I saw him, he was on the floor drawing pictures."

"Very good," he said. "And, I hope I wasn't being rude by asking."

"Not at all," she said. "I'm sorry you waited so long in vain for him earlier."

"Think nothing of it," he assured her. "Before we go in, may I ask one last question? Does Adam's friend have a name?"

"I think Adam called his friend Mr. Fuego," she said.

"Mr. Fuego?"

"Yes."

"Does Adam speak Spanish, Mrs. Gould?" he asked.

"Not that I'm aware of."

"So, he has no way of knowing that the word 'fuego' is Spanish for 'fire'?" he asked.

"I wouldn't think so."

"That's very interesting," he said. "Shall we go in?"

She unlocked her apartment door. When they were inside, she led the doctor to her son. Adam was sitting on the floor. He was drawing with crayons on pages that had been torn from a notebook.

"Adam," Carol said. "Do you remember Dr. Tseung?"

Adam didn't even look up from his work. "No," he said.

Carol cringed as she looked at what Adam was drawing.

"Hello, Adam," Tseung said. "You draw very well."

"Thanks."

"The man who is hanging by his neck," he asked. "Is that Mr. Schumacker? The man who hanged himself back in January?"

"Yes."

"I can tell," he said. "It really looks like him. I see you made his face very red."

"That's the color his face was when Dad got him off the balcony," Adam said.

"The man with the axe," he continued. "Is that Mr. Hilzak?"

"Yup."

"Have you ever seen Mr. Hilzak?" he asked.

"A couple of times."

"Does he scare you?" he asked. "Carrying that axe with the blood on it?"

Wrongful Secrets

"No," Adam said. "He's been dead a long time."

"That's right," he agreed. "He has. Listen, Adam. Can I talk to you about your friend Mr. Fuego?"

The boy finally looked up at the old man. "Why?" he asked. "Are you another cop?"

"No," Tseung said. "I'm a doctor. And I study ghosts and spirits. I just want to know what is haunting this place."

The boy glanced suspiciously over at his mother.

"Go on," she assured him. "It's okay, Adam. You can talk to him."

"What do you want to know?"

"Your friend," he began. "Does he live in the fireplace or does he travel all over the house?"

"He travels all over everywhere," Adam said. "He's always everywhere."

"But, he really likes the fireplace?" he asked. "Did he tell you why?"

"No," Adam said. "He just really likes it there."

"What does he tell you about people like the man in your picture?" he asked. "Mr. Fuego didn't like that man, did he?"

"No."

"Your Mom told me about wrongful secrets," he said. "Mr. Fuego doesn't like people who keep wrongful secrets. Is that right?"

"Yup."

"What does he say about those people?" he asked.

"He says people try to hurt other people when they keep wrongful secrets," Adam explained. "But what really happens is that in the end, people only punish themselves."

"Is that why Mr. Fuego kills people?" he asked.

"Mr. Fuego doesn't kill people," Adam informed him impatiently. "I just told you. In the end, people only punish themselves."

"Are you saying that man in your drawing hanged himself?" he asked.

"I dunno," Adam shrugged. "I guess."

"And, do you know what happened Friday night?" he asked. "Do you know about those people who burned in bed?"

"Yes."

"Did they punish themselves too?" he asked.

"Could be," Adam answered without emotion. "They're dead, aren't they?"

"How did they burn themselves?" he asked. "Mr. Fuego must help them punish themselves. What does he do to help them?"

"Mom?" Adam asked. "Can I stop talking to him now? Mr. Fuego doesn't like it when I talk about this stuff."

"Okay, Adam," Tseung said. "I promise I won't press you any further if you answer two quick questions. Alright?"

"What questions?"

"Mr. Fuego tells you what these people's secrets are, from what I gather," he said. "Your mom tells me you know what these people did. Does Mr. Fuego tell you to confront these people? Does he tell you to yell at them?"

"I'm not supposed to talk about that," Adam muttered meekly.

"Does Mr. Fuego scare you?"

Adam didn't answer. He just stared down at his drawings.

"Does he threaten you?" he asked. "Does he say he'll do something bad to you if you don't do as he says?"

"No," Adam began sadly. "He just…"

His voice trailed off. He never finished.

"Alright, Adam," he said. "That's fine. We don't have to talk anymore today. You were very helpful to me. Thank you for talking to me."

"That's okay."

"You were very good, Adam," his mother gently assured.

Just then, the apartment door opened. Leon entered the room.

"Oh, you're here," he observed. "Good. I was hoping I'd find you, Carol. Can you come help me downstairs please? We're getting swamped."

"Sure."

"May I speak privately with you two for a moment first?" Tseung asked.

"You'll have to make it quick," Leon said. "We're very busy."

"Of course."

They stepped out into the hall.

"Mr. and Mrs. Gould," he addressed. "My little talk with Adam offered not many surprises. As I suspected, it looks as if we are dealing with a glitch between the infinite forces that comprise Free Will."

"You got all that from this short conversation?" Carol asked.

"Again," he reiterated. "Adam did not give me definitive proof. But, what he told me only supported my thesis. The glitch is very difficult to read at this point. Compassion and Selfishness do seem to be in a battle for power. This is a focal point for the struggle that is the source of everything we know."

"What do you mean?" Leon asked.

"Free will exists because of want or need," he explained. "Everything we do, every decision we make is caused by a lack of something we either want or need. Thus, the need for free will was born. Food, shelter, love, friendship... everything we want or need. Even our excesses. Every action in our lives is caused by want or need. The two parallel forces run through us all the time. We make our choices based on whichever force we are more susceptible to. And according to Adam, we are meant to punish ourselves for our choices."

"Surely, that can't always be true," Leon stated.

"The consequences are not always immediate," he imparted. "That's obvious. People seem to get away with bad decisions all the time. That is where our sense of justice comes from. On an eternal scale, that is where our theories about Heaven and Hell come from. And if I interpret what Adam said correctly, we devise our own eternal Hell. One way or the other, I agree with Adam. Sooner or later, we all either reward or punish ourselves for our own decisions. It may be in a more roundabout way in many cases in most places. But, the consequences seem to be more direct when you get this close to a glitch in the forces."

"Do you still think it's dangerous for us to stay here?" Carol asked.

"That's a difficult question to answer," he said. "This place seems unsafe. It's definitely volatile. Your son is obviously scared of his friend. But, I think Mr. Fuego has bonded with Adam. He will protect the boy from harm,

I'm guessing. Still, there is a unique hunger in this site. A very unique, indelicate hunger. It feeds on everything that gets in its way. It preys on human weakness. The grand combustion I mentioned earlier is a theory that's hard to prove. I think it's going to happen, though."

Carol and Leon shared a concerned glance.

"And depending on how closely Adam bonds with these forces," he added. "He may eventually be able to use them to affect changes according to his will. Remember, the forces are primarily based on the concepts of Compassion and Selfishness."

"Like making a car break down if he wants?" Carol asked. "Adam can do that?"

"Possibly," he said. "At least that much. Probably even much worse! Why? Has something like that happened?"

"Well," Carol reluctantly replied. "Yes. I think."

"Then, this may have progressed even farther than I'd feared," he declared. "Who knows how far this will go?"

"Are you implying that Adam may someday be responsible for someone getting killed?" Carol asked.

There was a sense of fear in her voice.

"I hate to speculate on anything that drastic," he said. "There's only one thing I know for sure. If you keep this hotel open, more people will die! Even if your son is not to blame. People with secrets will come here. And, they will die!"

There was a grayish-purple underbelly to the puffy strings of clouds that rolled past the sunset like a silent parade. The west coast was not far beyond the spruce-laden hills that stretched out endlessly against a pink and violet horizon. After the deep orange sun vanished behind the plush veil of trees, it would soon take cover beneath the darkly regal Pacific Ocean.

Inside, there was a subtle charm in the place he had chosen.

…Almost a discreet elegance.

"This is a nice place," she commented.

"I was hoping you'd like it," he said. "It's a bit more of a modest family-style restaurant than we've been to before. Still, I'm glad you suggested Chinese."

"So am I."

"How's your Chow Mei Fun?"

"Very good," she said. "I always look for Chow Mei Fun when I try a new Chinese restaurant. Did you know that some Chinese places don't even offer it on the menu? I don't trust a Chinese restaurant that doesn't even have Chow Mei Fun."

"So," he ventured. "Do you trust this place?"

"So far."

"And you wouldn't mind returning here?" he asked.

"Not at all."

"Glad to hear it."

"Does this mean you have Chinese chefs in your list of connections?" she asked.

"Actually," he confided. "My friend in the kitchen here is named Tony Caravelli."

"That doesn't sound very Chinese," she said.

"I know," he said. "But, he's the best Italian-Chinese chef in the world. You haven't lived until you've tried his General Tsao's Chicken Parmesan."

They shared a laugh.

Her smile was delicate and enchanting.

"So, are there any Chinese cooks in this place?" she asked. "I'd like to think the food I'm eating is authentic."

"Sure," he said. "Most of them are. Not many of them speak English, either. I think Tony got this gig because he studied cooking for a while under a guy named Ling."

"That would help."

"And what's your take on Italian chefs in Chinese restaurants?" he teased. "Can you trust a situation like that?"

"I'll do my best to keep an open mind," she smiled playfully.

There was a deep profundity in her beautiful brown eyes. They could catch you off guard if you weren't careful.

"By the way," he said. "I've been meaning to ask. I hope it's not a sore subject. But, is your ex-boyfriend still bothering you?"

"You know, it's a funny thing," she said. "He called a few times this morning. He wanted to take me to lunch today. I told him to get lost. Then all of a sudden, he stopped calling."

"That's good, isn't it?"

"Normally, you would think so," she said. "I wouldn't have pegged him as the stalker type. But after his behavior since I dumped him, it seems unlikely that he would just stop the way he did. Maybe he got sick of the rejection. But, I can't help wondering if there was something more involved."

"What do you mean?"

Donald Gorman

"Well," she explained. "I got a call from him as soon as I got to work this morning. I told him to leave me alone and then I hung up on him. I turned around, and Adam was standing right there."

"Adam Gould?"

"Yes," she said. "I don't know how much he heard, but I'm guessing he caught most of the conversation. It struck me as kind of odd. He knew Spencer's full name even though I'm sure I never mentioned it to him before. And, he seemed rather curious about the fact that I wanted Spencer to leave me alone. You don't think it's possible…"

Her voice trailed off with fearful speculation.

"I doubt it," he assured her. "Sure, Adam seems to like you as a friend. But, you don't really believe those rumors about his supernatural attachment to the hotel, do you?"

"I'm not sure," she said. "On the surface of things, I'm not one who believes in ghosts and things. But, you have to admit the evidence seems to be mounting in that spooky place. Mr. Schumacker…and then the Hurds! And Adam always has some connection to the incidents. It's enough to make you wonder."

"Well," he said. "Even if you want to believe in that stuff, I thought the story follows the idea that these people were hiding some dark secret like murder. I don't think your ex falls into that category. Plus, I don't think Adam is supposed to have that much control over whatever ghastly forces that may inhabit the hotel. I thought the spirits are in charge. Here's another thing to consider: Aren't the victims always found on the premises? Adam couldn't do anything to Spencer unless the man was in the hotel.

Spencer has never even been to The Hillside Inn, has he?"

"Just once," she said. "When he picked me up for lunch."

"So, you see?" he assured her. "You have nothing to worry about."

"You're right," she said. "I'm being silly. I should just count my blessings that Spencer is finally gone for good… hopefully."

"Hey," he said. "Nobody can blame you for being scared after everything that's happened recently, Dawn. I get a little freaked out too, sometimes. It's hard not to. That is why I was thinking we should catch a movie after dinner. Something light. A comedy, perhaps."

"That sounds great."

The sweet look in those eyes nearly caught him off guard again. He would have to be vigilant as they finished their meal.

As promised, the movie was a light and pleasant distraction. She seemed to enjoy it.

Later that evening however, she mentioned that she couldn't believe she invited him up to her apartment for the first time after sitting through such pointless fluff.

For some reason, he would never forget that she said that.

"Don't get me wrong," she said. "It was a nice movie. And, I'm glad I saw it with you. It's just…"

Her voice trailed off.

"That's okay," he said. "You don't need to explain."

"Thanks," she smiled. "You don't have to work tomorrow, do you?"

"No," he said. "I usually have Mondays off."

"I'm off tomorrow too," she said as she sat beside him on the sofa. "I think I told you that I traded shifts with Maya. It's rare that I get a Monday all to myself."

"Maybe we could do something together," he suggested.

"Maybe."

The sound in her voice matched the look in her eyes.

"So, you're a girl of mystery, are you?" he asked.

"That's me," she said. "All veils and shadows."

"Veils and shadows, huh?"

He leaned over and kissed her. It lingered…then, another kiss.

Then another.

"What was that for?" she asked.

"I was just trying to strip away a shadow or two," he said.

"You won't be stripping anything away tonight, sir," she declared playfully.

"Pardon me for trying."

"Oh, I don't blame you for trying," she said. "But, trying and succeeding are two different things."

He leaned over and kissed her again. The kiss multiplied and gently amplified into a delicate dance of intermingling hungers.

"Now, what was *that* for?" she asked.

"What do you think it was for?"

She gave him a look.

"Probably the same as this," she whispered.

This time, she leaned over and kissed him. The dance gracefully continued along the silent, unrehearsed choreography of their shared and contrasting urges.

He still had an arm around her as he said, "I don't think so. If you and I were on the same wavelength, neither one of us would still be sitting upright on the sofa."

"Is that so?" she teased. "Why? What would we be doing?"

"Something like this."

The eloquence and discreet intent in their kisses slowly gave way to a primal passion. He kept kissing her long after he noticed that he was unexpectedly lying on his back.

She seemed more aggressive when she was on top.

It brought out the best in him as they immersed themselves in the moment.

"Why, Miss Wyler!" he exclaimed roguishly. "I'm surprised at you! I didn't know you were so brazen! Still, I must admit you look absolutely gorgeous from down here."

"Oh, Glen!" she giggled. "You're so transparent!"

"Transparent?" he asked. "I'm transparent and you're all veils and shadows?"

"Does the truth hurt?"

"I'm just shocked at your behavior, Dawn," he teased. "Especially after that movie."

"Actually," she explained. "The movie has a lot to do with it. I got all dressed up to go out tonight, didn't I? Well, a girl deserves to be entertained."

"Entertained?"

The veils and shadows consumed him as they kissed. They ran right through him as the delicate dance of their hungers grew to a simmering pace.

There was not much room for maneuver on the sofa. Still, he was on top when they came up for air.

Donald Gorman

"I work better from this angle," he said.

"You're not supposed to be working any angles," she softly replied.

"How come you get to have veils and shadows?" he inquired. "But, I don't get to have any angles?"

"That's just the way it is."

"So, what do I get to have?"

"Sincerity."

"Sincerity?" he asked. "Well, you've got nothing to worry about there. I'm loaded with sincerity. In fact, my angles are practically bursting with sincerity."

"Really?" she inquired.

"Absolutely," he assured her. "And anyway, whatever happened to 'entertainment'?"

"That's secondary."

"Secondary?" he asked. "How about if we give them equal billing?"

"We'll see."

A certain eloquence returned. A fiery grace continued to drive a choreography that was still spontaneous, yet rewarding.

The unique dance of their intermingling hungers was a dance that would last well into the most enticing hours of savage darkness.

It all seemed so familiar to him.

However, it still felt as if it was happening for the first time.

That cold! He could still feel the cold. It was a freezing cold that tore right through him.

And, the shack. Was it really so small? It looked so insignificant and poorly constructed.

But, he remembered it. In vivid detail. Even in the blatant dark of night.

It had been a second home. A sanctuary.

And of course, there was Trixie. She was so beautiful. So sexy. And so willing…to a point. She was the sweetest girl he'd ever known. But when she reached a certain limit, she wouldn't go any further.

He had loved her. That was love, wasn't it? He still remembered that love. It didn't seem like a memory.

It seemed fresh. It seemed new.

It was so dark that night.

So dark and so cold…when he took Trixie's hand and walked with her up the unlit staircase. She had a flashlight. There were already candles upstairs.

They were on the bed…kissing…making out…

Everything was fine. It was only natural to move forward.

She said no.

Still, they kissed…made out…

Everything was fine. It was only natural to move forward.

Suddenly, he heard screaming. Rich Kirsch was dragging him off Trixie. Everyone was acting as if he'd done something wrong.

What the hell was wrong with everybody?

Why was *he* the bad guy?

The girls were all upstairs consoling Trixie…as if being a tease and a slut was a reason to feel sorry for herself.

The guys were downstairs yelling at him. He knew what this was like. This had happened to him in California too. Girls get drunk. They get you worked up. Then they pull the plug.

And *you* end up being the bad guy!

People call the cops. Will she or won't she press charges?

For what? Because girls like to jerk you around?

Sure, he was drunk. But, he wasn't *that* drunk.

Was he?

Could it have been his fault?

Suddenly, there was a noise by the stairs. He slowly went over to investigate.

It was dark. It was cold. Even with his oil lamp, it was hard to see more than a few feet in front of him.

He knew there was nothing to be afraid of. Still, this shack had a way of getting inside your head.

He raised the lamp.

A grizzly, angry old face seemed to appear out of nowhere! There was an old man in outdated clothing standing before him. Shadows from the dim glow of the lamp accented the hostility in the old man's expression.

The axe in the old man's hands seemed larger than he remembered. And the blood dripping from its shiny blade made the whole sight even more terrorizing!

The old man glowered at him with a seething anger.

"You will become me!" the specter proclaimed. "You will be punished for your choices! Like me, you will know how it feels to punish yourself for the decisions you have made!"

The old man raised the axe over his head.

He screamed in horror as he stared at the menacing apparition!

He quickly stepped backward into the unknown darkness to escape.

Suddenly, everything around him erupted in fire. What was once darkness was now bright, scathing shades of yellow, red and orange. The flames whipped and lashed at him like merciless weapons of torture.

He took a fearful step backward.

Then, a figure rose up amid the perilous fire. He recognized her immediately. The bright, ominous light of the vicious flames accentuated her beauty. And the flickering shadows brought out the anger in her eyes.

She wasn't afraid of the fire this time. She seemed to revel in its comfort.

"Trixie!" he gasped. "It can't be!"

She glared at him from her fiery pulpit.

"You will pay for what you did to me!" she warned. "Make no mistake about it, Frank! You will pay! But, you have no reason to fear me! I won't be the one to make you suffer! You will punish yourself for the choices you have made!"

Then, four or five spires reached out from the ravenous flames like arms. They sped toward him as if they were tentacles meaning to grab him…even consume him with an indelicate hunger…!

He sprang up in the darkness.

Everything was quiet. Everything was pitch black.

There was no fire.

He was sweating and gasping for air. He was sitting up in his bed. Trixie wasn't there. She'd been dead for twenty years.

The motionless, sleeping lump beside him was Ashley. She was his second wife. The whole thing was coming back to him. His whole miserable life!

It had all been just a bad dream like all the others. Why did he allow these pangs of guilt to weigh on his conscience all these years?

It wasn't his fault! He did nothing wrong!

He wasn't going to surrender to guilt any longer!

He was going to live his life! He was going to his high school reunion! And he was going to stay in that damned hotel that they built over the ruins of Hell Shack!

He'd show them! He'd show them all!

There was absolutely no reason for him to feel bad!

No reason at all!

It was that time of year.

The weather was fickle and unpredictable. The previous day had seen over five inches of snowfall. However, this particular morning the sun was bright and warm. It was already nearly warm enough to melt the snow.

The sun was rising in the east. Long shadows spread outward towards the west coast. They were still trying to stretch far enough to reach the beaches. By the time the shadows shrank beneath the powerful sun, the white coating over the ground would begin to dwindle down into growing puddles and little streams along freshly plowed roads.

He was almost down to the bottom of his cup of coffee. He couldn't put the day off much longer.

She came out of the bedroom. As usual, she was beautifully dressed.

"Did you get a chance to think about what Dr. Tseung said yesterday?" she asked.

"What's there to think about?"

"His explanation of what's happening in the hotel," she reminded. "The forces, the grand combustion and how it might be dangerous for us to stay here."

"You're not going to take that seriously, are you?" he asked.

"Is there a reason why I shouldn't?" she asked. "Do you have a better explanation?"

"What makes you think I need one?"

"Are you kidding?" she pressed. "Where have you been the past three months, Leon? I've been here in this hotel…where people are dying and our son is turning into a zombie! Did you see those pictures Adam was drawing yesterday? Doesn't that concern you?"

"Sure, it would be nice if he was drawing flowers and rainbows," he said. "But, he drew Michael hanging from the balcony because he saw it. That was unfortunate, but unavoidable. He drew Hilzak because people like you won't stop talking about it. If people keep acting like this place is haunted, of course a seven-year-old boy is going to believe it."

"Are you blaming me for this?"

"I didn't start this conversation."

"Leon," she argued. "People are talking about what's going on here, because it's very real! People are dying! The police are still crawling all over the hotel!"

"The police have admitted," he reminded. "That they have no choice but to rule the Hurds' death as a freak accident. Their room was locked from the inside. There was evidence of smoking in and around the bed. They found a cigarette butt on the mattress. Michael killed himself because of the mess he was involved in. End of story."

"You don't really believe that," she insisted. "Nobody really believes that! Even The Chief of Police doesn't that!"

"Chief Farley has no choice but to face reality," he averred. "Which is exactly what you should be doing instead of listening to every crackpot who has snake oil to sell!"

"Dr. Tseung isn't a snake oil salesman!" she defended. "He's a legitimate expert on the supernatural! And he is genuinely concerned for our welfare!"

"How do you know he's legitimate?" he questioned. "How do you know he's even a real doctor? Anybody can say, 'My name is Dr. Nut Job! You have ghosts and spooks and your house is going to explode!' Why do you listen to these whackos?"

"Because I care about our son!" she declared.

"So do I!" he argued. "Even if you believe Dr. Nut Job, if the hotel bonded with Adam, it will protect him. He's in no danger! So if you're pushing for me to sell this hotel because some demented psycho says our building is possessed, your case has run out of steam!"

"What about the Proskys' car?" she persisted. "It broke down when Adam knew I wanted them to stay. You heard what the doctor said about that. Adam can control the forces that run through this hotel! Doesn't that bother you?"

"Someone's car broke down?" he scoffed. "Oh no! Call The X Files! People's cars break down every day! That's no reason to call an exorcist! I had a flat tire last month. Should I blame that on Adam too?"

"Don't be an ass!" she spat. "You know there are other issues with Adam!"

"Kids all go through phases," he reasoned. "There's nothing unusual about that!"

"Do all kids confront murder victims right before they die?" she inquired. "Is that unusual? Is that just a phase?"

"I wouldn't know," he said. "We haven't had any murder victims. All we've had is a coincidence or two."

"And, what about the possibility that Adam may someday directly be responsible for someone's murder?" she argued. "Is murder just a phase?"

"Will you stop talking about murder?" he snarled. "Nobody has been murdered! Nobody *will* be murdered! You're letting some fruitcake come in off the street and take advantage of your fears over a few freak occurrences! You want me to protect my son? How many times do we have to have this discussion? Everything we own is tied up in this hotel! Even if we decide to sell, it'll take time to find a buyer. And if Dr. Nut Job is right and a ghost blows up the building, it'll take even longer to find a buyer!"

"This is serious, Leon!"

"I know it is, Carol," he averred. "I take the safety of my family *very* seriously! Am I protecting my son if I move my family into a cardboard box on a street corner because some stranger walks up to me and tells me that spooks are going to blow up my home? Is that taking care of my family?"

"I'm scared, Leon!" she proclaimed. "I'm scared about what's happening to this hotel! I'm scared about what could happen to Adam!"

There was a hefty silence.

"I know," he said softly. "No one can blame you."

He approached her. He took her in his arms.

"You know I love you," he said gently. "Don't you, honey?"

"Yes."

"And, you know I love Adam," he continued. "Believe me. I only want what's best for both of you. And, I will always protect and take care of you both. It's what I live for. Trust me. There's nothing to worry about. And if any proof comes out that there's any danger to either of you in this hotel, I'll pick out the cardboard box myself. I'll even pick out the street corner where we can camp out. Then, we can all move in together. Okay?"

"That's not funny."

"I'm sorry," he said while holding her closely. "I know you're worried. But, I promise everything will turn out fine. Okay, sweetie? Now, let's get downstairs while we still have a hotel."

He ended the argument with a kiss.

For the next few days, the weather was bright and sunny. The warming trend continued. Green patches of grass widened across lawns and hillsides as snow melted away and disappeared. Birds sang from budding tree branches.

Spring was returning to Spruce Valley.

They hadn't used the fireplace for days.

One morning, he decided to clean it out a little. It wasn't the sort of task he usually did himself. He could always make someone else do it. And Carol always complained if he got dirt on one of his good suits.

But, it was a slow morning. The task needed to be done. He would be careful with the ashes. He didn't want to have to change clothes.

He opened the grate. He scooped a few shovels full of ash into a garbage bag.

Then, he stopped. Something caught his attention.

He studied it. He poked it with the shovel.

It was a blackened, charred mess. It looked as if it could have been a human ribcage.

A dull thud hit him right between the eyes. A headache started pounding at his temples.

He glanced around the room. No one seemed to be looking.

He poked it harder with the shovel. After a few pokes, the ribcage crumbled to smaller, indiscernible chunks of charcoal and ash. He kept poking and breaking up the pieces.

With a few more chops, the shovel hit something hard. It was a larger chunk of what looked like bone. It wasn't completely burned.

It could have been a piece of skull.

An eerie chill ran up his spine. A disturbing sensation of dread welled up in his stomach.

Who could this have been?

What could have happened this time?

He didn't even want to think about it.

He glanced around the room again. Luckily, there was still nobody around. It was a good thing he had told Jeffrey to stay at the reception counter.

It would be best if he disposed of this himself.

Donald Gorman

With a nonchalant sense of discretion, he shoveled the blackened debris into the bag.

Chapter 11
Alarming Behavior

Spring was always a beautiful, magnificent time of year in Oregon. The sun rose higher in the sky, bringing warmer temperatures. The environment responded favorably with plush, green grass, blossoming trees and colorful waves of breath-taking flowers.

Rain fed the rich earth and renewed the air with a refreshing dose of moisture.

April and May were pleasant months. The year was progressing in its natural course. Summer was just around the corner.

Winter was gone. And the disharmony of the recent past was easily forgotten.

There was no reason to remember what had happened at The Hillside Inn.

In a nearby apartment, a young couple sat at a kitchen table. Neither of them felt a need to dress up for each other. Waking up together had become a common occurrence.

"What's the matter, Dawn?" he asked. "Don't you like your eggs? You've been picking at them for the last twenty minutes."

"Oh," she muttered. "No. I'm sorry. The eggs are wonderful. You know I love your cooking. I guess I just have a few things on my mind."

"Like what?"

"I don't know," she shrugged. "I just wish we didn't have to keep this thing a secret. We've been seeing each other since March. Here we are in the second week of June and I can't even tell anybody that we're together. It's not right."

"I know how you feel," he said. "All this sneaking around was kind of fun at first. Now, I'm just getting tired of it."

"There's got to be something we can do," she said.

"If you have any plans," he said. "I'm willing to listen. You know how the Goulds feel about employee fraternization."

"I think we've gone beyond the point where you could call our relationship mere fraternization," she said. "Don't you?"

"Of course," he said. "But our definition doesn't matter. Leon is the one who signs our paychecks."

"Don't remind me."

There was a brief pause.

"Dawn?" he finally asked. "Are you happy…overall?"

She looked up at him with surprise.

"Yes," she said. She leaned over and gave him a reassuring kiss. "I'm very happy. I love you, Glen. You know that. What's this all about?"

"You just seem a little distant recently," he said. "That's all."

"I'm sorry, honey," she said. "Work is driving me crazy. My life has been kind of hectic. And, I guess this sneaking around is taking a toll on me."

"I understand," he said. "I don't mean to be sensitive about things. I just wish we were a little closer. I really keep hoping we could move in together."

"What?" she asked. "You want us to live together?"

"Why not?"

"We were just talking about why we can't," she reminded. "Leon and Carol would go ballistic."

"Oh, screw them!" he scoffed. "We're both great employees. They're not going to fire us over this. And if they do, they can go to Hell!"

"I can't afford to take that chance," she explained. "I need this job. I have bills to pay. I like having a roof over my head."

"You can have *my* roof over your head," he offered.

"What's the matter with my place?" she asked.

"Nothing," he said. "This is a nice apartment you have here. But, mine's bigger. And if you're worried about bills, they'd be much smaller if we were sharing them."

"That's a lovely sentiment, Glen," she said. "But, it's just not going to work. Not right now, anyway. It's already too difficult to keep us a secret. Living together would only complicate everything."

"But the way things are now," he argued. "We're constantly running back and forth. You're either at my place, or I'm here at your place. There's a lot more running around back and forth than there needs to be.

"That's part of what makes this so aggravating," she agreed. "But, there isn't any other way. Things have to stay the way they are, Glen. Surely you can see that."

"I suppose," he relented with a sigh. "Can we at least spend the day together today? It's one of those rare Mondays when we both have the same day off."

"I can't, sweetie," she said. "I'm sorry. I have a couple of job interviews this morning. If we're ever going to be able to let our relationship go public, one of us has to get out of the inn. And, I'd just as soon have it be me."

"Where are the interviews?"

"One of them is a maid's job at The Stratford," she said. "I also have two interviews for waitress jobs at a couple of restaurants."

"Wow!" he said. "You've been a busy girl. How did you line all those up for today?"

"It wasn't easy."

"Can we do something this afternoon?" he asked.

"I have a doctor's appointment at 2:00," she said. "I was lucky to get Dr. Kendall on such short notice."

"You're going to see a doctor?" he asked. "Is something wrong?"

"No," she said. "It's just a checkup."

"I see," he grunted with a disapproving tone. "So, not only do we not get to move in together, but I also don't get to spend any time with you today?"

"Please don't take it personally," she said. "The job interviews are for us. If one of them comes through, maybe we can move in together."

"Maybe?"

"Well, I'm not going to make any decisions until I see what I can do for a job," she explained. "You can understand that, can't you?"

"I guess."

"Things are going to turn out all right for us, Glen," she assured him. "And we'll get to spend more time together. I'm sure we will. But it can't happen until we straighten out a few things. If I get one of these jobs, then we can stop hiding our relationship. But we have to be careful until then."

"I know," he sighed.

"And when the time is right," she continued. "Maybe we can move in together. But I'm not going to even consider it 'til it becomes a realistic possibility. Okay?"

"All right," he said. "I get it. I don't mean to be testy. I'm just getting impatient with this shit. It's getting hard to deal with all this secrecy and running around trying to hide everything. I'm sorry, Dawn."

"I know, honey."

She kissed him.

"I'm not going anywhere, Glen," she informed him. "I promise. Be patient. Our time will come. Just don't rush it."

"You're right," he muttered. "I have to just stick it out. I'll be fine. I just wish I knew when it's all going to end."

She got out of her chair. She sat in his lap.

They shared a long, passionate kiss.

"Don't worry," she said. "Everything will go our way soon. I can feel it."

"I hope you're right," he said. "But judging by the way this year began, it's hard to be optimistic."

"Nothing's happened at the inn since March," she said. "What are you worried about? Do you think we're due for another disaster?"

"Somehow, it seems more than likely," he imparted.

"Well, if you really feel that way," she suggested. "Maybe you should start looking for another job too."

"Now that you mention it," he said. "That's not such a bad idea. Perhaps I will do a little job-hunting today while I have the chance."

It was approaching 10:00 in the morning.

They stood at the reception counter. As always, they were dressed in immaculate attire. They were both in a good mood.

There was nothing for them to quarrel about.

They greeted the man holding a suitcase with sincere smiles.

"Did you enjoy your stay, Dr. Tseung?" she asked.

"It was very pleasant, as usual, Mrs. Gould," he said.

"It's a shame you have to leave so soon," she said. "We always enjoy your little visits."

"As do I," he said. "But, I have to make a living."

"When will we see you again?" Leon asked.

"I'll try to make it back here in a month," he said. "But, I can't promise anything."

"We'll look forward to it," Leon said. "Whenever it is."

"We're so grateful to you, Doctor," she said. "Even with just a few short visits, you've done wonders with Adam.

He seems much happier. He even has more friends than he used to. The change has been remarkable."

"Your son is a fine boy, Mrs. Gould," he said. "He's just a little shy. He's very bright. And, I'm sure he'll be okay, given time. He just needs to open up a bit more. Of course, this hotel has had a negative influence."

"Thank God that's over with," Leon sighed.

"I would hardly say your problems are over," he corrected. "In fact, I hate to leave at such a crucial time. I can't help this nagging feeling that a major event is going to happen here very soon."

"Are you talking about that grand combustion again, Doctor?" Leon asked with a hint of skepticism. "You tell us this hotel is going to explode every time you come here."

"I don't claim that the hotel will explode," he explained. "I don't know what form the event will take. I just know the glitch in the forces is due for a confrontation."

"Is this like the paranormal seismic activity you mentioned?" Leon asked. "We're on a supernatural fault line and we're due for some spiritual earthquake?"

"I understand your doubt," he said. "I don't have any way to prove what I'm telling you. I have no way of knowing when or how it will happen. I don't even know what will trigger it. I just feel that something is going to happen."

"Well, I hope you'll forgive me if I don't run and hide under my bed," Leon said.

"That's okay," he nodded knowingly. "Just be careful. Keep your eyes open."

"We will."

Dr. Tseung paid his bill. Then, he bid a cheerful farewell.

When he was gone, Leon commented, "I have to admit I like that man. But, it drives me crazy that every time he comes here, he tries to scare us with his ghost stories. He always tries to tell us that spooks are going to blow the place up."

"I see what you mean," she agreed. "It always gives me the creeps when he starts with his tragic warnings of some upcoming disaster. Still, he's becoming a steady client. He spends money while he's here, and he never causes any trouble."

"He comes here," he explained. "Because he's like a vulture waiting for carcasses to turn up. He's dying to prove that he's right about this place."

"Does it scare you at all?" she asked. "It terrifies me."

"Should I tell him to stop?" he asked. "It doesn't bother me at all. I know he's full of crap. But, if it scares you, I'll talk to him."

"Don't bother," she said. "He's harmless enough."

"Just think about it," he said. "It's the middle of June. Nothing has happened since March. Just to cover ourselves, we told Adam to talk to us first if he ever feels the need to yell at any of our customers."

"And, Dr. Tseung really has helped Adam tremendously," she added. "He really is a good psychiatrist."

"That's true," he agreed. "We don't have any reason to complain. Things have gone well recently. There are no problems with the inn. The Doctor is a good, harmless, regular client. He just likes to tell ghost stories. I think we should just let it go. Listen when he talks, but don't take him seriously."

"I suppose you're right," she sighed. "His stories are a small price to pay for his patronage."

Wrongful Secrets

At that moment, their desk clerk returned to his post.

"I'm back, Mr. Gould," he said. "Thank you for covering for me."

"That's okay, Jeffrey," he said. "I'm glad you're back. I have other duties to attend to. It's been a quiet morning. I'm sure you can handle it yourself."

"I'm sure I can, sir."

"Then, if you'll excuse me," he said. "I'll be upstairs."

"And, I have to go to the dining room," she said.

"Don't worry," Jeffrey said. "I'll manage things here."

He was alone at the reception counter for a few minutes. It was very quiet.

Almost too quiet.

He occupied himself with a crossword puzzle.

Then, two people entered the lobby from the parking lot. They appeared to be a married couple in their late thirties. Neither of them seemed to be in the best of health.

He closed his book of puzzles. He displayed his most professional smile as they walked up to the counter.

"Hello," he said. "Welcome to The Hillside Inn. My name is Jeffrey Bartlett. How may I help you?"

"Hi," he said. "I'm Frank Bentworth. This is my wife, Ashley. I believe you're expecting us. We have reservations to stay here for the next three nights."

"Oh yes," Jeffrey said. "I remember taking your call, Mr. Bentworth. Delighted to see you. I've booked you in Room 29 on the third floor. I hope that will be satisfactory."

"I'm sure it will be fine," he said. "By the way, have Mr. and Mrs. Richard Kirsch checked in yet?"

"No," Jeffrey said while checking the registry. "We are expecting them, though. We have their room ready, but they haven't arrived yet. Are they friends of yours?"

"Yeah," he nodded. "Rich and I have been friends since we were kids. We're here for our high school reunion."

"That's nice," Jeffrey said. "I hope you have a wonderful time. Will you sign in, please? And, do you need help with your bags?"

"Yes please," he said. "Our bags are in the old shit-brown Chrysler sedan parked right near the front door. It's an old clunker, I know. But, Ashley's brand new Mercedes is too precious to take out of town. Besides, I may be good enough to pay for it…I'm just not good enough to drive it. Isn't that right, honey?"

"Don't start, Frank!" she snipped.

"I'm not starting anything," he continued. "I'm just saying that it's nice that I can afford to buy at least one of us a new car…even if I don't get to drive it."

"That's enough, Frank!" she grumbled. "You promised!"

"Sorry, dear."

"Ah…" Jeffrey stammered. He struggled to maintain his demeanor while ringing for a bellhop. "Let me get someone to help you with your luggage."

Just then, Frank turned around.

He saw the fireplace.

It was big and ornate. It sat dormant in The Den. It hadn't been used in months. Nobody was in The Den. Nobody was anywhere near the fireplace.

It just sat there…dormant and cold.

Still, somehow he knew.

Wrongful Secrets

Ten minutes later, the Bentworths were settling into Room 29. They unpacked a few items that would be necessary right away.

"I wish you wouldn't embarrass me like that in public, Frank," she said. "This is *your* high school reunion. Remember? Try to be a little pleasant, so we can both enjoy ourselves."

"I'm sorry, Ashley," he said. "You're right. This should be a happy occasion. I don't know what came over me. I really am in a good mood."

"Maybe it's just that you haven't had a drink in almost an hour," she jabbed.

"Don't be a wise ass," he griped. "If I have to be good, then so do you. Besides, you're not going to spoil my good mood. I'm starting to look forward to this. I haven't seen most of my old friends in years."

"I'm glad you're happy," she said. "By the way, did you get your good suit out of the back seat of the car?"

"Oh damn!" he cursed. "I think I forgot it."

"You're not going to just leave it there, are you?" she asked. "I don't want anything to happen to it."

"What could happen?"

"It could get stolen," she imparted. "Or even worse: wrinkled."

"Who would steal a suit?"

"Please, Frank," she insisted. "You don't want to go back to the tailor, do you?"

"No," he grunted. "I guess you're right. Okay. I'll go down to the car and get my suit. I'll be back in five minutes."

"Thank you."

He grabbed his keys from the night stand. He went out into the hall. He walked down to the elevator and pressed the button.

As he waited for the elevator, a song popped into his head. It was a song he hadn't thought about in many years.

As he waited, he began to sing under his breath.

"You're as cold as ice," he sang quietly. "You're willing to sacrifice our love…"

Suddenly, the elevator door opened. The only person inside was a young boy. He couldn't have been more than seven years old. The boy glared at him as he stood there.

It made him a little nervous.

Finally, the boy walked out into the hall. However, he kept staring at Frank as he stepped onto the elevator.

Then, the boy pointed an accusatory finger.

"You!" he growled. "It's really you!"

"What?" Frank sputtered. "Who are you, kid? Do I know you?"

"She's still here, Mister!"

"What?"

"She's still here!" the boy repeated angrily. "She knew you'd come back! She's been waiting for you all these years!"

"Who are you talking about, kid?"

"Trixie!"

Frank's eyes grew wide. His jaw dropped. His face turned as white as a sheet.

"W-what…? Wh-who…?"

"Trixie!" the boy snarled. "She's been waiting for you to return all this time! She knew you would! She's dying to see you! You have a lot to answer for!"

"H-how do you know…?"

The elevator door closed. The boy was gone.

Frank was still very pale.

A sick feeling began to grow in the pit of his stomach. The elevator slowly descended to the ground floor.

They were still holding each other by the front door.

"Well," she said. "That was an unexpected surprise."

"Why?" he asked. "I always kiss you when I come in."

"Yes," she admitted. "But not like that. What's the big occasion?"

"I got a job offer," he said. "I went to see a friend of mine at The Silver Swordfish. He said they were looking for a chef. I can get better hours and a bigger paycheck! I hit the jackpot!"

"Oh, Glen!" she smiled. "That's wonderful!"

She kissed him.

"I told them I have to give Leon two weeks' notice," he continued. "They said that would be fine. So barring any unforeseen circumstances, I'll be working for a friend of mine before the end of the month!"

"That's fabulous," she said. Her tone was not as ecstatic as she pulled away from him. "It's nice to hear things turned out so well so quickly. You certainly have a lot of friends in the business."

"What's the matter, Dawn?" he asked. "I thought you'd be happy for me."

"I am," she said with a forced smile. "I'm very proud of you, honey."

"Then, what's the problem?"

"My luck wasn't as good," she said. "I had three interviews today. None of them told me anything definite. But, the first interview ran long, so I was late for the last two. I won't hear from any of them for a few days, but I don't expect much."

"How bad can it be?" he asked. "They're only…"

He caught himself before he finished his sentence."

"They're only what, Glen?" she snipped. "Waitress jobs? Maid jobs? Unskilled labor? Is that what you're implying?"

"I didn't mean it like that," he said. "You know I realize how smart you are. You would be a valuable employee for anyone lucky enough to hire you. I just meant that it's only your first day of looking for a job. Even if none of those jobs pan out, you'll have plenty of other opportunities."

"You're right," she sighed. "I'm sorry."

"That's all right," he said. "By the way, how did things go with the doctor?"

"Fine," she said. "As far as I can tell. He said he'd call me with the results."

"Well, that should be a reason to celebrate," he said. "See? We should both be happy. We should go out to a really nice dinner tonight. What do you say?"

"You're right," she said. "That would be a great idea. I'm sorry I'm in a bit of a mood. It's been a long day. But, I'm very glad to hear you got a great job so quickly. We should go out and celebrate your good fortune."

They kissed. They kissed again. The kisses grew longer and more celebratory.

Eventually, they would go out to dinner.

But, it would have to wait.

It wasn't so much a decision. However, the celebration began in the bedroom.

"This is a decent place for a hotel bar," he commented.

"Yeah," he agreed. "Not bad. I don't think The Black Falcon had a bar in the old days. Did it, Frank?"

"I don't think so," Frank said. "Man! It's hard to believe it's been twenty years. I must say you're looking great, Bill. It's nice to see you."

"Thanks," he said. "It's great to see you too. I wish I could return the compliment. But quite honestly, you look like hell, Frank."

"Thanks a bunch, Ambrose," he said. "Life in California with five or six businesses that won't run themselves, one divorce with two brats and another wife that's trying to drive me to the poor house so I can't afford to divorce her fat, lazy ass will do that to you. At least, I'm still alive."

"I'm sure drinking helps."

"More than you can imagine," Frank said. "So how are you, Bill? I hear you got some cushy executive job working for a major airline."

"Yup," he said. "I'm a coordinating systems analyst for the whole west coast."

"Wow," Frank said. "Sounds impressive."

"Thanks," he said. "I'm proud of it. I have a lot to be thankful for."

"So impressive, in fact," Frank added. "That I'm wondering how I got stuck paying for the first round. I think it's your turn next time."

"Slow down, pal," he said. "The party hasn't even started yet. I just got into town. My wife hasn't even seen the inside of the hotel yet."

"Speaking of which," Frank said. "Where is your beautiful wife tonight?"

"Shopping," he said. "As soon as she heard Spruce Valley was big enough to have a mall, she commandeered the car."

"Before she even checked into your room?" Frank chuckled.

"She has a weakness."

"More of a sickness, I'd say," Frank laughed. "God bless you, Bill! It's nice to know I have one advantage over you. Even *my* wife isn't that bad!"

"Nancy has been wonderful, for the most part," he said. "I think she just wants a new dress for the big shindig tomorrow night. I'm supposed to meet her in our room so we can get ready for dinner tonight."

"I should probably get back to my Ashley, too," Frank nodded. "I'm sure she'll want to bitch about something for an hour or so before dinner to work up her appetite."

"You're such a charmer, Frank."

"Do we have time for one more drink first?" Frank asked.

"Why not?" he shrugged. "I'll buy a round. By the way, have you heard from Logan or Rich yet?"

"Not yet," Frank said. "I tried calling both hotels. Neither of them had checked in yet. It seems pointless to call their cell phones if they aren't even in Oregon. I'm not paying roaming charges for those two!"

"I don't blame you," he agreed. "They'll get here when they get here. Also…you know I have to ask, Frank. How does that Hillside Inn look?"

"It's a nice looking place," Frank said. "Those bastards did a great job building that site into a classy little hotel. And you wouldn't recognize Morris Hill anymore. It's all developed and civilized now. There's hardly a tree anywhere."

"It's called progress, Bentworth," he said. "And, I've got to give you credit. You've got a pair of steel globes to get a room in the hotel that they built over the burnt-out remains of our old Hell Shack. Any problems so far?"

"No," Frank said. "Well, not really."

"What does that mean?"

"To start with," Frank began. "I got an eerie feeling when I saw the fireplace. It was a big, beautiful fireplace. But for some reason, it just gave me the creeps."

"That's not surprising," he imparted. "I hear they built the new one right over the remains of the original fireplace."

"Is that right?" Frank said. He felt a familiar chill. "Well, that's not all. At one point, I was standing in the hall. All of a sudden, I started singing that old Foreigner tune *Cold as Ice*. It's the strangest thing. I haven't heard that song since that night when…"

He stopped talking as a queasy feeling returned.

"You know," Frank continued. "I've refused to play that song ever since that night. It always reminded me of what happened. It reminds me of Trixie. I haven't even thought about that song in years. Then, all of a sudden…"

"Well, sure," he nodded. "That hotel is bound to remind you of that night."

"I suppose," Frank said. "But then, this little kid appears out of nowhere. He told me that Trixie has been waiting for me all these years! He told me she's still there!"

"Who was the kid?" he asked. "Did he actually call Trixie by name?"

"I never saw the kid before," Frank said. "But, he knew Trixie by name. That's what was so freaky about the whole thing. He just said Trixie was waiting for me. Then, he disappeared. It really gave me the creeps!"

"Could you have imagined it?"

"Possibly," Frank conceded. "It's the most rational explanation. I tell you, Bill. For a moment, I began to regret my decision to stay in that place."

"Maybe you should move out."

"No," Frank shook his head. "I don't think that'll be necessary. I don't think I need to do anything drastic…"

Suddenly, Frank felt the sensation of waking up. He had that groggy feeling, as if returning to consciousness. He moaned. He tried to open his eyes.

There was a sense of light before him. He felt woozy.

It took some effort. But, he finally opened his eyes.

Everything looked foggy. He could perceive a source of light. A ceiling lamp, perhaps.

He glanced around. Things were starting to come into focus.

He didn't recognize the room. But, it was definitely a hotel room.

The last thing he remembered was talking to Bill Ambrose. They were in the bar at The Black Falcon. That was the hotel where Bill was staying. This must be his hotel room. He remembered Bill suggesting that they go upstairs to wait for his wife.

That was all he could remember.

At this point, he could feel that he was sitting in a chair. He still felt a bit drained.

He called out, "Bill?"

There was no answer. How did he get here?

"Bill?"

There was still no answer. What had happened?

"Come on, Ambrose!" he shouted. "What the hell?"

There was still no answer. His senses were returning.

He could feel something in his lap. He looked down.

His eyes grew wide. His face went pale. He screamed in terror.

Where did that axe come from? How did it get in his lap? What was dripping from the shiny new blade?

Was it...blood?

The axe looked like the one he'd seen in the hands of Mortimer Hilzak.

No! It couldn't be!

"Bill!" he shouted. "Answer me, damn it!"

The silence made the hairs on the back of his neck stick straight up.

He gingerly picked up the axe. He slowly rose to his feet.

The double bed was off to his left. There was a big-screen TV. The furniture was tasteful and elegant.

No one was there.

There was a room off to his right. The door was open halfway. He could see tile.

It must be the bathroom.

Cautiously, he made his way over to the bathroom door.

As he approached, he glanced down at the floor. His heart stopped.

He let out a blood-curdling shriek.

The axe fell out of his hands. It hit the carpet with a dull thud.

He screamed again. He couldn't stop screaming for a whole minute.

Panic raged through his brain. Panic and confusion made it impossible to think.

How had this happened?

He wasn't capable of such an act. He had no reason to do such a thing.

It couldn't have been him? Could it?

Something needed to be done. He grabbed his cell phone. He hit the speed dial.

A voice on the other end answered, "Hello?"

"Logan?" he asked. "Where are you?"

"Bentworth?" said Logan. "Is that you?"

"I don't have time for stupid questions," he said. "This is an emergency! Where are you?"

"I just checked into my hotel room about five minutes ago," Logan said. "Vanessa and I are unpacking a few things. Why? What's up?"

"So, you're at the hotel?" he asked. "You're at The Black Falcon?"

"Yeah," Logan said with concern. "Why? Where are you? You sound terrible. What's going on, Frank?"

"What room are you in?"

"Room 304. Why?"

"I think I'm in your hotel," he stammered. "I need you to come up here right away."

"You *think* you're in the same hotel?" Logan asked. "Don't you know where you are? How much did you drink today, Frank?"

"Don't be an asshole, Tetweller!" he barked. "This has nothing to do with drinking! This is deadly serious! I have an emergency, and I need you right away!"

"All right, Frank," Logan said. "Calm down. I'm sorry. What's the emergency? What room are you in?"

"What room?" he asked. "I don't know. Let me look."

He walked to the front door of the suite.

"What going on, Frank?" Logan asked. "What's the problem?"

"You're not going to believe it, Tetweller!" he said. He was practically gasping for breath as he opened the door. "I don't believe it myself! Oh my God! I don't fucking believe it! I'm in Room 507. Get up here now, Logan! Please!"

"What's this all about, Frank?" Logan asked. "Talk to me!"

Frank took a moment to compose himself. He closed the door to the room. He was nearly sobbing.

"Bill Ambrose is dead!" he finally stammered. "He's dead on the bathroom floor! His wife is too! They're both dead! And I think I may have killed them!"

"What?"

"Ambrose is dead!" he repeated. "He and Nancy have both been hacked to pieces like chainsaw massacre victims! There's blood splattered all over the bathroom! Oh my God! I've never seen anything so horrid in my life!"

"Jesus, Bentworth!" he gasped in shock. "What are you talking about?"

"Just get up here, Tetweller!"

He hung up.

He fell into the nearest chair. He was in a daze. He stared straight ahead for a minute or two. Then, he was overcome with grief and guilt.

He began sobbing into his hands.

He was still crying a few minutes later when there was a loud knock on the door.

"Bentwoth!" a voice called as the knocking continued. "It's Logan! Open up!"

He stood. He crossed the room and opened the door.

"So, what's the story, Frank?" Logan asked as he entered the room. "What's going on here?"

Frank closed the door as Logan stared with wide eyes at the bathroom floor.

"Holy Christ!" he gasped. "What the hell, Frank? What the fuck did you do?"

"I d-don't know w-what…"

"Son of a bitch!" he sputtered. "Look at this mess! I knew your drinking was getting out of control! You've pulled some crazy stunts before! But even for you, this behavior is…well, frankly…it's alarming!"

"Cut it out, Tetweller!" Frank insisted. "This has nothing to do with drinking!"

"Well, I hate to break it to you, Bentworth," he quarreled. "But, this sort of thing isn't normal! It's beyond sick! It's beyond twisted! It's…it's alarming!"

"I don't know what happened, Logan," Frank explained anxiously. "I'm not even sure I did this! In fact, I'm almost sure I didn't! I couldn't do something like this! Hell! How could I do this to Bill? How could I do this? Oh God! How could I?"

"Where did you even get the axe, Frank?"

"Will you shut up, Tetweller?" Frank grumbled. "I don't need stupid questions right now! I need you to help me clean up this mess!"

"You want me to clean up your mess?" he asked with genuine surprise. "Again?"

"Well, what the hell, Tetweller!" Frank argued. "I can't just leave them here like this! They'll lock me up and throw away the key! I can't go to jail for this!"

"Why didn't you consider that while you were chopping them to bits, you freaking idiot?" he angrily inquired.

"I told you," Frank reminded impatiently. "I don't even remember doing this! I'm not even sure it was me! But if anybody sees this, I'm screwed!"

"I hear you!"

"Damn it, Tetweller!" Frank snarled. "Are you going to help me or not?"

"All right," he said. "Calm down. You've obviously had enough excitement for one day. Don't worry, Frank. I'll help clean up your mess. Just like I always do. It's a good thing you didn't get too much blood on the carpet. You realize this makes me an accessory to murder, don't you? Where can we get a mop around here?"

"How are your stuffed shells?" he asked.

"Delicious," she said. "I love the food here."

"I'm glad."

"Thanks, Glen," she said. "This really makes me feel better. I needed a night like this."

"Well," he reminded. "It's like I told you. I wanted you to help me celebrate my good fortune."

"I'm happy things are turning out so well for you," she said. "And I'm glad you didn't take me to The Silver Swordfish. I'd hate to think you're taking advantage of your employee discount so soon."

"What kind of scoundrel do you take me for?" he poked.

"Actually," she said. "I'd label you as more of a rogue than a scoundrel. Are we going somewhere after dinner?"

"Sure," he said. "Why not? This is a celebration. Would you like to see a movie or something?"

"That would be nice," she said. "How about *Summer's Sweet Journey?*"

"A chick flick, huh?" he said. "Sure. Okay. Tonight is all about making you feel good. And, I want to thank you too, Dawn. These past few months have been great. You're the best thing that's happened to me in a long time. And now that I have this new job, it'll get even better. Tomorrow when I tell Leon I'm leaving, we can stop hiding our relationship. We can finally go public. And, we can finally move in together."

"Aren't you jumping the gun a little bit?" she asked. "I never said that I was ready to move in with you."

"What?" he asked. "I thought your only problem with moving forward was the snag caused by Leon's employee dating policy. Now that I have another job, there's no reason to keep this thing a secret anymore."

"It's not a question of secrecy," she explained. "I just don't know if I'm ready."

"Why not?" he asked. "We've been together for three months. I thought everything was going well. It's been a wonderful three months for me, aside from all this running around and hiding everything. I thought it was going well for you too."

"It is," she assured him. "This has been a great few months. I love you, Glen. I really do. I just don't want to rush into anything. And, I don't want to be pressured into moving in with anybody without thinking about it first."

"What's there to think about?" he asked. "You just told me you love me, Dawn. And you know I love you. So, what's the problem?"

"We never discussed any of this," she said. "This is not the kind of decision that I'm going to take lightly."

"I'm not saying you have to start packing tomorrow," he said. "But, we should be able to start making plans, shouldn't we?"

"What's your hurry?"

"The hurry is that I love you, Dawn," he explained. "We've been keeping this whole thing so hush-hush since the beginning. I'm tired of lying and hiding this from people. I want to get it out in the open and proclaim my love for you from the highest treetop. I've felt imprisoned by secrecy for so long, I just want to break free! I want us to be free to move forward like any normal couple."

"All of that will happen when it's time," she said. "I'm not going anywhere, Glen. I'm committed to this relationship too. But, I can't tell the Goulds that we're a couple yet. I don't have another job lined up yet. I'm still stuck there for the time being."

"Okay," he nodded. "We won't tell them for two weeks. I can hold out that long. By then, you might even have another job. But in the meantime, we can at least discuss the idea of living together. Can't we?"

"Let's wait until things are more settled," she suggested. "Okay? Let's see how we look when we've gone public for a while. Let's wait and see how things look when they've aired out in the light of day."

"Aired out?" he asked. "What are we talking about? Laundry?"

"Can we please discuss this later, Glen?" she asked. "I'm just not ready yet."

"Fine!"

The mood was a bit more bleak through the rest of their dinner. And the movie was exactly what he expected: an endless torture sentence designed for women, so they could poison their minds and punish their boyfriends.

He was not very happy as he drove her home from the theater.

As they neared her building, she asked, "Are you alright? You haven't said much since we left the restaurant."

"Never felt better."

"Are you coming in with me?"

"Why?" he muttered. "It's not as if it's *my* place. It's not as if we'll be sharing a place anytime soon!"

"Are you still moping about that?" she asked. "Please don't be like that, Glen. I told you I just need time to think about it."

"That's great!" he snapped. "You go to your place and think about it! I'll go to my place and think about why my girlfriend doesn't love me enough to move in with me!"

"Why are you taking this so hard?" she asked. "I'm just asking you to be patient."

The tires screeched to a halt as he stopped the car in front of her building.

"I'm tired of being patient," he complained. "I've been patient for three months. I've snuck around, hid things, pretended you mean nothing to me in front of everybody I know…I'm just sick of it."

"Look at me, Glen."

He turned to face her. Those eyes always knew how to grab him and tangle him in her web.

"I promise you, sweetie," she said softly. "It will happen. We'll move in together eventually. Maybe even someday soon. I just need time. I love you, Glen. I really do. Please be patient. Please? For me?"

Those eyes wrapped him up like a doomed fly in her web.

"Okay," he sighed. "I guess."

"Thank you, honey," she smiled. She kissed him. "Will you come inside with me now?"

"No," he muttered. "I really would prefer to be alone right now."

"Are you sure?"

"Yes," he said. "I need some time to myself."

"Are we okay?"

"We will be," he said. "I think. I just need to sort things out."

"I love you," she said. She kissed him again.

"I love you too, Dawn," he said. "Good night."

He watched her leave the car. He watched her walk to her door. When she disappeared inside, he drove away.

Donald Gorman

He drove slowly. The darkness outside couldn't match the darkness of his mood.

His sleep was troubled.

It had been an unpleasant evening. Ashley had wondered how he had gotten blood on his clothes. At dinner, everyone kept asking where Bill and Nancy were. Logan grew increasingly uncomfortable as the night progressed.

Finally, it all ended.

He was tossing and turning in his sleep. He had insisted on staying at The Hillside Inn. He was not going to cower in the face of rumors about ghosts and spooks! He wasn't stupid!

This place was a demon. It was a demon from his past that he needed to face. It was a demon that he was determined to face head-on!

His sleep was troubled. He tossed and turned in bed.

Murky flashbacks drifted through his thoughts. Vacant, hollow memories danced through his brain.

He could see Bill's face. The sheer panic in Bill's eyes as the axe plunged deep into his chest…again and again…

He didn't want to swing the axe. But, he couldn't let it go. He couldn't stop it from driving deep into Bill's torso…again and again…

He could hear Bill's screams as a muffled, distant plea for mercy.

"What are you doing….please stop, Frank…for the love of God…please stop, Frank…please…"

He was compelled to keep swinging the axe because Bill wouldn't stop screaming. When Bill was finally quiet, he stopped swinging the axe.

Everything was at peace.

Then, Nancy entered the room. She came in unexpectedly. She started screaming when she saw the body on the floor. He went over to explain. He just wanted to calm her down. But, she wouldn't stop screaming.

Even when he began swinging the axe again, she just wouldn't stop!

He just wanted to calm her down. However, no matter how many times he buried the axe into her trembling body, she just wouldn't stop!

He didn't want to hurt her. He just wanted her to be quiet.

So, he kept swing the axe…

…and swinging…

…and swinging…

Finally, all was silent. He looked down at the motionless, bloody bodies.

Everything was at peace again.

Then, the entire room erupted in flames. He stepped back in fear as the entire room became alive with a raging, furious fire. Angry flames lashed toward him. They crackled and threatened with a menacing glow.

Suddenly, a girl's voice called to him. It was a sweet voice that nearly sang his name.

"Frank?" she said. "I've been waiting for you."

He stared in horror as she stepped out of the flames.

"Trixie!" he gasped in terror. "No! It couldn't be!"

Donald Gorman

"I've been waiting for you all these years, Frank," she said sweetly. "I knew you'd come back to me. I just knew it. I've been dying to see you again. Just *dying* to see you."

"Trixie!" he stammered. "Please don't! You know I never meant for this to happen! Please, Trixie! Don't!"

"Now we can be together again, Frank," she said sweetly. "Together forever. Just like it was always meant to be."

"No!" he shrieked.

He sat up in bed. He was gasping for breath. He was sweating profusely.

Everything was dark around him. Everything was silent. It had all been just a dream.

He felt something in his lap. He looked down... slowly.

His face grew pale as he recognized the axe resting on his thighs. The blood dripping from the blade must've been fresh. He'd cleaned it before.

He let out a bone chilling scream.

Then, he stopped himself. He didn't want to wake Ashley. He slowly turned to look at her. As he figured, his wife was lying beside him in bed.

Still, his eyes grew wide. He began to scream uncontrollably.

There was no reason not to.

Even though her eyes were open, it was obvious that Ashley was never going to wake up again!

Chapter 12
Compulsion and Combustion

The sun proudly decorated the bright blue morning sky like a badge of honor. It was a warm and pleasant morning, even for the middle of June. A light breeze skirted atop lush green grass and slid between full, leafy tree branches. The occasional cloud lolled about briefly as if trying to catch a tan.

You couldn't ask for a better way to begin the day.

They were getting ready to go downstairs. He needed just another minute with his cup of coffee. Then he could go to work.

"Did you get Adam off to the school bus on time?" he asked.

"Yes," she said. "Everything went fine. He only has half days this week anyway. Remember? I told you school will be over for the summer next week."

"That's right," he said. "You did mention that. I'm not looking forward to having him home all summer long."

"He's been making new friends these last few months," she said. "Perhaps he'll have places to go."

"That would be nice," he said. "I wish we had thought to sign him up for day camp or something."

"It's a bit late for that now," she said. "Are you ready to go to work?"

"Just about," he said. "I'm tired, and I have a stiff neck. I didn't sleep well last night."

"Why not?" she asked. "Are you sick?"

"No," he said. "But, I do feel a bit edgy, as if something is about to happen. Did you hear any screaming last night?"

"What? Screaming?"

"Yes," he said. "I could've sworn I heard a few blood-curdling screams last night. Then, it stopped. I went out into the hall to investigate, but then I didn't hear anything else. I figured it was probably a bad dream. So, I went back to sleep."

"What time was it when you heard the screams?" she asked.

"I don't know," he shrugged. "Two or three o'clock, I guess."

"Maybe you imagined it," she suggested. "You were probably right about it being just a bad dream. Perhaps Dr. Tseung's stories are starting to get to you after all."

"That could be it," he said. "It has been a bit too quiet around here lately. Given the recent past, maybe I'm just waiting for our next big disaster. I shouldn't expect negative things. Everything's been great these past few months. I think the tragedies are over. We have nothing but smooth sailing ahead."

"That's the spirit, Leon," she smiled. She gave him a kiss. "Everything's going to be fine. Are you ready to go downstairs?"

"Yeah," he sighed. "I guess it's that time."

A few minutes later, they were down at the reception counter.

"How are you this morning, Jeffrey?" he asked.

"Fine, Mr. Gould."

"How does the day look so far?" he asked.

"Not too bad," Jeffrey said. "Most of the rooms are full. Five couples are leaving today. Four families are scheduled to arrive. And, may I say you look stunning today, Mrs. Gould?"

"Thank you, Jeffrey."

Leon was looking over the names in the registry. Suddenly, he stopped.

"Is something wrong, Mr. Gould?" Jeffrey asked.

"No," he said. "It's just this name. A guy who signed in here yesterday. His name is Frank Bentworth. For some reason, I could swear I've heard that name before."

"An old friend, Mr. Gould?"

"I don't think so," he said. "I don't think I know him. But, that name sounds awfully familiar. What did he look like?"

"I don't know," Jeffrey shrugged. "Late thirties, I suppose. Five foot ten. Putting on weight. Dark hair. Just starting to go bald. I think he'd been drinking. Why?"

"I'm not sure," he said distantly. "Nothing specific. I wish I could remember why that name sticks in my head."

"Mr. Gould?" said a female voice. "Can I talk to you for a second, please?"

He came out of his daze. He recognized the maid standing before him.

"Yes, Dawn," he smiled. "What can I do for you?"

"May we speak privately?"

"Sure," he said. "Come with me to my office."

She followed him to the office. Once they were behind closed doors, he asked again, "Okay, Miss Wyler. What's the problem?"

"The problem is Jeffrey Bartlett," she said. "He's always flirting with me and hitting on me. I've told him to stop a thousand times. But, he just won't leave me alone!"

"Has he gotten that bad?" he asked. "I can see you're upset. Does it really bother you that much?"

"Yes," she said. "He's relentless! I reminded him of your rules. I told him I'm spoken for. I've tried everything I can..."

"Alright, Dawn," he interrupted. "I get your point. I'll speak to him. I promise. Now is there anything else?"

"No," she said. "That ought to do it. Thank you, Mr. Gould. I'm sorry to trouble you."

"That's okay."

She felt a little better as she left his office. There was another maid waiting for her in the hall.

"Hi, Rita," she said. "Are you here to talk to Leon?"

"No, Dawn," Rita said. "I'm here to talk to you. I saw you come in here. You were very short with me this morning. You're letting Jeffrey get to you. You didn't go into the kitchen for your usual morning bagel. Are you alright?"

"I'm fine," she said. "I'm sorry if I was rude to you. It's not your fault. I just have a lot on my mind."

"I figured you were avoiding the kitchen on purpose," Rita surmised. "Could it have something to do with a certain Mr. Cummings, perhaps? Is there trouble in paradise?"

"Uh…" she stammered. "Trouble in paradise? What are you talking about?"

"Oh come on, sweetie," Rita said. "Who do you think you're talking to? It's me: Rita! I know you and Glen have been seeing each other for months."

"What makes you say that?"

"I'm no fool, Dawn," she declared. "Your love for him is written all over your face. Even now, I can see it."

"You're crazy!"

"Okay," Rita said. "I understand why you want to keep it quiet. That's why I haven't said anything. And, don't worry. Your secret is safe with me. I just thought you might need a friend to talk to."

The sincerity in Rita's eyes spoke to her.

"Okay," she acquiesced with a sigh. "There's nothing to tell, really. He's just sick of keeping everything a secret. We both are. He got a job as a chef at The Silver Swordfish yesterday. He's supposed to put in his notice with Leon today. He asked me to move in with him."

"He wants you to move in with him?" Rita gasped. "That's great! Isn't it?"

"I guess it would be," she said. "If I was ready. I just can't face it right now. I'm trying to find another job myself. There are the pressures of this place, the anxiety of keeping this a secret…not know how long it will last. I'm just not ready."

"Did you tell him that?"

"Yeah," she sighed. "He got mad. Do you believe it? I seem to have a strange effect on men. My last boyfriend didn't want to let go when I dumped him. He kept calling me and harassing me for a couple of days. Then, he stopped all of a sudden. I thought he finally grew up. Then over the next few weeks, a number of his friends called me. They were wondering if I'd seen him. Apparently, when he finally got the idea that we were over, he disappeared. He must have left town without a word to anybody. Is that unreal or what? Why are guys always so screwed up?"

"I don't know, honey."

"Glen told me he'd be okay," she said. "But, I wish he'd talk to me. I wish he would just be patient. I wish he wouldn't have refused to come in with me after our date last night."

"Sounds like a real head case," Rita diagnosed. "Would you like me to talk to him?"

"God, no!"

"Don't worry, Dawn," Rita assured her. "I'll use all my tact and discretion. You've got nothing to fear."

"I wish you wouldn't," she said. "He's already in a mood about keeping this a secret. If he thinks I talked to you, he's going to be really pissed off."

"Don't worry," Rita reiterated. "I'll handle it."

She made her way over to the kitchen.

"Hi, Glen," she said. "Can I talk to you privately for a minute?"

"Well," he said. "I'm kind of busy, Rita. Can it wait?"

"Not really."

"Okay," he sighed. He followed her to a discreet corner in the dining area. "Make it quick. What's up?"

"First of all," she said. "I hear you got a job at The Silver Swordfish. Congratulations! That should be a great gig. I'm going to miss you, though."

"Thanks, Rita," he smiled. "That's sweet. I'll miss you too."

"Next," she continued. "I know Leon can be a bitch to work for. Some of his policies about employee relations seem kind of unfair. They can lead to sneaking around and all sorts of bullshit. But, some girls are worth a little extra effort. Wouldn't you agree?"

"Oh shit!" he snipped. "How much do you know?"

"Don't get mad," she said. "Dawn didn't tell me anything. I figured it out on my own. I have a radar for true love. And you two have been shooting off signals for months."

"If Leon finds out…"

"He won't," she assured him. "He's clueless. And now that you're getting out of here, things will be able to move along in time. I know sneaking around has been hard. And Dawn's going to need a little room to breathe. It's been hard on her too, you know?"

"I know."

"Give her time, honey," she said. "She loves you, Glen. Good things will come when they're ready. Okay?"

"Yeah," he sighed. "I know. I love her too. I'm just sick of the secrecy."

"She is too."

"I realize that," he said. "I'm just tired of the stagnation. Don't worry. We'll be fine. I just needed some time to think. Does anybody else know about this?"

"Pearl suspects, I think," she informed him. "But, she won't say anything. You're in the clear. I have to get back to work now. I just want to leave you with one final thought about our little Miss Wyler. Some girls are worth the extra effort."

"You're right," he smiled. "And Dawn really is worth it. Thanks, Rita."

"You're welcome, Glen," she smiled back. "And congratulations on the new job."

"Thank you."

She gave him a hug.

"You better treat my girl right," she warned playfully. "Or I'll kick your ass."

"I can believe it," he grinned.

With a sweet smile, she hurried off to work.

But, nobody noticed the boy hiding in the shadows. Somebody didn't go to school that day.

❧

Frantically, he hit the speed dial on his cell phone. He waited for a response.

"Logan?" he said. "It's Frank! I have a big problem!"

"Bentworth?" said the groggy voice on the other end. "What time is it?"

"It's about 8:30," he said. "I know it's early, but it's an emergency!"

"Call Kirsch!"

"I already did," he said. "He's not answering his phone."

"Maybe that's because we're not used to drinking like you anymore," Logan said. "We're not used to hangovers."

"Will you cut it out, Tetweller?" he snapped. "This is an emergency!"

"What is it now, Bentworth?"

"It happened again!" he stammered. "Ashley's dead!"

"What?"

"You heard me!" he said. "Ashley's dead! She died just like Ambrose! It looks as if I did it! But, I swear I don't think it was me!"

"You got to be kidding me, Bentworth!" Logan barked. "What the hell?"

"I swear I don't know what's going on, Tetweller!" he begged. "This isn't me! It's this place! It has to be! That freaky kid said that Trixie was waiting for me! I'm starting to think he was right! Trixie really has been here waiting for me all these years! She's behind this! I just know it!"

"Will you calm down, Frank?" Logan said. "You're not making any sense."

"Just get over here, Logan," he implored. "Please! I need you!"

"Alright, Frank!" he grumbled. "Quit whining! I'll be over as soon as I take a shower and find some clothes. But, I have to tell you I'm getting real sick of this crap!"

"Thanks, buddy!"

He hung up. He leaned back in his chair. He was very tired.

He hadn't slept a wink since he'd found Ashley. She was still where he found her.

He closed his eyes.

It seemed very dark. He remembered this darkness.

It was a nighttime darkness. Only a few gaunt wisps of stark moonlight splashed against her body from the window.

Ashley was still breathing then. He could see her clothes move along with her breathing. He just stood by the bed and watched her.

She rolled over. He could see her face better. She looked so peaceful.

So peaceful.

It was almost a shame that he was holding that axe. It was almost a shame what he had to do.

"Ashley," he whispered.

She stirred a little.

"Ashley," he repeated.

She didn't respond.

So, he raised the axe over his head. He watched her face for a moment.

...her sleeping face.

Then, he brought the axe down on her with all his might. That got a reaction!

She opened her eyes as the blade cleaved her flesh.

He kept chopping...and chopping...and chopping as if splitting a load of soft firewood that bled.

Even after she stopped moving, he just kept chopping...

Finally, he stopped. He stood quietly. He stared at the body. It looked so still and peaceful in the shadows and pallid splashes of moonlight.

Torn, shredded, still...and so peaceful.

Then with blood dripping from the blade, he carried the axe to the door. He was careful to open it quietly.

Mustn't disturb the neighbors.

The hallway was lined with inadequately spaced night lights. The occasional glow of these scant lights gave an eerie quality to his path. Shadow dominated light as he walked.

It didn't matter. He didn't need to see. He cautiously made his way down the hall.

It felt as if he had traversed this path before. He just walked...very quietly.

Mustn't disturb the neighbors.

Blood still dripped from the shiny blade.

The beautiful stairway stretched out before him. It was just where it was supposed to be. He started to walk down the steps to the second floor.

There was an old man on the stairs. A farmer. It didn't bother him to see the old man. He had seen him before. Although it was the first time he'd ever seen that farmer without an axe in his hands.

This time, *he* held the axe, as he walked downward....

...Down to the second floor.

The same dim, eerie lighting met him on this floor. Still, he knew his way down the hall. He walked slowly, with a deliberate stride. He walked steadily to Room 8.

He was still carrying the axe. A few drops of blood still dripped from the blade.

The blood dripped quietly.

Mustn't disturb the neighbors.

Finally, he found himself standing in front of the door to Room 8.

He reached out to the doorknob. It felt cold in his hand. It turned easily.

Somehow, he was not surprised that the door was unlocked.

He pushed the door open. He entered the room. As expected, everything was dark.

He closed the door for privacy. It was easy to find the bed. The rooms were nearly identical. Besides, this room seemed to have borrowed the same gaunt wisps of stark moonlight that had illuminated the bed in Room 29.

Donald Gorman

He walked over to the bed. He looked down at the two bodies sleeping under the covers. He recognized the faces of Rich Kirsch and his wife Felicia.

They looked so peaceful as they slept.

So peaceful.

It was a shame what he had to do. He didn't want to. He needed to.

It was a compulsion. He couldn't help it.

He raised the axe over his head. He raised the axe quietly.

Mustn't disturb the neighbors.

Suddenly, he thrust the axe downward into Rich's chest! He began chopping and chopping and chopping!

He couldn't stop himself!

He just kept chopping and chopping!

The splattering of blood pleased him.

It made it easier to keep chopping…

…and chopping…

…until he heard a loud knocking sound.

He woke up in a chair. The loud knocking continued. Ashley was still lying motionless beside the axe on the bloody bed.

The loud knocking continued.

"Come on, Frank!" shouted the voice outside the door. "It's Logan! Let me in, you fool! You're the one who called me! Remember?"

He jumped up and rushed to the door. He opened the door and allowed Logan to enter.

As he closed the door behind him, he cried, "Oh God, Logan! Thank God you're here! I don't believe what's happened! I don't freakin' believe it!"

"Oh damn!" Logan sputtered as he stared at the bed. "What the hell, Frank? What the fuck is wrong with you? This has just got to stop!"

"I swear to God I didn't mean it, Logan!" he whimpered. "I swear to God it's not me! It's this place! That spooky little kid was right! Trixie's here! I know she is! She's behind all this! I know it! Oh my God! I don't believe this is happening!"

"Get a hold of yourself, Bentworth," Logan advised. "You have to pull yourself together. Trixie has been dead for twenty years!"

"Don't you think I know that?" he sobbed. "I killed her! My God! I killed her! And now, she's getting even with me! I've carried the guilt around with me all these years! I've tortured myself and everyone around me! And somehow, that wasn't enough! Trixie's here, Logan! And, she wants to get even with me!"

"I'm going to slap you, if you don't pull yourself together," Logan warned. "How much did you drink already today, Bentworth? It's only 10:00 in the morning!"

"This has nothing to do with drinking, Tetweller!" he argued. "I haven't touched a drop! Damn it, you bastard! Don't you get it? This isn't me! I didn't do this! Trixie is behind all this! She's making this happen!"

"Get your head out of your ass, Bentworth!" Logan shouted. "Trixie isn't making anything happen! She's dead!"

"How many times do I have to tell you?" he desperately insisted. "I know she's dead! I know I killed her, you fuck! I didn't mean to kill her! But, I did! I never wanted to kill Ambrose and his wife! But, I couldn't help it! I was compelled to do what Trixie made me do! I didn't mean to kill Ashley! I didn't even remember doing it until after I called you! Just like I didn't remember killing Rich and Felicia 'til after I called you!"

"What?" Logan gasped. "Rich and Felicia too?"

"God!" he sobbed. "I don't know! I think so! I didn't even know 'til a few minutes ago! But, I think I did! I think they're dead too!"

"That's just great, Bentworth!"

"I told you I didn't mean it!" he sobbed. "I don't even know if they're really dead! I just had a few foggy visions! Flashbacks, I suppose! I don't even know if they're real! If they are real, then I'm not responsible! It was a compulsion, Logan! A compulsion brought on by Trixie!"

"A compulsion, huh?" Logan spat. "You are some piece of work, Bentworth! Do you feel any compulsions now, you piece of shit? I swear if you feel any compulsions towards me, I'm going to beat your brains in! Do you understand me?"

"Yes."

"Call Rich again," Logan advised. "See if he answers. If he doesn't, we'd better go down and check on him."

"Okay."

He took out his cell phone. He hit the speed dial. He prayed for a response as he listened to ring…after ring…after ring…

After a minute, he said, "There's no answer."

"Wonderful!" Logan grunted. "I'd better go to his room. I want to see exactly what we're dealing with."

"Let me go with you," he said. "I need to know."

"Haven't you done enough, Bentworth?"

"Can't you hear a word I say?" he insisted. "I don't even know if they're dead! I didn't kill them! Not on purpose, anyway! If this really happened, I need to know! I need to see what I've done!"

"Alright, Frank," Logan sighed. "Let's go. But, leave the axe here! I don't want you to feel any more compulsions! You hear me?"

"Don't worry," he anxiously agreed. "I don't even want to go near that thing!"

"What room number are they in?" Logan asked.

"Room 8 on the next floor down," he answered.

"Okay," Logan muttered. "Let's get this over with."

They discretely left the room. Frank locked the apartment door.

As they walked down the hall, he pointed out, "Look! That looks like a few drops of blood on the carpet. That's not a good sign."

"That's just marvelous, Frank!"

"You know?" he theorized. "It occurs to me that maybe Old Man Hilzak never actually meant to kill his family. Maybe it really is this place. Maybe there's something about this place that compels people to act in disturbingly unnatural ways."

"That's a lovely story, Frank."

"I mean it," he said. "Maybe this place is just evil or something."

"The only thing that's evil about this place," Logan grumbled. "Is the drunken asshole that's walking down the hall. Just stop talking and take me to Rich."

They descended down the stairs to the second floor without a word. Then, they followed the numbers on the doors to Room 8.

Donald Gorman

Logan knocked once or twice. "Rich?" he asked. "Are you in there? It's Logan."

"I don't hear anything."

"Great!" Logan grunted. "So, how do we get in?"

Frank reached out and turned the doorknob. The door opened without a hitch.

"Of course," Logan said. "I should've known."

They each took a breath for courage. Then, they cautiously entered the room.

Both men stared in horror at the sight on the blood-covered bed.

"Son of a bitch, Frank!" Logan gasped. "What did you do? Just hack them both to pieces in their sleep? I knew it was a mistake to let you stay in this hotel! I knew this place was going to get to you! You've gone absolutely insane!"

He didn't reply.

"Frank?"

Logan turned around to face his troubled friend. His face turned pale as he saw the look in Frank's eyes.

"What the hell, Frank?" he gasped. "I thought you left the axe upstairs!"

"I did!"

"Then, how did you…?" he sputtered. "Put the axe down, Frank! Put it down! Damn it, Frank! I'm not kidding! Put the axe down!"

As he buried the axe deep into Logan's chest, he cried, "I'm sorry, Logan! Oh God! I'm so sorry!"

Logan screamed as the axe sank deep into his chest the second time.

Frank was weeping as he swung the axe again and again. He just couldn't stop. He heard the screams. He saw the blood. Still, he kept chopping and chopping until

Logan was just a motionless, silent, bloody mass on the floor.

Then, the entire room burst into flames. The walls, the floor, the furniture, the door… everything was engulfed in angry, hostile, impetuous flames.

He cried out in terror. Tears were still streaming from his eyes.

He was trapped. There was no escape.

Suddenly, a child stepped out of the fire. The boy could not have been more than seven years old.

"You!" Frank gasped. "You're that creepy little kid from yesterday! Who are you?"

"Who I am is not important," said the boy. "I knew you would return here, Mr. Bentworth. I have always known. Trixie has been waiting for you all these years!"

For being so young, the boy's voice seemed awfully deep. But, Frank had more immediate concerns.

"Please believe me!" he begged. "I never meant to kill her! I never meant to hurt anyone! I'm sorry!"

"I'm not the one you need to apologize to, Mr. Bentworth," the boy said. "You made your choices. You chose selfishness over compassion. You chose to serve yourself instead of those closest to you. You never paid for what you did!"

"I *have* paid!" he insisted hysterically. "I've carried this guilt with me for twenty years! I've paid plenty!"

"No!" the boy demanded. "Everyone around you has paid! You indulged yourself in alcohol and hedonism! You have served yourself while others have paid the price!"

"I know!" he sobbed as he dropped to his knees. "I've destroyed everything and everybody I've ever touched. Oh my God! Please forgive me!"

"I cannot forgive you," the boy imparted. "It is not my place. It is usually the destiny of any person who chooses to follow the path of selfishness over compassion that they are condemned to punish themselves for their lack of judgment. It is on this basis that selfish people devise their own Hell. And it was on this premise that the concept of Hell was invented. The French philosopher Jean-Paul Sartre said that Hell is being locked forever in a room with your friends. Well, Mr. Bentworth…you have killed all of your friends!"

"Please no!" Frank begged. "I didn't mean to! I didn't mean for any of this to happen!"

"According to Dante's classic tale *The Inferno*," the boy continued. "The sign on The Gates of Hell ends with the inscription, 'Abandon all hope, all ye who enter here!' Well, Mr. Bentworth…you have just stepped through The Gates of Hell! It is the Hell that you devised for yourself! You can abandon all hope now!"

Frank didn't have time to wonder how the boy's voice got so deep…or how a young boy had access to such a vocabulary…or how the kid was quoting people like Dante and Jean-Paul Sartre.

He just cringed and cowered as the fires boomed and crackled. Flames whipped and lashed at him. It was almost as if the fire was deliberately trying to reach him.

Then, he heard a voice speak to him from amid the vicious blaze. It was a sweet, familiar voice. It was a voice that scared him to tears.

"Hello, Frank," she said sweetly. "I knew you'd come back to me."

The girl stepped out of the fire. She was dressed just as she had been the last time he'd seen her. She offered him a genuine, endearing smile.

"Trixie!" he sputtered. "No! It can't be!"

"I've been waiting for you, Frank," she said sweetly. "I've waited for so long."

"Please believe me, Trixie!" he implored. "I'm so sorry for everything! I never meant to hurt you! I never would have hurt you! Please forgive me, Trixie! I'm sorry! Oh, my God! I'm so very sorry!"

"You tried to rape me, Frank," she said sweetly. "Then, you left me to burn in a fire that you started. Then, you walked away without reprisal because you lied to the police."

"I never tried to…" he stammered. "It was all a mistake! I was just a kid, for God's sake! Please, Trixie!"

"Now it's *your* turn to burn, Frank," she said.

The fires tossed and convulsed in a menacing manner. They moved closer as they devoured everything in their path.

"No!" he screamed.

Suddenly, a big hole opened in the floor with a loud crash. There was a long, narrow staircase that descended down into the hole.

He looked down into this simple chasm. There was no light. It was brutally dark down there. The hole and the stairs seemed to go down forever. But as the flames closed in on him from all directions, he had no choice.

He quickly began to run down the narrow, crumbling cement steps.

The fire seemed to follow him as he ran. The flames appeared purposeful, threatening and malicious. They taunted and lashed out at him as they followed him downward.

They afforded just a dim light as he ran without the benefit of a banister.

"Run!" Trixie's voice laughed from above. "Run, Frank! Run for your life!"

There was no end in sight. The stairs extended ever downward. And, the flames were intentionally following his vain effort to escape.

However, he had no choice! He just kept running downward.

He kept running...

...and running...

...and running...

She still felt a little depressed. She pushed the cart with her cleaning products up to the door of Room 29.

She sighed as she took out the key. She opened the door. She wasn't really paying attention as she pushed the cart into the room.

There was no reason to worry about Rita. Rita wouldn't tell anyone her secret.

However, she hoped Rita wouldn't screw things up when she talked to Glen.

After a moment, she looked up. Her eyes travelled over to the bed.

Her eyes grew wide as she focused on the bloody surprise lying on the sheets.

She screamed.

Wrongful Secrets

The terrible sight sickened her. Yet, she couldn't look away. Her whole body trembled. She wanted to run away. However, her legs wouldn't move.

She took out her cell phone. She dialed the front desk.

After a few rings, a familiar friendly voice answered, "Hello. This is The Hillside Inn. Carol Gould speaking. How may I help you?"

"Mrs. Gould?" she sputtered. "I'm glad it's you!"

"Is this Dawn?" Carol asked with concern. "What's the matter, dear? You sound upset."

"I just went in to clean Room 29," she explained shakily. "I walked in and…and…oh God! You need to come up here! We have a problem!"

"What sort of problem?"

"A woman's been killed!" she stammered. "Well, hacked to pieces, really. It's…oh God! Please come up here right away!"

"Alright, Dawn," Carol said. "Don't move. I'll be right there."

Carol hung up the phone. She turned to the young man beside her at the reception counter. "Jeffrey?" she said. "I have to go up to Room 29. Dawn tells me there's a problem up there. If you see my husband, let him know. Okay?"

"Sure thing, Mrs. Gould."

She took a deep breath for courage. Then, she walked to the elevator. A sick feeling began to rise in the pit of her stomach.

She couldn't believe it was happening again. She should have known that the peace in this hotel was only temporary!

He was in the dining area. Preparations for the lunch rush had already begun.

His cell phone rang. He answered, "Hello?"

"Hello," said a friendly voice on the other end. "Is this Mr. Gould?"

"Yes," he said. "How may I help you?"

"Hi, Mr. Gould," she said. "This is Mrs. Novak with The Spruce Valley Elementary School. I hope it's okay to call. This was the only number I could find for you. I called because I was wondering if your son was feeling better."

"Adam?"

"Yes," she said. "I know he's out sick today. Is it anything serious?"

"Adam?" he repeated with confusion. "Out sick? That's news to me. My wife told me she put him on the bus this morning."

"That's funny," she said. "Adam never came in this morning. When your babysitter called, he mentioned that Adam had a bad cold or something."

"Babysitter?" he asked with growing concern. "We don't have a babysitter, Mrs. Novak. We take care of our son by ourselves."

"But, Mr. Gould," she explained. "I could swear that the man who called said he was Adam's babysitter. He said Adam was sick and wouldn't be in today."

"Did this babysitter give his name?" he asked.

"Yes," she replied. "He said his name was Mr. Fuego."

"Mr. Fuego?"

"That's right."

His face turned pale. There was a lump in his throat.

"Thank you, Mrs. Novak," he stammered. "I'll be in touch."

He hung up. He rushed out to the reception counter.

"Jeffrey?" he asked anxiously. "Where's my wife?"

"She went up to Room 29," Jeffrey said. "Dawn Wyler called her. Apparently, there's a problem up there."

"What kind of problem?"

"She didn't say."

"Have you seen Adam?" he asked.

"No," Jeffrey said. "Isn't he usually in school this time of the day?"

"Something strange is going on," he declared. "Who's registered in Room 29 right now?"

"Well, let's see," Jeffrey said while glancing at the book. "It's Mr. and Mrs. Frank Bentworth."

"There's that name again!" he stated impatiently. "Bentworth! Where have I heard that name before?"

"Was he a guest here before, Mr. Gould?" Jeffrey asked.

"No," he said. "That's not it. It's something..."

He stopped. His muscles grew tense.

"Of course!" he declared with recognition. "That's it! Frances Bentworth! Police Chief Farley told me that Frances Bentworth was the high school kid who burned down the old Hilzak house twenty years ago! When those three girls were killed!"

Suddenly, the entire building shook with a loud explosion.

"My God!" Jeffrey exclaimed. "What was that?"

Instinctively, Leon ran out of the building. He wanted to see the extent of the damage.

Tall flames shot insolently out of the windows on the east side of the third floor. The ruthless blaze hurled thick flumes of smoke up into the air.

"Son of a…!" he gasped.

He ran back into the building.

"Jeffrey!" he called. "What room did you say my wife was in?"

"Room 29," Jeffrey said. "Dawn said there was a problem up there."

"Damn it!" he growled. "That's exactly where the fire is! Oh no! Carol!"

Loud fire alarms began sounding all through the building.

"Jeffrey!" he shouted over the alarm. "Get everybody out of the building!"

"Right, Mr. Gould!"

"And grab Adam if you see him!" he instructed. "I'm going to start on the third floor! I've got to save my family! I've got to get to Carol!"

People were already beginning to fill the lobby. There was a growing air of anxious curiosity.

Glen ran into the lobby from the kitchen. "What's going on?" he asked.

"My wife and Dawn Wyler are trapped in Room 29," Leon shouted over the alarm. "And the third floor is on fire! I'm going to try and save them! Get everyone out of the building!"

"Oh my God!" Glen gasped. "Dawn!"

Chapter 13
Punishing Yourself

Finally, he reached the bottom of the narrow staircase.

It seemed as though he had been running forever. He was out of breath. He was standing on a solid, flat surface. The fire had fallen back behind him.

Everything was very dark. Everything was eerily silent.

He was trying to catch his breath. It was still difficult to feel as if he was safe. He glanced around. There was nothing visible in the brutal, belittling darkness.

Suddenly, monstrous flames sprang up from the floor all around him. The tall fires erupted with a thunderous roar. They bobbed and swayed, assuming threatening postures as they illuminated the dank, dismal room.

There was a certain dungeon motif to his surroundings. Cinderblock walls were decorated with chains and restraints. A few of the restraints still had rotting corpses hanging from them that may have at one time been human.

Cobwebs covered everything. The stench was unbearable.

However, the scariest sight was the girl standing right in front of him.

"Trixie!" he stuttered. "Not again! Please!"

"Welcome to Hell, Frank," she said sweetly.

She had always had a beautiful smile. And in the dodging shadows and fierce orange firelight, her smile took on a decidedly disarming quality.

"Please don't, Trixie!" he begged. "You know I never meant to hurt you! How many times do I have to apologize? I'm sorry, Trixie! I'm truly sorry for what happened! For God's sake! Please don't do this to me!"

"I'm not doing anything to you, Frank," she explained with that beautiful smile. "I didn't put you here. I didn't tell you to try to rape me. I didn't tell you to burn down the Hilzak house. I didn't even tell you to walk away without getting punished by lying to the police. I didn't do any of that, Frank."

"I didn't try to rape you!" he insisted.

"This is the wrong place to argue that point, Frank," she said sweetly.

The fires boomed and shot high up into the air. The intense yellows and malicious reds lashed and mocked him as he began to weep.

"This is all one big mistake!" he cried. "Please listen to me, Trixie!"

"It's too late for talk, Frank," she said sweetly. "What happens to you now is not up to me. I didn't start these fires. Everything that is happening here has been constructed by you. You have always had the ability to choose between your own selfish interests or caring for others. You had your choices, Frank. You made your choices. Your choices put you here. Your choices built these flames."

"No!" he implored. "There must be a way out of this! Please! Have mercy!"

"Mercy is an act of compassion, Frank," she explained with that beautiful smile. "Compassion is a choice. It's an option you have never chosen. It's an option that is no longer available to you, sweetheart. It is the destiny of anyone who chooses Selfishness over Compassion that they will someday punish themselves for choosing unwisely. Your day has come, Frank. Your only choice now is how you will punish yourself."

"What do you mean?" he asked with a sense of desperation.

That creepy boy stepped out of the fire.

Frank began to sob openly with fright.

"As I said," the boy reminded in that deep, intimidating tone. "Jean-Paul Sartre quipped that Hell is being locked forever in a room with your friends. Here is the room, Mr. Bentworth. And here are your friends."

One by one, his friends stepped out of the raging, furious flames:

Joining Trixie Sinclair were Kimberly Johnson and Cheyenne McCall.

Frank fell to his knees as he saw the three girls who died twenty years ago in the fire standing side by side.

Next, Bill Ambrose stepped out of the flames with his wife Nancy.

Then his wife, Ashley Bentworth.

Next, Richard Kirsch stepped out into the open with his wife Felicia.

"This isn't fair!" Frank begged. "I didn't mean to kill any of these people! It wasn't me! It was this house!"

Lastly, Logan Tetweller stepped out of the flames.

"No!" he wept hysterically. "You can't blame me for all this! It's not right!"

"It's not right what you did to these people," the boy said. "It's not right what you've done to everyone you knew. It's not right that you have walked away without punishment for every wrong choice you have made."

"Please, Trixie!" he implored. "I was just a kid! I've been paying for this all my life! Logan! Ashley! You know I've paid!"

"Here are your friends, Mr. Bentworth," the boy repeated. "The only question that remains is how you will join them. You built this fire to punish yourself, Mr. Bentworth. Here is your final choice. Do you choose the fire you opted to build? Or would you like to die as you lived: taking the easy way out?"

The boy pointed to somewhere behind Frank. With wild eyes, Frank spun around to see what the boy was pointing at.

There was a tall stepladder. Beside the ladder, a rope with a noose dangled from some indiscernible place in the darkness overhead.

"No!" he screamed in terror. "Please! No!"

All his friends started walking toward him. As they walked, the scorching fires followed.

"Choose, Frank," Ashley said.

"It's time to make a choice, Frank," Cheyenne said.

"No!" he shrieked as the tears streamed down his face.

"At least, you get a choice, Frank," Rich said. "We had no choice."

His friends and the ferocious flames all closed in on him.

Frank jumped to his feet. He slowly began to back away from them. He took a few steps backward toward the noose.

"Why is this all on me?" he defended desperately. "We were all there at the Hilzak place! Logan! Rich! Bill! We all hid the truth! We all used the same alibi!"

"It was *your* alibi, Frank," Rich reminded. "We were protecting *you*!"

"Besides, *we've* already paid, Frank," Bill added. "You've seen to that!"

"We have all paid the price for being your friend!" Logan said.

"Now it's your turn to pay," Kim said.

As they approached, Frank took a step backward.

"This is all wrong!" he insisted. "We were just kids! We made a few mistakes!"

They kept walking toward him.

He took a few steps back. His foot accidentally kicked the ladder. There was nowhere left for him to go.

Seething, vicious flames quickly surrounded the ladder.

The fires shot at least seven feet into the air. The brilliant yellows and vivid reds danced, teased and taunted him as they grew higher.

Frank was stranded with nothing but a ladder and a noose for company. It was obvious that he had no chance for escape.

He screamed in absolute horror.

Various voices whispered at him.

"Choose, Frank. How will you punish yourself? At last, there is no wrong choice."

"Choose, Frank…"

He climbed the ladder slowly…one rung at a time.

"Please no!" he sobbed as he climbed.

The angry fires teased, taunted and lapped at his flesh.

"Choose, Frank…"

He stepped up to the rung that put him in perfect position for the noose. He was sobbing openly as he put the noose around his neck.

"Please don't make me do this!" he wept. "Please, Trixie! Stop this!"

The hostile flames drew in closer to the ladder. There was nowhere to go.

"Choose, Frank…"

The fires were white hot. They burned his flesh as they flailed and flogged at his sweaty face and hands. The noose fit perfectly around his neck.

"Choose, Frank…"

He gave one last frantic screech.

Then, he stepped off the ladder.

―✠―

The fire alarm was still blaring loudly. People ran out into the halls. They raced toward the staircase and elevator.

"The elevator won't work during a fire alarm," he warned.

He directed people to the stairs.

"Please remain calm," he instructed. "Walk down the stairs in an orderly fashion. Nobody will get hurt if you keep your heads."

He wanted desperately to get off the second floor. The woman he loved was still upstairs. She could be hurt. She could be dead!

He knocked on doors. He entered rooms. He checked for stragglers. He ushered guests toward the stairs.

Three dead bodies in Room 8 didn't even phase him. It was fewer people to worry about evacuating. Getting up to the third floor was all he cared about.

He could only hope Leon had successfully reached the girls.

He could only pray that they were still alive.

When he was reasonably sure that all the living guests were off the second floor, he bounded up the steps to the third story of the building.

The whole east half of the building was a wall of fire.

Leon was helping an old couple out their room. It was possibly the last room that could be accessed on this side of the ferocious blaze.

"Did you find the girls?" he asked hopefully.

"No," Leon said. "They must still be in Room 29!"

"Damn it!" he grumbled impatiently. "We have to get them out of there!"

"I know that!" Leon barked angrily. "My wife is in there! I've called but nobody answers! Chances are, they won't make it!"

"They have to!"

"Please get the Wilsons out of here safely," Leon requested. "I'll deal with this."

He looked at the old, feeble couple. He didn't want to leave Dawn behind. Still, he knew where his duty lied.

"Of course," he said politely.

He struggled to be patient as he helped the guests to the stairs. As they began their descent, there was a loud explosion behind them. He turned to look.

The wall of flame suddenly started moving quickly toward the staircase.

"Oh shit!" he exclaimed.

There was no time for delicacy. The men excused themselves before carrying the old couple down to safety. Once downstairs, Jeffrey got the Wilsons out while two men rushed back upstairs.

"What are you doing, Glen?" Leon asked. "The third floor is a lost cause! Even I know the chance of saving those girls is practically zero! But, I can't leave Carol behind! Get out of the building! You were a great help, but you've done all you can!"

"I'm not leaving those girls!" he demanded.

They ran halfway up the stairs to the third floor.

Then, they stopped. They stared with wide-eyed dismay.

The roaring, treacherous fires had nearly reached the stairs. The ravenous flames could be seen from where they stood devouring the whole floor.

"God, no!" Leon muttered. "Not my Carol! I can't lose her like this! I won't!"

He was in no mood to console Leon. He had his own reason to be depressed.

"You can't do this!" Leon shouted at no one in particular. "I won't lose Carol!"

Wrongful Secrets

The chef wished his boss would just shut up. He wasn't the only one with a broken heart. He couldn't believe his last words to Dawn had been a silly, meaningless argument about moving in together.

It felt as if his stomach had turned into one, big, heavy rock that was crushing everything else inside him.

There was absolutely no chance that the girls could have survived.

Suddenly, a young boy stepped out of the fire. There was a dark intensity in his eyes that startled the two men on the stairs.

"Adam!" Leon shouted. "How did you do that? What are you doing here? Get out of the building!"

"I am not your son, Mr. Gould," the boy informed with a disturbingly deep voice. "But, don't worry. Adam is safe for the moment."

"What's going on?" Leon asked. "Where's my wife?"

"Mrs. Gould and Miss Wyler are both in Room 29, as you suspect," the boy said. "They are both alive at the moment. But, they don't have much time."

"What's this all about?" Leon asked.

"Don't you understand, Mr. Gould?" the boy said. "This is The Grand Combustion that you have been warned about. You were told. Yet, you chose to ignore it, because it interfered with your selfish plans."

"What?" he asked. "What do you mean?"

"As you have been told," the boy explained. "This is a site where the concurrent forces that comprise the infinite entity known as Free Will often conflict with each other. We don't need to run through the reasons why this happens right now. There isn't time. But as you may have surmised, this present friction was triggered by the return of Frances Bentworth."

"So, what do you want from me?" Leon asked. "I had nothing to do with his return."

"Mr. Bentworth only triggered the current friction," the boy expounded. "But when the conflict was set into motion, all conflicts within the system of Free Will on this site were brought into focus. You have been warned a number of times that this hotel is sitting on an unstable location. Yet despite numerous warnings, you chose your precious hotel over the safety of your guests, and even your own family!"

"Are you kidding me?" Leon argued. "A bunch of nuts tell me that ghosts are going to blow up my hotel? And I'm supposed to take that seriously?"

"Michael Schumacker offered proof," the boy said. "So did Christopher and Jennifer Hurd. Not to mention the man's body you found in the fireplace. Do you even know who that man was, Mr. Gould? Did you care how he got there? Did you bother to find out? No! You just hid him from the world, so no one would threaten the existence of your precious hotel!"

"This is my business!" Leon insisted. "It's how I provide for my family! I didn't want the cops crawling all over this place again!"

"His name was Spencer Robinson, Mr. Gould," the boy continued. "And nobody even knows he's dead because of you! He offered more evidence that this place is a danger to your family! You intentionally kept your own wrongful secret, just so you could place your hotel above the welfare of your family!"

"This hotel *is* the welfare of my family!" he argued. "If I lose this hotel, how am I supposed to feed and house my wife and child?"

"You don't need to feed and house the dead, Mr. Gould," the boy stated. "Your selfish justifications may have convinced you why it was acceptable to ignore your family's safety so you could have your hotel. But it is your selfish justifications that built this fire. And now you will punish yourself for your selfish choices. Because of your selfishness, you will lose both your hotel and your wife!"

"No!" he begged desperately. "You can't do this! If you're supposed to signify Justice, it isn't right! Carol doesn't deserve to die for my choices!"

"You're right, Mr. Gould," the boy agreed. "She *doesn't* deserve to die for your choices. And if you learn to truly believe that soon enough, you may just save your wife! The time has come to choose, Mr. Gould! Which is more important? Your hotel or your wife? Only when you truly choose your wife, will you be able to save her!"

"But, I *do* choose my wife!" Leon argued. "I always did!"

"If that's true," the boy reiterated. "You will make your way through the fire that was created by your selfishness."

"What about Dawn?" Glen asked.

"Apply what I've been saying to your own situation, Mr. Cummings," the boy said. "You have made your own selfish choices. You spurned and hurt a woman who loves you for purely selfish gain."

"What are you talking about?" Glen pressed. "I just got a little upset because she wouldn't move in with me.

I said I'd get over it. It's not like I broke up with her or anything! I didn't do anything to her!"

"Arguing your petty semantics and justifications with me won't put out that fire that you created, Mr. Cummings," the boy said. "Choosing Miss Wyler's needs over your own selfish interests is the only thing that will get you through the fire."

"You can't possibly..." Glen began.

"Listen to me, gentlemen," the boy interrupted. "You both created this fire with your selfish decisions. If you cling to your selfishness, your fire will be the means by which you punish yourselves. Only by choosing not to be selfish will you find your way through these fires of your creation. I wish you good luck, gentlemen."

The boy turned around. He walked back into the fire.

"No, Adam!" Leon shouted. "Don't go in there!"

It was too late. The boy was gone.

The two men looked at each other with confusion.

"What do we do now?" Leon asked.

"I don't know about you," Glen said. "But, I'm going after Dawn! I'm not leaving her here to die!"

"But, how?"

"I don't know," Glen insisted. "But, I don't care what happens to me! I'm not leaving her in that room!"

As he marched up the stairs, it almost seemed as if a small passage opened up in the center of the flames.

"You're right!" Leon averred. "I don't care about this place! You can burn the whole damned hotel to the ground, for all I care! I'm not going to lose my Carol!"

As he approached the intimidating blaze, he began to sweat. The fires seemed to jeer and taunt him as they flailed and danced before him. He tossed his expensive suit coat and tie to the stairs.

The fire was dangerously hot.

But, he could not leave Carol in that room!

Glen knew it was impossible to make it through the blaze. But, saving Dawn was more important than anything in the world!

He concentrated on how he'd rather die than leave Dawn in that fire as he stepped into the fire. He tried not to look at the daunting, mocking flames that seemed intent on swallowing him as he moved steadily onward. The fires thrashed against him. He could feel their scorching heat as he advanced bravely toward Room 29.

The occasional sting and burn of the merciless flames tore against his flesh.

It was like being in an oven. Those fires wanted to roast him like a Thanksgiving turkey.

But, he refused to stop. He pressed onward.

"I don't care what happens to me!" he shouted into the fires. "You can't have my Dawn! I'm going to get her out of this hellhole if it kills me! Do you hear me? Do what you want to me! But, you can't have my Dawn! I won't let you take her, you bastard!"

The fires seemed to leave him just enough room to slip between them as he concentrated on putting Dawn's safety above his own.

Leon coughed as he got a lungful of smoke.

The vengeful blaze whipped against his face and clothing. He felt a distinctive, painful burn on the back of his hand. With fire all around him, it was difficult to be sure he was even travelling in the right direction.

Still, sheer instinct drove him to move forward.

Donald Gorman

He didn't know how there always seemed to be just enough space to squeeze between blazes. And, he didn't care. He just focused on saving his wife as he moved down the burning hall.

"You're not going to take Carol away from me!" he called to the flames. "It's not going to happen! I don't care about this hotel! Burn the whole damned building to the ground, for all I care! But, you're not getting Carol! I won't let you!"

And there always seemed to be just enough of a path between the fires to fit through.

Finally, both men made it to the end of the hall. They couldn't see each other. But, both men could read the number 29 before the burning door fell to the floor.

The doorway was clear. However, the entire room was one big barricade of fire.

Suddenly, a figure appeared in the door. It could only have been the image of Mortimer Hilzak.

The old farmer looked angry as he glared straight ahead. He assumed a threatening stance as he blocked the door.

However, not even the axe daunted Glen in the least. Somehow, he knew the hotel was testing him. He was not going to give up on his mission.

"Get out of my way, you son of a bitch!" he warned.

As he stepped into the doorway, Hilzak disappeared.

Leon could barely see in front of him. But, he could make out the figure of Glen making his way through the door. It gave him the courage to enter the room.

Menacing fires were everywhere. However, he could here coughing above the intimidating roars of the blaze.

He practically pushed the flames out of his way. There was a small clearing in the fire. Carol was on her hands and knees in the clearing. She was coughing from the smoke.

There wasn't much time.

"Carol!" he shouted.

She managed to look up.

"Leon?" she coughed. "How…?"

"Don't worry, sweetheart," he averred. "I'm getting you out of here!"

Likewise, Glen found Dawn huddled in a shrinking break in the flames. She was choking from inhaling the thick smoke that filled the room. There was no way to get to the blazing windows.

"Take it easy, Dawn," he called. "I'm going to get you to safety!"

"But, Glen!" she choked. "How did you…? There's no way…the fire!"

"Don't worry about it," he instructed. "Just keep your eyes closed and don't think about it. Don't think about anything except how much I love you and that I'd die before I let this fire take you! Do you understand?"

He quickly scooped her up in his arms.

"Let's go!" he asserted.

"But, Glen…" she coughed. "The fire…!"

"Don't think about it," he repeated. "Just close your eyes and trust me!"

He practically barreled back out into the fire with Dawn in his arms.

"Trust me," he assured her. "Everything's going to be fine. I don't care whether you move in with me or not, sweetie! I don't give a damn about anything! As long as

Donald Gorman

you love me, I'm the happiest man in the world! Take your time. I won't push you into anything. Just don't die on me, honey! Stay with me! Nothing matters except keeping you alive! You're everything to me! Please remember that!"

The flames kept raging all around him. They lapped and whipped at his face and arms. He could feel the raw pain as the fires singed his arms and legs.

Still, he strode bravely onward towards safety.

When he reached the stairs, he could finally breathe again. He carried Dawn quickly down the stairs. She coughed and wheezed and clung tightly to him as she struggled for breath.

The flames seemed to be restricted to the third floor.

Moments later, Leon emerged from the blaze carrying his wife in his arms. She was choking and gasping for air.

As they hurried down the stairs, they were met by a group of nearly ten firemen carrying hoses and axes.

"Did you get everyone out?" the head fireman asked.

"I think so," Leon replied. Somehow, he knew Adam was already safely outside.

"Do you need any help?" the fireman asked.

"I think we can manage," Glen called over his shoulder as he continued down the stairs with Dawn in his arms.

"There's an emergency medical team outside," the fireman called to the men who wouldn't stop running toward the exit. "They can treat you for smoke inhalation."

Neither man stopped racing until they were outside. As they set the women down on the ground, all four of them coughed and tried to clear the smoke from their lungs.

They took no notice of the many people and emergency vehicles assembled in the parking lot. They just sat down and struggled to breathe.

Moments later, a heavy rain started pouring down from above.

A steady rain was still falling over what was left of The Hillside Inn the following morning.

It made it easier for Leon to hammer a sign into the mud. The sign read "For Sale By Owners". There were no people, ambulances or fire engines. There was no fire.

Rain was all that broke the silence.

Leon and Carol shared a single umbrella in the parking lot.

"You're doing the right thing, Leon," she said.

"I know that now."

She smiled.

"You know, I can't help but wonder," she finally added. "Which one of the forces finally won the conflict?"

"Well," he ventured. "It's probably best if we don't ask. But since you and Dawn are alive, and rain put out the fire…I know what my guess would be."

A car pulled into the parking lot. It took a spot near the Goulds' vehicle not far from the building. A young couple got out of the car.

They each had their own umbrella.

As the young couple approached, Carol welcomed, "Glen! Dawn! It's nice of you to stop by. How are you feeling, Dawn?"

"Much better, thanks," Dawn said. "A few minor burns. I'm still a bit shaken up. But, I'll be okay. How are you, Mrs. Gould?"

Donald Gorman

"Wonderful," Carol said. "I never got to thank you or commend you for your act of heroism, Glen. Thank you for all you did."

"Think nothing of it," Glen said. "Just doing my part. Plus, the world seems like a better place with you and Dawn in it."

"That's nice of you to say," Carol beamed.

"We just came to see you off," Glen said. "We wanted to say thanks for everything and good-bye."

"We're sorry it turned out this way," Leon said. "Will you be alright?"

"Without a doubt," Glen assured him. "As I told you, I'll be starting my new job at The Silver Swordfish soon. It will mean more money for me."

"That's great," Leon said. "How about you, Dawn?"

"I've put in a few applications," Dawn said. "The job hunt will go on until something comes through. I'm sure something will turn up. In the meantime, I'll be moving in with Glen."

"I told her she didn't have to," Glen said. "I told her she didn't need to rush into anything before she was ready. But, she insisted."

"I think that's marvelous," Carol smiled.

"How long have you two been seeing each other?" Leon asked.

Glen and Dawn shared a nervous glance.

"About three months," Glen finally admitted.

"If I'd known," Leon smiled. "I would've fired you both."

"Believe me," Glen said. "We know."

"I'm glad we never found out," Carol said.

"How about you two?" Dawn asked. "You're selling the inn? Are you going to be alright?"

"We'll do okay," Leon said. "The hotel was insured. Most of the third floor was destroyed in the fire. But, we can stay with my brother downstate until we get things settled. It shouldn't be hard for us. We made a fortune once. We can do it again."

"So, exactly what happened here yesterday?" Dawn asked. "How did the fire start?"

"Well, I'm sure the insurance company and fire inspectors will have their own theories," Leon admitted. "They're still investigating. But according to Dr. Tseung, a grand supernatural reaction was caused by the return of Frank Bentworth."

"He was the boy who burned down the Hilzak house twenty years ago," Carol added.

"Police Chief Farley came over yesterday," Leon explained. "The body you found in Room 29, Dawn, was Bentworth's wife, Ashley. And, Glen? The three bodies you saw in Room 8 belonged to Mr. and Mrs. Richard Kirsch and a Logan Tetweller. According to Chief Farley, Kirsch and Tetweller were allegedly with Bentworth when the Hilzak house burned down. A fourth boy named Bill Ambrose was also allegedly involved in the Hilzak fire. All four of them are in town for their high school reunion. Ambrose and his wife were staying in another hotel."

"Farley thinks that staying at The Hillside was more than Bentworth could handle," Carol continued. "Ambrose and his wife are missing. Farley figures Bentworth totally went nuts when he came back here. He must've killed everyone involved, along with whatever wives were present. And then, he killed himself. Bentworth was found hanging by a noose from the balcony outside of Room 8. Even Farley says it looks like a suicide."

"Wow!" Glen commented. "That's rough!"

"It was enough for me," Leon said. "I have my family. That's all I need. I'm ready to bail on the hotel business."

"Thankfully," Carol added. "We didn't lose anyone else. All our other guests and staff were accounted for after the fire."

"Well, that's good news at least," Dawn commented. "But speaking of family, how's Adam?"

"He's fine," Carol said. "He's in the car. He doesn't remember a thing. He doesn't even remember Mr. Fuego. Dr. Tseung says that as long as we keep him away from Morris Hill, Adam will probably never remember any of the unpleasantness."

"Mom!" Adam called from the car. "I'm hungry!"

"Okay, honey," she called back to him. "We'll be leaving in just a few minutes."

"You know," Glen suggested. "I was just going back to my place to make us some breakfast."

"That's *our* place," Dawn corrected playfully.

"Excuse me," Glen smiled. "*Our* place. You're welcome to join us for breakfast, if you'd like."

"That would be wonderful," Carol smiled. "Adam has always loved your cooking, Glen."

"He's a good kid," Glen said. "He's always welcome."

"Thank you, Glen," Leon said. "That's very kind. We'll be there in half an hour or so. And, Dawn? I can have a letter of reference ready for you by tomorrow. Any assistance you need in finding a job, I'd be delighted to help. I know people."

"Thank you, Mr. Gould," Dawn said.

Wrongful Secrets

"So, we'll see you for breakfast at *our* place in half an hour?" Glen affirmed.

"See you there," Leon said.

The young couple turned and walked back to Glen's car.

As they passed the Goulds' vehicle, Adam stuck his head out of the window. "Are you guys leaving?" he asked.

"Yes," Glen said. "But, your mom says you can come to our place for breakfast."

"Cool!" Adam beamed. "I love your French toast and sausages, Glen!"

"I'll make 'em special just for you, buddy," Glen smiled.

"Excellent!" Adam smiled. "Will you be there too, Dawn?"

"I wouldn't miss it, honey."

"Awesome!" Adam said while waving. "See you soon."

"We'll see you, sweetie," Dawn said.

The couple walked back to the car. They closed up their umbrellas and got in. Glen started the car. The engine came to life like a dream.

Large raindrops continued to pelt his windshield. He just sat for a minute with the motor running.

"Are you okay, Glen?" Dawn asked.

"I will be," he said. "How about you, honey?"

"I'm sure I'll be just fine," she smiled.

She rested her head on his shoulder.

He gazed out his window at The Hillside Inn. To him, it looked like a forlorn little sand castle that was being drenched in the surf. Half of the third floor appeared to have already been washed away by an incoming tide.

The 'For Sale' sign looked very, very wet in the pouring rain.

ABOUT THE AUTHOR

Donald Gorman was born in Albany, NY on September 25, 1961. He grew up in the nearby small town of East Greenbush. He attended Columbia High School and graduated in 1979. He now works for The State, and resides in upstate NY. His fascination with the horror genre began at an early age while watching slasher movies in the '70s. He has been known to say, "I find the swift, blinding, gratuitous violence and carnage very soothing and relaxing. Nothing calms me down after a long hard day better than senseless bloodshed...and lots of it!" But, he's probably just kidding. His other six books with Authorhouse offer more proof of his commitment to the grotesque and morbid hostility. Be sure to look into: *The Brick Mirror*, *The Waters of Satan's Creek*, *Macabre Astrology*, *A Grave in Autumn*, *Deliciously Evil: A Cookbook for Killers*, and *The Red Veil*. We all hope he will be scaring us for many years to come.

Printed in the United States
120288LV00001B/10-12/P